To
Nancy...
Thought you'
enjoy reading
short stories. Min...
chapter 19 and is a "W...
to Hell's Jutche pigeons and the
power of love. Please let me
know what you think.
Meanwhile hope all is well
and I send my love.
Peace
Jane
5/2023

Our Magical Pandemic

OUR MAGICAL PANDEMIC

Stories of Love and Whimsy in Lockdown

Edited by Jeff Ourvan

Stone Tiger Books

Cover and Jacket design by Kristine Scheiner

ISBN: 979-8-9858240-8-7

Published by Stone Tiger Books
225 E. 35th Street, Ground Fl.
New York, NY 10016

Fun was cancelled, unsafe or came with all these parameters that somehow, well, took the fun right out of it. If you miraculously could get your hands on fun, you needed to keep it under wraps or face unwanted judgment and scrutiny. Are you aware of the risks?

—Forbes, December 2021

CONTENTS

Foreword

This is an anthology of original short stories depicting moments of love, whimsy, fantasy, and humor during the Covid lockdown. Ranging from works featuring zombies, vampires, and aliens to others about Zoom meetings, romance, and, yes, pigeons protesting for justice, this volume aspires to capture moments of spontaneity, quirkiness, and awe amid the most wrenching social upheaval of our times. For those of us fortunate enough not to succumb to the virus, especially in the pandemic's fearsome early days, *Our Magical Pandemic* is a paean to the beauty and courage we managed to find within: life went on, and art, as it does, resolutely emerged.

All the storytellers herein have been affiliated with The WriteWorkshops, a New York-based community of authors who together strive to hone their craft and bring their creative works to publication. The Workshops operate out of a cozy storefront on Manhattan's East 35th Street that was at one time a plumbing supply shop but more recently a massage parlor (or, "massage parlor," more likely). Prior to the pandemic, the space had evolved into something of a writers' salon – workshops almost every evening, the single room packed and spilling out to the street for open mic nights and readings evoking the ambiance of a low-ceiling, college bar.

By March 15, 2020, however, all this – like everything else the world over – came to a screeching halt. Over the weeks that followed,

New York's streets were deserted, schools and businesses shut, and our once-cozy WriteWorkshops community shifted online. Many of our writers in these early days suffered from devastating cases of Covid, some of which lingered into "long Covid." Thankfully, in our community, no one lost their lives, although of course, at the time of this writing, well over a million Americans have died from the virus – nearly seven million people worldwide.

Still, the urgency within The WriteWorkshops to complete our novels, memoirs and short stories mounted. The idea of a volume of short stories was proposed: since we can't get together physically to read and critique our works, why not collect our stories into an anthology? Moreover, now that we're all camped out on Zoom, our community comprised numerous writers from outside of New York – from the United Kingdom, from Spain, from Canada and beyond. Why not include these members of our growing family in a collection as well?

The theme was left wide open: write the story you want to tell but either set it within, or refer to, the lockdown; don't dwell on the real-world horror of the disease; and make it fictional. The 20 stories that ended up in this anthology were written by 20 diverse and talented writers – several have been published by major imprints, some have appeared in numerous prestigious journals and anthologies, and others are debuting in this volume.

This resulting book is a flowering of artistic perseverance in the midst of, for most of these writers, some formidable personal obstacles. I, for one, subscribe to the words of the Buddhist philosopher Daisaku Ikeda: "Art is the liberation of the humanity inside yourself." These stories reflect just that.

JEFF OURVAN

New York, N.Y.
March 2023

1

STUCK ON ME

by Ashley Williams

After riding almost an hour from the Bronx in a congested and polluted subway, I can finally take a breath of fresh air. Midtown Manhattan never fails to overwhelm me. The night is a bit nippy, but the sky is clear and calm. My little sister, Emmy, and I walk arm in arm, weaving through the bustling crowd. She sneezes under her purplish tie-dyed mask as we step over a puddle of grubby water.

"Bless you," I say.

She sniffles. "Thanks."

"You good?" I ask, raising an eyebrow.

"Yeah, sis. That came outta nowhere. Probably from that nasty ass subway ride."

This morning she woke up full of ginger and pep, belting lyrics to the infamous Erykah Badu. Our parents forced me to take Emmy to her show tonight, because she's my little sister who always gets what she wants. She's been looking forward to this concert for months.

Since the pandemic, we've been trapped at home for a year, waiting for life to get back to normal. Once the vaccines were developed and administered, people scrambled for them, regardless of the side effects, just so we can get back to our day-to-day lives. If that was all I needed to roam freely and experience normalcy as we know it, I did not hesitate. Don't get me wrong; Covid is still at large. New York City mandated everyone to be vaccinated to enter any arena. Of course, there are some people against the vaccines, claiming the government is using it to track us. I don't believe any of that nonsense, so I went ahead and got the Pfizer shot. I was sick after the second dose for a few days, but that was to be expected. It took countless conversations trying to convince my sister about getting her vaccine.

That's because Emmy is afraid of needles. As a child, we had to hold her down for her doctors to give her any type of shot or they would have to put her to sleep. She's very stubborn and naive in that way. She said she can only endure one shot, so she settled for Johnson & Johnson.

We're three years apart. I've always seen Emmy as an annoying tic that doesn't go away, like tagging along when she wasn't invited, spying on my phone conversations, not borrowing but actually stealing my new clothes and jewelry, tattling on me whenever she got the chance, and using her excuse as the baby to always get her way. Once she turned eighteen and already began her first semester of college, I watched her mature into a young woman. Maybe our sisterly bond will grow closer as we blossom into young adults. Here's to hoping . . . miracles are possible.

"Make sure you look out for your sister now." My parents' warning still rings in my ears. She's the youngest and possibly the favorite because of her beauty and charisma. Either way, they say that every time we go anywhere.

Emmy pulls out a tissue from her sweater pocket, removes her mask and blows hard. She wipes her nose, then glances up at me and smiles, revealing her deep dimples.

I wrinkle my nose. "You're so gross, Em. Ugh, I wish you stayed home."

She nods toward a homeless guy urinating by a trash can. "Whatever! It's just allergies. Anyway, I wouldn't want to miss all this action. . . ."

The disheveled man finishes urinating, then leans over the trash can, vomiting. My stomach starts to churn, and I'm beginning to feel anxious.

"Don't stare. C'mon. Let's get moving. I want to put much needed space between us and that guy."

She fixes the natural puff on her head. It's wrapped in a colorful scarf. She wanted to dress very bohemian tonight for the concert. I scope her up and down. My baby sister is all grown up. Her fitted red dress hugs her curves in all the right places. She's wearing some glitter eye shadow, making her look very classy. An emerald stone hangs from her dainty neck, on a thin gold chain. Mom's gift for her graduation. It suits her well, the crystal symbolizing youthfulness and growth. She may look grown but her mind is still so naive.

She clutches my arm tightly. "Di, chill. I know you'd rather be here with one of your boring and weird friends, but I'm way more fun. This night is gonna be lit!"

I sigh. "Just don't embarrass me tonight, deal?"

She dramatically clutches her chest. "Me? Never!"

I know sarcasm when I hear it. I roll my eyes.

We turn the corner on Sixth Avenue, and Emmy leaps up and down like a little kid in a candy store. "There it is! Radio City, baby!"

I turn away as if I don't know her. "Girl, act like you get out much. White folks are staring at you."

"Shut up, Diamond! You sound like Mom."

When our parents first got together, they grew up in the Bronx projects. With aspirations of making it out the hood, they valued fancy clothes and accessories, claiming the look made the man. My mom had an obsession with jewels, collecting them, working with them to eventually become CEO of a high-end jewelry company. So it was no surprise when she named us both after their favorite stones. Emerald, Emmy for short. And Diamond. In school, we used to be called the Diamond sisters even though I was the only one actually named Diamond.

We walk through the entrance of Radio City Music Hall and are directed to take out our IDs and vaccination cards. The security officer lingers on Emmy, looking her up and down.

Emmy sneezes loudly.

The officer glares before taking her card, then huffs impatiently. "It's another J&J. Do I let her in?" he speaks into his walkie-talkie.

A muffled voice answers him back. "How does she look?"

Emmy places her hands on her hips. "What's wrong? I just sneezed. It's allergies from the train ride."

I quickly come to her defense and confirm, "She's vaccinated. Do we have a problem?"

He rolls his eyes and waves us through. "She's good."

I swing my arm through hers, pulling her inside the lobby.

"That was close." Emmy sighs.

I shake my head. "If you had gotten Pfizer like I told you, he wouldn't have been looking at you like that."

"That was kinda weird, though, right? What's wrong with J&J?" Her almond-shaped eyes look up at me, seeking answers.

I had to transform into big sister mode. I take her hand. "It's fine. We're in. Don't worry."

Emmy's giddy and animated as she gapes about the lobby.

"True. We're here! We made it! I'm so excited. I can't wait to see what she's gonna wear onstage. She always looks so fly."

Her skin feels warm, and I fake a smile. I don't want to ruin her happiness. She was looking forward to this moment for weeks, sending me GIFs of Erykah Badu and blasting her albums in her room.

It's also my first time at Radio City. The walls are huge and wide in yellow and red regal wallpaper. Red carpet covers the floors and wide staircases. People flood the brightly lit room with lines wrapped around the lobby. We shuffle through the crowds, looking for what section our seats are in. It's packed like sardines in here, as if people forgot not long ago six feet apart was a thing. Sometimes I wish it still was. Food shopping has recently become unpleasant again as people, still wearing masks incorrectly, stand too closely while grabbing their milk and cheese. I'm very squeamish when it comes to germs and people and crowds. I've always avoided busy places, especially during the beginning stages of the pandemic, but now that more and more people are getting vaccinated, the city is becoming lenient with the rules. But people are still getting sick.

Then, I drag her down the carpeted stairs toward the bathrooms.

She squeezes the back of my arm, a nervous habit she's done since she was a kid, to the point where I have bruises. Battle wounds. "Ugh," she says. "It's even more crowded down here. I don't have to pee. Hurry up."

"Girl, you better try. I don't want to hear you saying you need to go and make me miss any of Erykah Badu's performance!"

She groans. "Yes, Mom." I hate when she calls me that because it reminds me of how much I baby her and act like our mother.

I enter the nearest stall and unzip my one-piece jumper so I can stoop over the toilet. I finally relieve myself and instantly feel at ease. Suddenly, I hear a gargled cough coming from the stall beside me. It's deep and full of phlegm. I gag and hold my breath.

Someone makes a comment out loud. "How disgusting."

Another voice responds. "Right? I bet it's that Johnson & Johnson thing going around. They should only allow people who got Pfizer or Moderna in."

This virus has affected everyone differently, and I can't wait until the world can go back to normal—before masks, vaccine mandates, and remote learning. I feel bad for my sister experiencing her first year in college through remote learning and not being in person.

I finish up and leave the stall and wash my hands at the sink. I'm able to identify the two women who were speaking earlier. One is tall with straight hair and pale skin. The other was an older woman, probably in her fifties, in red pants and a matching fedora. I lean in closer as I wash my hands and stare at myself in the mirror.

"Yeah, I heard about that. People with the J&J shot are still getting sick. Pus around the nose, throwing up blood, and even acting crazy. Is it contagious?" the one in the red asks.

"I don't know, but they should be banned from entering. I don't have time for that!"

They both giggle and walk out the bathroom together. I think about Emmy. Why would they offer that vaccine if it causes those types of effects? These vaccines are so new, and there wasn't enough time to research them fully, with millions of lives at stake. Who knows what all the side effects are? The person who was in the stall next to me approaches the sink; her eyes are droopy and her face is gray, like the undead. She glances at me in the mirror and excuses herself, blowing her nose. "Sorry about that. Don't worry, I'm vaccinated."

I wonder, *Yeah, but which one?*

"I love your outfit, by the way."

I smile and thank her. I feel bad for judging. Those women don't know what they're talking about. She's not throwing up blood or acting crazy. She's being a normal person who happens to be sick.

I calm myself down and stare in the mirror again. I'm feeling my all-black jumper with the long pants. My pretty brown braids match with the outfit perfectly, and I'm glad I decided on flats and not heels for this evening. I'd be in pain already before the concert even starts. My eyes fall to my amethyst necklace, hoping the healing properties protect me tonight with understanding, wisdom, and strength. I also brought a few more crystals in my purse, like my rose quartz for finding love, which I probably won't have luck with Emmy hanging around, and my black obsidian for protection. Feeling satisfied with gussying myself up, I saunter out to the hall and look around for Emmy. The floor is full of people, and I don't see her anywhere. I grab at my purse and pull out my phone to call her. It goes straight to voice mail. Great.

I lean against a wall and begin texting furiously. In a burst of energy, a group of paramedics stampede through the crowd with someone being rolled out in a stretcher. There was a cloth over the person's face, but that wasn't enough to deter the attention of the rest of the crowd. I watch as the paramedics head toward the elevators in the back as someone pinches the back of my arm.

"What the—!" I shout.

"Got you!"

"Emmy, I'm gonna kill you. You could easily be kidnapped out here."

She sucks her teeth. "Stop being dramatic. Are you ready? Let's find our seats."

Holding a hand to my fast-beating heart, I try to relax. But I can't seem to shake this eerie feeling, like something is off. From the person in the stretcher to the sick lady in the bathroom, things seem more abnormal than usual.

We head upstairs and are directed to rows KK, eight rows from the stage. A parade of sneezes ring out of Emmy, and people near us stare in disgust.

"She has allergies," I repeat, then lean in and whisper toward my sister. "Dang, girl! You good? People are gonna kick us out thinking you have Covid or that J&J thing going around. . . ."

"What J&J thing?"

I pat her hand. "Nothing. Don't worry about it. Just get your shit together."

Twenty minutes later, the lights dim and a band begins to play smooth R & B music. I rock side to side in my seat, closing my eyes and feeling the rhythm. I'm in my element. I've been listening to R & B all my life and always felt this deep connection to it. Like my ancestors calling me, talking to me, soothing me. I stand and wave my hands in the air. I repeat some affirmations to myself and grab at my rose quartz and black obsidian crystals in my purse, hoping Erykah can charge them with her beautiful voice and style. *I don't chase. I attract. What belongs to me will simply find me.* I can already feel a strong energy overtake my body. Then finally, the moment that everyone is waiting for, Erykah walks out onstage wearing an oversized gray fur coat and a tall brown hat, with sparkly silver platform shoes.

The crowd screams and cheers as she belts out her first note. My heart warms and I stand, dancing in place. Emmy and I are giddy like little schoolgirls. The band plays the first few beats, and she's playing our favorite song, "On and On." I get lost in the music and feel like I'm floating and high. The bass is pumping harder. I can feel it reverberating in my chest.

These lyrics I've listened to over and over again for years hit differently tonight. Maybe because it's a live performance or maybe it's my excitement about seeing her in person, but I'm singing along and feeling as if she's reaching my soul.

I can almost see a spirit emanating from her, flying into the audience. A powerful presence hovers over us, and I clutch my crystals in my palms. The bass is beating harder and I can barely feel my own body. The air feels thick, pushing me down. My chest is heavy. I begin to choke. A chilling sensation crawls down my spine. Something falls at my feet and I jump back, startled. I turn to my left and Emmy is laid out on her chair with her head back. Her legs are kicked out and her foot landed on mine.

I rush to her aid and smack her cheeks, calling her name. "Emmy! What's wrong? Wake up!"

The person beside her is also helping me to revive her. We carry Emmy out the aisle as the bass of the music pounds against our eardrums. Once we make it out of the aisle, Emmy collapses into the wall and falls to the floor. I lean her up against the wall. Someone brings her a bottle of water. I remove her mask and try to pour some water into her mouth. But I gasp. The person who was originally helping me jumps back and runs away from us in horror. Emmy's nose and mouth are covered in red sores and puss. I almost throw up but swallow it.

What the hell is happening? I try to shake her awake but she doesn't move. A loud shriek, which sounds different from the cheering, echoes in the distance. Then more shouts and the ceiling rumbles over us as if a boulder is rolling down a mountain. I realize it's people rushing out from the mezzanine upstairs. A body falls from above, crashing into the aisles below. The band stops playing and Erykah stops singing. Security rushes to the stage, protecting the starlet as they flee, while some people scream and run for the exit.

Emmy and I are being trampled. I shield her body with mine. I holler into her ears. She's coming to slowly but is coughing up blood now. My heart beats out my chest, and I don't know what to do. People scramble like rats, and I try to flag someone down to help me carry Emmy out. One tall, dark man with a uniform picks her up into his arms and barrels toward the exit as I follow. We squeeze through gaps and finally make it out of the theater and onto the street. He places her down gently.

"Are you okay?" he asks. The panic in his eyes terrifies me.

"Please don't leave us. Can you help us?" I plead, clutching onto his uniform.

After glancing back and forth at the chaos spilling out into the streets, he shakes me off as a cluster of people separate us. I place my hands under Emmy's arms and hoist her up. "Please, Emmy. Move your feet. We need to leave!"

Her head is tilting this way and that like a newborn baby. We stumble down Fifty-First Street. I try my best to hold her, but she's barely walking. I try to steer away from the crowd and turn into an alley. We trip as I try to get her onto the sidewalk, and she tumbles onto the hard ground.

I fall to my knees. "Emmy! Please get up. Baby, please! I can't help you." Tears, snot, and dirt stain my face.

She begins coughing up blood again.

I clap my hands. "Emmy, talk to me! Stand up! Please!"

A crunching noise disturbs my prayer.

I look off into the darkness. I don't see anything. "Emmy, come on. Please. Can you walk?"

Her legs are wobbly, but she tries to stand.

I swing my arm around her waist to hold her up. She leans her body against mine, and I try to drag her. The crunching sound gets louder, and I pause. Emmy's sliding down and I try to catch her. "Emmy, please!" I whisper.

The crunching stops.

"What the hell is that?" I ask out loud.

A deep moan surfaces along with the shuffling of feet.

Behind a parked car, a slender figure with wobbly legs peeks out, like Emmy's. A limp bloody body lies beside the figure, its intestines spilling out of its stomach, bloody and stringy. I gag and my eyes widen at the lanky body hobbling toward us. It's the same homeless guy from earlier. But how?! His clothes are grimier than before, covered in blood stains. Red sores pock his face. Blood is dripping from his mouth.

I wail and tremble as I continue to drag my sister's limp body. "Emmy, you gotta wake up!"

He begins moving faster toward us and I'm stepping away as swiftly as I can, dragging Emmy. "Emmy, no. Please! I need you!"

The homeless guy is reaching for us, with smeared, bloody hands and thick dark nails. I dodge the other way and accidentally drop my sister. She's coughing and laying in her own bloody vomit.

"Emmy, get up! Get up!"

But her body is too weak. She slinks facedown on the asphalt, motionless. I cry over her body. The homeless guy gets closer and I try to kick him away. He reaches for me again, and I sprint down the block, leaving my hobbled sister on the ground. Panting and out of breath, an image of my life flashes before my eyes. Mom, Dad, Emmy, and I at a picnic in Central Park a few years ago. Smiling, laughing, holding each other. Family. Normal. I slow down in my tracks. I need to go back for Emmy. She needs me. I'm her big sister. I'm supposed to take care of her. I start to run back but immediately wish I didn't.

I see her.

I close my eyes, then open them again.

It's still there.

It won't go away.

The zombielike homeless man and my baby sister, Emmy, are kneeling down by the limp dead body, clawing into it and chewing gloppy chunks of flesh.

.

2

BREATHE WITH ME

by Derlys Gutierrez

The wailing of ambulance sirens was now the soundtrack to Harold's day. In the first couple of weeks of the lockdown, he noticed the sound approaching as the ambulances neared his tiny apartment, then noted how it diminished as they sped away. Although he worked in a tall building in Times Square, he had chosen to live in a small town across the Hudson River so he could travel easily into the city and then escape its crowds at the end of every long workday. Lockdown seemed to have made that decision less consequential, since there was no escape no matter where one lived.

In the weeks since everything closed, he had become immune to the noise as he made his usual breakfast: eggs over easy, but not too easy; turkey bacon crisped just so; and seedless rye bread, lightly toasted. Harold cleaned as he cooked so that nothing was out of place by the time he plated his breakfast and folded his lanky frame into the cushioned chair on the right side of his two-person dining room table.

The kitchen was as small as Harold was tall. He had once laid on the black-and-white-   tile floor to prove to himself that his semibald head touched one wall and his feet touched the doorway on the opposite side. Six feet two inches precisely: Harold liked to know that things were exact. The stove had two gas burners and a tiny oven that would fit the small ham he planned to soon cook for Easter. This year it would be just him, and he was trying to calculate exactly how much food to order online so he would have enough leftovers for one day. Harold didn't like waste, but he also didn't like leftovers older than thirty-six hours.

The refrigerator that didn't fit in the kitchen stood in the equally small living room on the same side of the wall as the fifty-five-inch-wide flat-screen TV that Harold paid extra to have mounted on the wall. The twenty-plus years of living in this tiny apartment and the years of being in the military had taught him to maximize tight spaces. To the right of the kitchen lay the bathroom, which, thankfully, had a tub large enough to accommodate Harold's long legs. Since lockdown began, he found that languishing in lavender-scented bubbles soothed his jangly nerves. His Navy buddies would laugh at him if they knew what he was up to.

Directly across the bathroom, precisely two steps away, was the door to the bedroom. It hung slightly askew, which bothered Harold every time he walked into the room. Inside, in the very center of the room, his bed was neat and tidy, with the corners of the sheets perfectly squared beneath a hunter-green coverlet. Two pillows stood at attention by the headboard—one for Harold's head and one to hug throughout the night. A two-drawer nightstand on the right side of the bed held his reading glasses, a self-help book about sleeping habits, a tall reading lamp, and a coaster for his water glass. In the days before lockdown, Harold's slippers sat in a straight line on the floor by the nightstand during the day, but now they left his feet only for baths and bedtime.

One wall of the bedroom was occupied by a narrow closet with folding doors. Harold's few shirts and slacks were arranged by color and season so they'd be easy to find. These days, he preferred light cotton sweatpants and a polo shirt, since there was no reason to dress up for work anymore. No one saw the bottom half of his body in Zoom work meetings.

The other wall of the bedroom had two tall windows facing the street. Forest-green blackout curtains that matched the bedspread kept out the glare of the street lamps at night. In the morning, Harold pulled back the curtains and opened the windows so he could hear the birds singing. He had noticed that birds were louder now. He wasn't sure if this was a result of being able to hear them better since he was home or whether nature was rejoicing vociferously that humans were finally back in their cages. Whatever the reason, he felt like he was certainly caged now. Birdsong outweighed people chatter, but he was nevertheless a little stir-crazy without going to an office filled with people.

Harold spent his days listening to the dire news of illness and death, the daily count growing as quickly as his paranoia about germs. The rest of the day was spent on monotonous meetings where his boss vainly attempted to rally the team's morale while people obviously scrolled through their phones or tapped away on their laptops ordering food, alcohol, or exercise equipment online.

On one of the now-countless *Groundhog*-like days, as he sat through another boring PowerPoint presentation, Harold's eyes wandered to the blank walls in his apartment. Prior to lockdown, he had fancied himself a nature photographer in training and enjoyed solitary hikes with his Canon Sure Shot. He had never printed his photos, preferring to keep them to himself in a continuous slideshow setting on his laptop. Figuring no one would ever be interested in looking at them anyway, he didn't bother to spend money on paper and frames. But on this particular day, something about the sound of ambulances and birds got to him, and he yelled, "That's enough!" even though his Zoom call was not on mute. His coworkers cried out, in unison, "Harold, mute yourself!" So he did, and immediately proceeded to take himself off video and searched on the internet for a place where he could print photos and have them framed. He also ordered a level and placed all the requests on rapid delivery. He coughed as an excuse to leave the meeting early, and logged off before anyone had a chance to object.

Two days later, much to his surprise, Harold received a package that contained exactly what he had ordered. The black-and-white frames and the vibrant colors of his nature photographs were evidence that, sometimes, he could actually get what he desired. On the bit of wall space left over by the large television set, he arranged the frames in perfectly straight lines thanks to the level.

Weeks later, even after the parks were reopened and people were out walking their dogs five times a day, Harold remained steadfast in his obsession with remaining safe. He ordered all the basic necessities online—groceries, toiletries, laundry services – as everything was available without him needing to step outside.

With every passing day, Harold's separation from the world became more acute. He resorted to not showing his face on Zoom work calls. Instead, he used a selfie photo as a replacement for his live face. He told his boss he simply did not feel well enough to be on camera. The persistence of online meetings had left his team tired, and, after a while, no one even bothered to ask Harold to get on camera. He had the delivery people leave packages outside his door so he wouldn't be in touch with any living being. The smaller his world became, the less he felt the need to interact with anyone. The few friends he had were so tied up in their own dramas that they stopped calling Harold. It made no difference; he wouldn't have answered anyway. The only conversations available were about the increasing number of deaths worldwide, and how much worse it was going to get before it got better.

Thus, Harold stopped speaking at work and communicated through emails only. Essentially, he ceased interacting with the humans remaining in his world. The only thing left for him to do was gaze at his photographs. They, alone, offered peace.

After breakfast and before lunch, between lunch and dinner, and in the space between dinner and bedtime, Harold sat on the sofa in the living room staring at the dark television and at the photographs of the flowers. He devised a practice where he would focus on a picture long enough to create the shadow of the flower, and then he'd look at the blank television screen so he could see the shadow there. The first time he discovered this game, he did it for a little while and then got up to order something online.

But as the hours and days passed, he found himself itching to finish preparing his meals so he could spend more time staring at the photographs. They emitted a constant hum, like a sibilant s hanging in the air permanently. Harold could hear it above the sizzle of eggs in the frying pan in the morning. He could sense it in the ripples of the water in his bathtub, making him skip baths. He resorted to five-minute showers, barely washing the important bits.

He ignored the call of sleep and stayed on the couch in the living room. Less to clean up in the bedroom, he thought. He skipped work, finding the Zoom meetings too distracting from his perpetual new job of focusing on his flowers. They were his children and needed tending.

One evening, after the sun had set and the room-darkening blinds were pulled tight across the living room windows, Harold heard it. That voice. At first it was soft and gentle, a seductive invitation.

"Harold *dearesssssssst*," it said. "Come *inssssssside*."

Harold rubbed his ears, convinced he was hearing the neighbors next door.

The voice repeated its call. "Darling Harold. Come with *ussss*."

Harold stood up and walked toward the frames. The voice was loudest from the largest frame, the one with the purple flowers—the hyacinths.

"Harold, it would *pleasssse usss* for you to come with *ussss*."

With the reverberation of the letter *s*, Harold saw the picture swell, and he heard a pulsating sound, like a heartbeat. *Pum-pum, pum-pum. Pum-pum, pum-pum.* The closer Harold got to the photo, the louder and faster the beat. *Pum-pum-pum-pum. Pum-pum-pum-pum.*

The glass in the frame arched toward him, becoming convex, like a pregnant belly. *Pum-pum-pum-pum-pum-pum-pum-pum.* The faster the beat, the rounder the glass, the wooden frames straining against the miniature nails that held their corners fast.

Mouth agape and his head cocked to the side, Harold reached out his right index finger to touch the glass, when he felt his fingers dip into a jelly. Inch by inch, his hand started to disappear. Startled, he pulled his hand back abruptly, and then he heard the voice repeatedly calling his name.

"Harold!" It commanded him, and he was powerless to object. He put both hands against the picture and leaned his forehead on it until his entire body was immersed.

For the duration of the blink of an eye, there was darkness with no sound. Then all the noises of the world crashed onto Harold. Car horns, tires screeching, people yelling, children laughing, doors slamming shut, street vendors hawking their wares: "Hot dogs!" "Kabobs!" "Take a picture!"

"Hey, buddy, watch where you're going!"

Times Square? Why was he in Times Square? How did he get here? *There's a pandemic. We're all supposed to be masked and social-distancing—staying safe.* These were his thoughts, but these people seemed unaware of the death-knell that pealed all around the world. They were going about as if nothing had happened. How could this be?

Harold jumped when a guy pushed him aside on the sidewalk near the M&M store entrance. The M&M store—the bane of his existence when he worked in person in the city. The multitudes of tourists who were determined to take home chocolates wrapped in a hard candy shell had always made Harold want to work anywhere else. Something about the creepiness of the candies having legs, hands, and faces made him squirm.

But the crowd near the M&M store had grown, and Harold was pushed inside the door by the throng.

Everything was so loud, he could barely breathe. There was no room to move away. No social-distancing. No masks. Only ear-splitting noise, the sweaty skin of strangers touching his own, and the smell of unwashed bodies in the heat. Harold felt bile in his mouth and gagged, wanting to vomit, just like when he was a child. He feared he would throw up on someone's shirt as he tried to get out of the line to find a bathroom.

A woman in a white short-sleeve blouse with the M&M logo above her right breast yanked his arm and pulled him into an empty corner of the store. Before she started dragging him, he looked at her face and found lilac eyes made brighter by the curls of red hair bouncing off her shoulders. Even her eyebrows were red and full. In a daze, Harold lowered his head to look at her hand on his bare forearm and noticed the softness of her palm. He hadn't felt a woman's skin in so long that he was shocked at how lovely it felt. She smelled like hyacinths.

Once they were ensconced in the corner, she put both of her hands on his shoulders and gently guided him so his back was against the wall. She moved toward his right ear and whispered, "You're safe here, Harold. I promise I won't leave you alone, sweetheart." She pronounced the *s* with a sibilant and long sound that surprised Harold at the same time it soothed him.

The woman moved her head back, locked her eyes on his, and whispered, "I've been waiting for you, Harold. I'm so glad you're finally here."

Harold opened and closed his mouth, incapable of uttering words and emitting only a ragged noise in response.

"Breathe with me, Harold," she continued.

Not questioning why, he obeyed. He inhaled and exhaled in time with her, unable—unwilling—to take his eyes away from hers. They were a tropical sea of lilac and sunshine, and he walked into them as one steps into warm water, delighting in the embrace of a lover who's finally returned. There was no light, no sound; there was only the nothing and everything of being with her.

After a few moments, the woman blinked and broke the spell. Harold could hear the tumult of people in the main area of the store, the clatter of overhead speakers blaring out announcements of sales, and he once again felt claustrophobic.

She grabbed his hand and pulled him toward a door at the end of a hallway. They exited and ran down stairs with metal handrails. There were lights on the steps in case of a power outage. Funny that he was noticing these details at the same time he sensed the warmth and strength of her hand. As they descended what seemed like dozens of flights, he realized he was not frightened at all. In fact, he didn't care where they were going. He only wanted to be with her and the scent of hyacinths that surrounded her.

As they approached a landing, he pulled her hand to stop.

"What is it, dearest? she asked. "We're almost there."

He noticed again the pronounced sibilance of her *s* sound. He smiled at how endearing that was. He reached for her waist and brought her toward him. Without thinking or asking, he lowered his head and kissed her full lips, hard at first, but when she responded by opening her mouth like the petals of a flower, he softened the kiss, and once again fell into her gentleness, her embrace, her delicious welcome. They stayed there for an eternity and a few seconds at once, until she broke the connection.

"Yes, that was . . . that was . . . lovely. I've missed you."

"I've missed you also," he said, "but I don't know you."

She smiled, showing bright white teeth perfectly spaced and small. "Oh, but you do know me. You just don't remember me in this form."

He cocked his head to the side, trying to assemble his thoughts and understand what she was saying.

She continued without explanation. "We don't have time to sort that out now. We have to get out before we're discovered." She took his hand in hers again, and they resumed their descent.

He willingly obliged and, following her, asked, "Where are we going?"

"To the lake."

"What lake? Is it underground?" At this point, he was open to anything, as long as he was with her.

"No, but the escape is just a couple of flights down." She stopped briefly. "Are you okay? Do you feel out of breath?"

Grinning, he pulled her toward him again.

"I'm perfectly happy, as long as I'm with you."

He heard himself say the words but didn't realize they came from his mouth. He remembered the old Harold, the one who didn't leave the house, and wondered where he had gone.

As if listening to his thoughts, she moved away from him again and continued walking down.

"That Harold is gone. You left him back in the apartment."

The statement halted him, goose bumps spreading all over him. "What does that mean?"

For the first time, the woman sighed with exasperation. "Harold, we've no time for explanations now. We must hurry or the door will close, and we'll be stuck here forever. I'll tell you the whole story when we get to the other side."

She turned back to the stairs, and he allowed himself to be pulled, not knowing how to answer such a dire statement. *The door will close? The other side? Where is she taking me?*

The woman charged down the stairs now, her pace quickening, almost frantic. The fragrance of hyacinths grew stronger with every step.

Soon enough, they reached the bottom of the stairs and found themselves in front of a wooden door, ancient and braced with iron bands and an iron lock. From the pocket of her long lavender skirt, the woman pulled out a key.

The tremors in her hand rattled the key in the lock, making it difficult to open. She stopped and breathed deeply, looked at Harold with love in her eyes, and again inserted the key into the lock and turned. This time the door opened, revealing a short corridor bathed in light and the sound he'd heard from the picture frame. *Pum-pum-pum-pum. Pum-pum-pum-pum.*

At the end of the corridor was an opening, like the mouth of a cave, high on a cliff overlooking a lush valley of wildflowers with a cool stream running through that led to a huge lake, sunlight glinting like diamonds on the water. Just outside the opening, a long set of stone steps led down to the valley. The stairs beckoned both of them to descend.

The woman pulled Harold by the hand. "Come with me, dearest. This is our gateway to freedom. See the lake down there? I have a house where we can live happily together. Join me."

Harold saw the light in her eyes. He wanted so much to go with her. He yearned for her touch, her presence. Instinctively, he knew she had gifts he would cherish. But this place where they were going – how could he be sure it would be safe? It was unknown. It could be dangerous. Everything about this woman seemed unreal, like a dream. Even if he trusted her, he'd have to give up everything he knew: comfort, rules, order. And what if he didn't like her fantasy? How could he get back to what was real?

The woman squeezed his hand and brought it to her lips, kissing it sweetly, pressing her cheek against it before she gazed into his eyes again. "Dear one, the portal is open only for a moment. We must make haste. You can't deny you love me. Please don't waste this chance to be happy." Tears welled up in her eyes.

He felt afraid again, not sure whether to run with this wild woman or stay put. "I don't even know your name, yet I can't bear to see you cry. Or to leave you."

She sighed and pointed to the valley. "I have no name. I am whoever you want me to be, but if we don't go through the door now, I will never see you again." She paused to take a breath. With a sob, she added, "And I can't bear the pain of only watching you from the wall anymore."

Harold squinted at the sunlight, which seemed to pulsate with a beat that was frenetic now. *Pum-pum-pum-pum. Pum-pum-pum-pum. Pum-pum-pum-pum. Pum-pum-pum-pum.* "Am I dead? Is that heaven?"

She pointed again and yelled, "Harold, we must go now! We have only seconds before the door closes. You must trust me!"

With resignation and regret, he caressed her velvety cheek with the palm of his hand. He paused for a split second, then pushed her abruptly as he stepped back. She fell to the floor and reached out her arm. He heard her yelling "*Noooo!*" while he continued backward, his eyes locked on hers.

The door slammed shut with a heavy thud.

She was gone, and he was left alone in the semidarkness, making it difficult to see the door any longer. He stepped backward some more as the light dimmed into nothingness.

A few seconds later, warmth nuzzled his face, and he recognized it as the presence of light. He hesitated opening his eyes, afraid the brightness would cause him pain. He stood there, his feet unmoving and his body wavering side to side as if he were surfing. He stretched his arms out, not knowing what else to do, but he sensed he should be doing something to understand what had happened. He suspected he had been dreaming but wasn't sure if he was awake now or still sleeping. He then heard a television droning the news, the loud sound assaulting his senses even more acutely than the light. When he could no longer tolerate the noise, he opened his eyes and saw he was back in his living room, in the same spot as when he'd left it: in front of the wall with pictures. Except that now one was lying on the floor, the frame broken, and the photograph ripped where the glass shards of the frame had pierced it in half.

It was his favorite photo—the one of hyacinths in the park before the pandemic. He let out a sharp cry as he bent down to pick it up, and tears streamed down his cheeks, falling like raindrops on the wood floor. He didn't notice them while he stared at the photograph, remembering the kiss of the sensuous nameless redhead. He could still taste the sweetness of her lips and smell the fragrance of her skin. Holding the picture to his chest as if to relieve the unspeakable pain in his heart, he sat down cross-legged on the floor and remained there, immobile for hours.

As sunshine abandoned the room to moonlight, Harold finally stood up, his back stiff and his legs wobbly. He carried the picture to the dining room table much as one carries a dead baby bird, and he made a mental note that, in the morning, he'd tape the back of the photo and keep it secure in a book in his nightstand drawer.

Then he walked to the hallway closet, picked up the broom and dustpan, and cleaned up the mess. He noted the gaping hole left in the wall and promised himself he'd order another frame to fill the vacuum.

He lowered the volume of the television, then headed to the bathroom so he could lay in the tub amid lavender bubbles. It was, after all, time for his daily bath.

A few days later, Harold drank his coffee while sitting on the sofa, staring at the emptiness of the wall where the hyacinth photo used to hang, ignoring the sound of the Zoom meeting that was occurring without his participation. He briefly considered joining the work crew but decided not to. Surely they didn't miss him anyway. With the last sip, he took the cup to the kitchen sink and washed it. After drying it and putting it back in its spot in the cupboard, he returned to the living room, where he picked up the new frame and brass picture lamp that had arrived the night before.

He had had enough sense to order a picture lamp that was battery-operated and worked with a remote control so he could turn it on and off while he sat on the sofa. He measured out the wall space with meticulous care and installed the brass lamp so that the frame would be completely washed in light. He proceeded carefully, laying the frame on the same nail that had held the hyacinth. He straightened it out, and, when he was satisfied that all the frames were level again, he returned to the sofa to examine his handiwork. Harold imagined a certain sadness in the photos that remained, almost as if they missed their prior companion.

He then went about his ordinary day, almost congratulating himself at the solution he'd found. Serenity and silence. After all, a blank piece of white paper bathed in light inside a frame would cause no further trouble.

3

AT LEAST FIVE

by Christopher Ragland

Jim's fist clenched on the object in front of him, the uncertainty of the situation playing havoc with his mind. His right eye twitched as he cast his mind back through recent events, desperate to remember, to know, what the truth was. His temple throbbed with the strain. He just couldn't remember, and that ambiguity shot through his mind like a knife. How many times? Dammit, how many?!

How many times *had* he wiped down the bag of chips? Four? Five? The Clorox wipe squeezed in a death grip in his right hand, he looked at the shiny wrapping in his left, its fresh gleam seeming to mock him, and snarled. Four or five? Think, think! Four or five? Had he done it . . . ?"For god's sake, Jim, what the hell are you muttering about? You're not singing that damn happy birthday song again, are you?"

Jim's head shot up, his train of thought shattered by the interruption. He hadn't realized he'd been speaking aloud, but one look at Susan's face confirmed he had. Glaring at him from across the room, her disgusted countenance speared him with the power of an actual lance, the book she'd been reading forgotten in the palpable loathing flowing toward him, a bitterness she did nothing to hide.

It was nothing new. They hadn't been good, hadn't been happy, hadn't been *them* for years. But with the past year of enforced togetherness, the multitude of cracks in their relationship widened into

31

chasms, gulfs that now seemed impossible to cross.

And the largest of all was the cleaning. In Jim's mind, they couldn't be too safe. There was a virus, a deadly pathogen, floating around, and he would do whatever he could to protect him and Susan. So of course, he washed his hands far longer than ever before. And without fail, he wore a double mask anytime he stepped outside his front door. And if he was being honest, he was known to spend a good five minutes scrubbing the doorbell anytime it was pressed. God knows what germs the unclean delivery guys brought with them; he could practically see the spike proteins on every Amazon box!

But what he saw as the acts of a loving husband, she saw as a descent into compulsive behavior that approached madness. Issues that would have been mild complaints now took on epic proportion. Compounded with the forced time together, their marriage was hanging on by a thread, and even that thread seemed to be fraying.

With a huff, Susan went back to her book, sinking into the large armchair that she loved so much by the window. Jim still remembered buying that chair. They'd only been married six months. One look at the smile on his young bride's face as she'd fallen into its plush embrace and he'd sworn to move heaven and earth to make it hers. The fact that it was the better part of his monthly pay check at the time didn't matter; he would have paid anything to make her happy.

Jim couldn't remember the last time he'd seen her smile. A grimace, a glare, a snort of derision, all were commonplace, but her smile, the smile he'd fallen in love with, the smile that even on his worst days filled him with warmth and peace, was sadly absent.

It didn't used to be this way. Their first five years of marriage had been bliss. They'd traveled. Spent countless nights at dinner parties and birthday celebrations. Their house rang with life and laughter, from game nights to Super Bowls and everything in between. And he'd loved every minute of it. He'd loved every minute of her.

But as the years passed, it all started seeming like too much work. The restaurant was so far away. The party would go till late, and he needed to be up early for work. Plane tickets were so expensive. Susan always wanted to go to the newest exhibit, see the latest movie, or simply jump in the car and drive somewhere, but Jim began to resent it. He'd still go to the party, take the vacation, see their friends, but it annoyed him more and more. And Susan knew it.

In the beginning, she tried to find a happy medium. She'd meet the girls so he could stay home. Choose places that were an easy drive away. Only ask him to go to the movie theater when it was a film she knew he'd like. But after a few years, even this seemed too much. He said no more, and Susan slowly stopped asking. He couldn't understand why she was so desperate to constantly be *doing* things, what sense of identity she was chasing with her endless activity, what hole she was trying to fill. She couldn't fathom why he seemed to want to be old before his time, to waste away at home, seemingly content to shut himself off from all the world had to offer. Why he was happy to miss out on so much fun and joy because of what amounted to minor annoyances. Resentment grew and grew, and the gulf between them widened.

Even so, they might have made it if not for Covid. They'd formed an uneasy peace, she living her life and he living his, and though the chasm between them never shrunk, at least it stopped growing. But now, unable to escape those things in each other that they both found so maddening, the gulf seemed too wide. It was as if she forever leaned away from him, even at this moment as she sat in a chair. Jim sighed. Maybe it'd gone too far. Maybe this was it. Maybe . . .

Ding-dong.

The chime of the doorbell shattered his reflection, both his and Susan's gaze flicking instantly to the front door, the wipe in his hand twitching as the urge to cleanse the now sullied metal rose up in him unbidden.

"Can you get that, please?" Susan asked, the acidity of her tone belying the politeness of her words.

"Well, I guess, but . . . ," Jim stammered, holding up the chips and the wipe, ". . . I'm kind of in the middle of something, so, um"

"You and your incessant cleaning!" Susan barked, leaping to her feet and slamming her book down on the chair cushion. "Fine. I wouldn't want to take you away from your favorite thing in the world. I'll get it."

Without waiting for a reply, Susan stalked around the corner. Though she was out of his sight, Jim could follow her journey by her stomping, angry footsteps as she strode to the door. They stopped a second before he heard the heavy wooden front door swing open. And in a pleasant voice—a tone he hadn't heard in weeks, if not months—Jim heard her say, "Can I help you?"

Unable to bear the kindness beyond his reach, Jim returned his attention to groceries. Putting down the chips and moving on to a carton of orange juice, he began his slow, thorough cleaning of every inch of the cardboard.

However, before he'd managed to wipe down even one side, he heard a scream from the door, a wail of terror, and the squealed word, "Jim!"

Sprinting toward the door, not even realizing that, in his haste, he still held the juice and wipe in his hands, Jim skidded down the hallway, his heart thundering in his chest. Rounding the corner, his rapid heartbeat stuttered at the sight in front of him.

His wife, tears in her eyes and mouth wide in fright, stood stiffly in front of a tall, gaunt man, his left arm wrapped around her, pulling her in close. But it was his right hand, the hand clenching the knife pressed into Susan's neck, that took Jim's full attention. The man's eyes bugged out, bloodshot and manic, and the hand that held the knife trembled. Jim could see he was barely more than a kid, early twenties at a push. His wispy mustache and pitiful attempt at a beard just barely hid the obvious signs of acne, and his long hair, pulled into a ponytail, looked to have never been washed. Licking his lips nervously, the kid's eyes darted here and there.

"Give me your money, man, or I cut this bitch's throat!" he yelled, the severity of his threat lessened by the squeak in his voice at the end. "I swear to god I'll do it. Don't mess with me!"

Never taking his eyes off the knife, Jim lowered his hands, his posture unthreatening. "Take it easy. Nobody has to get hurt. I can get you money. Just put the knife down."

"No way, old man," the kid snarled. "You get me my money right now or this bitch gets it! I'm not playing around! Don't test me!"

"Nobody's testing you," Jim cooed, his tone low and calm. "I'll give you all I've got. Just don't hurt her, okay? I'll give you everything. Just let me go get it." At a brusque nod from the assailant, Jim turned to grab his wallet.

"That's right," the boy crowed. "Fucking pussy," he sneered, spitting at the floor at Jim's retreating form . . . and making his fatal mistake.

Jim's shoulders, slumped before, straightened. His head rose. Turning on his heel, Jim glared at the invader and addressed him in a voice filled with thunder. "Did you just spit in my house?"

Taken aback by the sheer malice in Jim's eyes, the kid stumbled, pulling Susan with him. "Easy, man," he stammered. "Take it easy or I cut her throat! Don't come any closer. I swear I'll do it!" As if to prove his seriousness, he pressed the blade closer to Susan's neck, the sharp edge dimpling her fair skin.

Rather than being cowed by his threat, Jim's eyes blazed even hotter. His grip on the juice and wipe tightened till his knuckles shone bright white with the strain. In a voice throbbing with rage, Jim growled, "Did you, in the middle of a respiratory pandemic, just spit in my house? Without a goddamn mask?!"

"Chill, man," the attacker squeaked, thoroughly terrified now by Jim's ire. "Just chill." The hand holding the knife shook even harder.

"Are. You. Even. Vaccinated?" Jim ground out, biting off each word.

The sneer on the boy's face told Jim all he needed to know, but what he heard next clinched it. "Fuck no! I ain't putting that Bill Gates shit in my body."

And with that, Jim snapped. With a flick of his wrist, he flung the sodden wipe at the intruder, the sudden movement causing the assailant to jump back, releasing Susan.

And giving Jim the opening he needed.

Before a speck of fabric even hit the floor, Jim had the full juice carton behind his head. With a yell, he hurled the pulpy missile toward the thug who dared to invade his home. His aim was true, and before the kid knew what happened, four pounds of cardboard struck dead center on his forehead, knocking him back, reeling, into the still-open door behind him.

Jim leaped the distance between them, moving faster than he had in twenty years, and tackled the smaller man, blasting the air out of his lungs as they crashed into the linoleum of the entryway. Jim grabbed his shirt and lifted him up before smashing the goon's head back down onto the hard floor, bouncing as it hit.

As he lay there, dazed, Jim snatched a disposable mask from a box kept on a table by the door and mashed it down over the boy's face. Looping the straps around his skull, he knotted them quickly, securing the mask as tight as it would go. Then, he grabbed a fistful of the man's hair, yanking his head up. "How! Dare! You! Bring! Your! Unvaccinated! Unsanitized! Unclean! Self! Into! My! House! And! Threaten! My! Wife!" he screamed, punctuating each word with a fist to the man's face. His arm worked like a piston as he mashed the kid's features. With the mask over the intruder's face, Jim couldn't see his handiwork, but he heard the crunch of a nose breaking, the snap of teeth, and he watched the blue mask turn a dark crimson.

His breath coming in gasps, Jim continued to hammer at the man's face until a gentle touch to his shoulder and a whispered "That's enough, Jim" brought him back to his senses. With a last growl of disgust, Jim let the attacker's head drop to the tiled floor. The snuffly breathing proved he was still alive, but consciousness had long since fled.

Jim stumbled to his feet, his face still gripped in a fierce scowl. Again, he felt the soft touch. He turned toward it, toward that gentleness filled with warmth, toward Susan. Looking down into her face, the anger, rage, and pain fled from him, blown away by the love shining from his bride. "You were magnificent," she whispered, but her eyes said so much more. He'd fought for her, fought in a visceral and instinctive manner that he could now see was what she'd pined for, for years, and despaired of ever seeing.

For a moment, they were back at the beginning. Back to the time where everything he did delighted her. When everything she did made him love her more. A time when Sundays were for sleeping in and making love. When he rushed home from work every day just to spend one more second staring into the face of the person on this planet who made him happier than he ever dreamed possible. When the world was an adventure to be experienced together.

4

A SHAPE THAT HAS NO NAME

by Monica Wendel

Of course, the planes weren't going to explode on their way to JFK. But we liked watching them just in case.

"Don't you remember on 9/11, how they said that the buildings were bombed?" King asked.

"You remember 9/11?"

King had that look in his green eyes, dreamy yet determined, that I'd known since high school. The look when he declared that mushrooms were fertilized by dead fish and therefore were not vegetarian, much less vegan. Or the look when he announced that the Ant Liberation Front (ALF) was responsible for the release of Mr. Murphy's ant colonies.

King turned to face me, leaning on his side. "I remember 9/11. I remember tons of stuff from that age. When I was two, I fell down the stairs and peed blood in my diaper. I remember my mom changing it."

I didn't believe him, but I liked pretending. "There's another one," I said, pointing at the sky.

The plane was low, and in the early morning light, its belly looked soft and pink as a puppy's. King took my hand as I lifted it and pinned it gently to the roof. The black tar held April's warmth. I knew what he wanted: He wanted to fuck one more time before the sun came up. He liked racing against time, running late, and he liked almost being caught.

But King didn't ask me to have sex. He held my hand and looked at me for a long time as we listened to an ambulance call down Flushing Avenue on the way to Woodhull Hospital. We had been up all night together, and his eyes were as pink as the bellies of the planes. I listened to the unguarded silence the siren left behind and wondered what he was seeing. Then King spoke. "Belle, do you want to come to Marion with me?"

That was the thing about King. On the J train, he put his hands up my skirt, and in the Chicken Hut, he wanted me to touch him by the wall while everyone else danced to Big Freedia. And when I didn't want to, he told me about the girls who did want to, who had done it, at some point in college or high school, way before we started: Katie and Olivia, Meredith, and the other Belle. He liked telling me how good it was with them. Which was why he wanted to do it with me. "Who's Marion?"

"Illinois. Where Darius is," he said, his face hardening at the sound of his brother's name.

"The jail?"

"The prison."

"Oh," I said, searching his face and trying to understand why he was asking me. "Um, I don't know. When?"

King leaned over me and checked his phone. "He's being released in six weeks, and it's a two-day drive. We'd leave on May 20."

"I can't," I said, relieved. "I have my final teaching practicum then."

"So do it online," King said, loosening his grip on my hand.

"The schools will be open by then," I said. "Right? I'm pretty sure I'll have to go in. Do you want to ask, like, Tatiana?" Tatiana was my roommate, and besides being prettier than me, she was also much, much smarter.

"Maybe, Belle." He checked something on his phone. "It could be, you know. Kind of an adventure."

I took a breath and tried to connect myself to him. My head never worked right around King; I was too swept up in the ocean of him. We'd met in high school and orbited each other for years, never quite part of the same friend group. I'd see his green eyes across a flood of people in the cafeteria, and something deep inside me would bend; water shaping itself over the continental shelf. "Maybe," I said. "Are you sure it wouldn't be weird?"

"Why would it be weird?" King pulled his shirt on. "I should get going."

"Okay." Another siren sang down Flushing. It felt like they never stopped. "I'll see you later."

King left, and I logged onto Google Classroom. My students didn't have the resources to log on to the classroom at certain times, so everything was asynchronous.

There wasn't much to do. Yesterday, in the bitterness of isolation, I had made a week's worth of worksheets and uploaded them. I'd also made a video about how to make an abstract drawing and uploaded it to YouTube and Google Classroom. It wasn't clear if any of them had watched it. If they even could watch it.

How long would this last? I looked out the window onto the driveway, feeling inside me the loneliness that only the classroom took away. There was a buzzing warmth to elementary schools, to kids, that I couldn't find anywhere else.

And so I missed the kids—not just missed them, but missed them physically. I missed their skinny arms and the way their bellies paunched out. I missed the way they couldn't say Rs, and I missed the way they talked while they ate, with their hands pinwheeling and their eyes growing huge with concentration.

But I didn't have any theory to back up my feelings. King, Tatiana, the people they introduced me to—they all stood for something. They all had purpose. They believed in anarcho-feminism, and ecoprimitivism; they knew the intricacies of squatting. They could tell you what was wrong, and their theories could explain why, and then they had a solution. Meanwhile, I was scrounging for new markers and debating the best size of crayons for three-year-old fingers. I was wiping muffin crumbs off sticky faces and giving hugs. I didn't know if I was fixing any problems or making them worse; I didn't know if I was showing kids love or teaching them how to obey a fucked-up institution.

The closest I came to believing in something was believing in King. Following him into dumpsters. Helping him organize fundraisers for his brother. Serving drinks at the performance space at the John Bosch House.

Tatiana interrupted my wallowing. "Hey," she said, leaning against the door. "You working right now?"

I looked at the screen. The cursor blinked on an empty Google Doc. My whole fucking life depended on Google. "I don't know," I said. "I was thinking about making a podcast that the kids could listen to."

"Come to my office with me," Tatiana said, her Russian accent as crisp as my parents'. "I'm going to 3D-print masks."

I stared at her for a second. She wore all black and dyed her dirty blond hair black, too. But you wouldn't know that unless you lived with her. I was the only one who saw her roots. "Seriously?"

She nodded. "Hammer is providing us with the supplies. You can use his bike because it has a trailer. We'll ride the plastics there, print them using the code, and give them to Woodhull."

I looked at her and blinked, wondering for a moment what it would be like to be heroic. To be Hammer and know how to steal from Home Depot. To be Tatiana and know how to 3D-print masks. To be King and drive across the continent to pick up Darius. To be anyone, anybody, but myself. "Are we taking the Williamsburg Bridge or the Manhattan?"

"Williamsburg," she said.

"Sure," I said, closing out of the Google Doc. "Just let me get dressed."

We called our house the John Bosch House because of some tiled lettering on the front stoop, but it was really two houses. The main house had seven bedrooms over three floors, a classic Brooklyn brownstone. We lived in the garage behind and to the side of it—Tatiana and I upstairs and Hammer downstairs, next to the performance space. Before the pandemic, it had felt like one house. In the mornings, I'd prop my door open before leaving to student teach, and Hammer would slip in at 6:00 a.m., just as he was coming home. We took turns bringing home dumpstered juice and Whole Foods treats.

But with the pandemic, we had cleaved. Or maybe I had.

Tatiana and I unlocked our bikes from the performance space and pushed off down Willoughby Avenue. We rode slowly, pacing ourselves, pulling the heavy supplies on trailers on our bikes. The Williamsburg Bridge crested, and without speaking, we nodded at each other and stopped at the top.

The J train passed by, rattling the bridge. I hoped no one else would be riding near us. What if someone came too close and we breathed in their air? Below, the water was choppy and green; above, the sky gray and damp.

Tatiana took out a water bottle, and I checked my phone. We had one downhill to get to Delancey, then it was flat crosstown, then the hills of the Upper West Side, then Tatiana's office at Columbia. Tatiana noticed me looking at my phone. "Did you see what King posted?" she asked.

"No," I said, my stomach sinking. I opened up Instagram. "*Photo dump*," his caption read. I scrolled through the ten photos. There were the bare branches of the tree you could see from outside my window, not filtered black-and-white, but looking desaturated in a cloudy sky. Empty Times Square.

And Tatiana.

Tatiana on the other side of a dumpster, their hands reaching for the same apple. Tatiana on our roof, staring up at the planes. A screenshot of Tatiana facilitating a prison support Zoom meeting. I swiped right and right again. Finally, I appeared on the last slide—our ankles, tangled together. "When did you guys hang out on the roof?"

Tatiana put her phone away and closed her water bottle. "I'm not sure. It might have been when you were in Florida."

Fucking Florida. I had my cousin's wedding in West Palm Beach in February, during midwinter break. "Oh, that's cool." My hands were shaking. I rubbed them on my shorts and stared at the holes in my black tights.

"Is it, though?" Tatiana laughed. "We went to the fundraiser at the Knockdown Center. It took forever to get back. The bus never came, and we had to walk the whole way home."

I looked down at the East River. King must have slept over; where else would he have slept? But did he sleep on the floor or in Tatiana's bed?

It always felt easy to distance myself from my body while having sex with King. It felt better that way. He was attentive but also precise; I couldn't help feeling, while we were having sex, that I could be anyone; that the basic anatomy was the same from person to person and what he was doing wasn't so different.

But sleeping in bed together felt different. That was when I could look at him and see him vulnerable, his eyelids turning purplish. The moments when he didn't have to be King of anything. It took a long time before he fell asleep with me. I loved the gentleness of his breathing and how he slept with his arms crossed, as though he were covering himself.

The thought of him having sex with Tatiana was not so bad. I had already accepted it. But the thought of him sleeping in bed with her felt like a betrayal.

I kicked the pedal of Hammer's bike and watched it spin in the air, moving but going nowhere. "I might go to Illinois with him. To pick up his brother from prison."

Tatiana nodded slowly. "You better prepare yourself. Prison is another world."

"I know," I said, even though I didn't.

She leaned over the bridge. "What about your students?"

I laughed an empty laugh. It sounded more like a cough, which then, of course, freaked me out. "I didn't just cough," I said. The waters lapped at the feet of the bridge. "I haven't really been able to get in touch with them. They're too young to have laptops or phones. Some of them have tablets. There's not really much you can do through a screen."

"You just seem so happy when you're teaching." For some reason, her accent kicked in strong, and each syllable was musical. "Is there any other way you can connect with them?"

"I don't know." And it felt then like my students had sailed off somewhere, had been abandoned. That I had abandoned them. I shook my head. "Yeah, maybe. I'll try to figure something out." I put my foot on the pedal. "Wanna keep riding?"

"The *world* won't end," said King. "Humans will end."

We were in a lush Pennsylvania hollow, one of those places where the Allegheny Mountains dip into valley. "You don't think that humans will destroy the earth?" I asked. The green outside was encompassing but fragile, a mist that might dissolve at any moment.

King scoffed at this. "With any luck, humans will kill each other, and the dolphins will take over."

"Unless we kill all the dolphins first." I gazed at his profile. "Wait, really? You think the world will be okay?"

"If you were on a life raft, and it was you and a cow and two other people, who would you throw off the life raft?"

I knew this was a trick question. "The cow."

"See?" He thumped the steering wheel with his hand. "But the cow won't kill anyone. The people on the life raft would kill animals. The cow wouldn't."

"That's true," I said. "So do you not like people?"

He shrugged. "I don't think their lives are worth more than any other lives."

The rolling hills were making me nauseated—that, and I was expecting my period. Today or, if not today, tomorrow. We'd been on the road now for five hours, and we were making terrible time. First, King was late picking me up. Then he wanted to see the field hospital set up in Central Park. Then we hit construction outside of Harrisburg. "I have to puke."

"Again?"

Right. That was the other thing making us late.

The car rumbled to the side of the road, and I sprinted out to the tree line. Only bile was left in my stomach. I sat down, dizzy, and took a sip of ginger ale. Tears came to my eyes, but I brushed them away. I was supposed to be helping King, not having him take care of me.

My hands shook. I felt like shit.

"You okay?" King asked when I made it back to the car.

I nodded. "Sorry."

42

"It's okay," he said, but his voice was flat.

He pulled out onto I-76, and I willed my stomach to calm down. "What were we talking about?"

"I dunno," he said, chewing his lip, suddenly looking worried.

"I'm sorry," I said again. "It's just— I haven't been in a car in a long time—and—"

"It's not that." He took his hat off and put it on the dashboard.

"Oh," I said, wondering then what it was.

"Did you know that Darius has a job already?"

It was weird to hear King call his brother Darius. This whole time, he'd existed as part of King, like one of King's limbs—or a phantom limb. Missing but felt. Always present but invisible. "Wasn't that part of his release? Like the condition of release?"

King's face was tight and twisted. "He's doing PR for the ACLU."

"Isn't that—isn't that—" I took a sip of ginger ale. "I mean, isn't that a good thing?"

"It's not fair," said King.

"Of course not," I said reassuringly. "He should never have been in prison."

"Not that." King sped up and passed a double tractor trailer. "That now he has a job. And I'm still stuck in the same place I've always been."

"You want a job?"

"He's coming out of prison, and he's got a support network; he's got people rooting for him; he's got me coming to pick him up. And I've spent the last three years making all that happen. What do I have to show for it? Nothing."

I thought back to the benefit show I had helped King put on in the performance space. Booking bands, buying alcohol, counting bills at the end of the night. And that was on top of King's GoFundMe. "You've done so much for him."

"My parents' house is double mortgaged to pay for his lawyer. They do everything for him. And I'm expected to do more."

"I'm sorry," I said lamely.

"Sometimes I wonder what my life would look like if it had been me in prison."

"Are you . . . jealous? That he's in jail?"

I didn't mean for my tone to sound accusatory, but King grew silent, a silence I could only read as anger. Finally, he spoke. "I thought you'd understand, Belle." We rolled over more hills. "And it's prison, not jail."

"I'm sorry."

"Stop apologizing."

I didn't know what to say to that. There was nothing to say. I looked out for a signpost, any sign, besides mile markers. I remembered when the feds were first investigating Darius. They subpoenaed all the electronics in King's house, so he lost his laptop our senior year of high school. He had to write his papers in the library. He never told me that; I found it out through friends.

And that was how all the information came. Rumors, drips, texts. Sometimes facts drifted to the surface: an article in NPR about Darius's case and what it meant for the Earth First! movement or King quoted in the *New York Times* about his brother's gentle nature.

"If I had been in prison instead of him, what would we be?"

"What would . . . who be?"

"Us," said King. "Would we be together?"

I stared out the window, but the mountains gave me no answers. Were we together now? But I knew what he meant. He wasn't my partner, but he wasn't my nothing, either. We were something, even if we hadn't defined it. I tried to picture myself organizing a GoFundMe, planning a concert fundraiser, posting pictures and updates from prison. I tried to picture myself being that person—King's person. I tried to picture myself and King together without his physical presence. Without sleeping in bed together and waking up together. Without his fingers on my thigh and my hands reaching.

Would I have waited for him? For how long?

Would I go three years without sex? Would I schedule my life around his phone calls? Would I go to Marion, Illinois, every other month to see him for a few hours two days in a row?

I glanced over at King, his olive skin and strong features. His parents were outsiders in Belle Harbor, Persian Jews who somehow didn't make it over the Gil Hodges Bridge to Brooklyn. My parents, the few times they saw him, asked me if he was an Arab. I decided to lie. "Yeah," I said. "You'd be getting sick of me sending you letters," I joked. "And books."

King relaxed into the seat cushions. Then he reached out and took my hand as I asked him to pull over, once again.

That night, King wanted to have sex in the hotel room, but I was spotting. "It's light," I said, relieved.

"I don't care," he said.

And then he was bloody, and I pretended it was my first time.

King fell asleep, and I touched the blood that had flowed out from me when we had sex. It didn't look like normal period blood. *Have my period but the blood looks weird*, I googled. Nothing about pregnancy came up. So I was probably not pregnant. I put my phone away and looked at King's face.

The first time I slipped into a dumpster with King, I couldn't believe the sense of possibility. Here was capitalism, wealth; here were eight-dollar juices still sealed. And just beyond, I could make out the Manhattan skyline.

If he had been in prison, not Darius, then I would have a sense of purpose, I thought. I would know what was right and what was wrong. Because right now, I couldn't figure it out. I wasn't an ecoprimitivist; I didn't want a world where kids died from cancer because we were against technology. And I wasn't an anarchist; hadn't Occupy Wall Street dissolved? Some of the older activists had been part of that, and when they talked about it, I wondered, if it was so wonderful, so powerful, why it hadn't changed anything. Why we weren't doing it again.

And I wasn't a socialist, either. Because the services that were supposed to help my students hurt them—like the homeless shelters and ACS. In Bed-Stuy, when I saw those wheat-pasted black signs that said, *They separate kids from their parents in Brooklyn, too*—I found myself nodding. Fuck liberalism. Fuck the idea that the government is going to help you.

But who was I if I didn't believe in anything? It made me nothing. A shadow of King. A sidekick. A housewife in training decorating a Pinterest-ready classroom.

King rolled over in his sleep, and I looked at his body. I felt addicted to it, wanting him even as he slept. Was my emptiness how he liked me—why he liked me? Maybe this was the answer. He could fill me, over and over again, and pour me out, and I would fit the shapes that he wanted.

I went to the bathroom. The blood was already gone. I tried not to think about what that meant. If it meant anything at all.

"Sir, I cannot let you in." The prison guard slapped King's driver's license down. "This license expired two years ago." Her mask hung loosely around her chin.

King's jaw set. I watched a vein pop out of his forehead. "We need to secure his release."

"Sir." The word was a whole sentence, saying everything. "I cannot release Inmate 56835 to you without a valid form of identification. If you cannot provide me with identification, there is nothing that I can do."

"I have something," I said. "I have ID."

The guard swung her head slowly. "Ma'am, you are not on the approved list."

King scrolled through his phone. "Here is a copy of my passport," he said, holding the phone up to the plexiglass barrier.

The guard's eyes flickered over the screen. "I cannot accept a copy of a ID. You need the original."

King's eyes bored into hers. "We drove two days to get here."

"I'm sorry to hear that, sir." She did not sound sorry.

"Is there any way I can get on the approved list?" I asked. King rolled his eyes. I guess I said something dumb.

The guard almost looked sympathetic. "Ma'am, the list needed to be submitted six weeks in advance in order for the Department of Corrections to run the necessary background check."

"So what now?" King broke in.

The guard looked at me, and I tried to look as harmless as possible. "If no one is authorized for the release, then Darius will depart today in a prison van for the Greyhound station and will be provided with a ticket to his destination as well as forty dollars to cover incidentals."

"Thank you," I said. "I really appreciate it."

King visibly flinched. "Where's the Greyhound station?"

"It's fine," I said, touching his arm. "I can find it on my phone."

"You have a blessed day, ma'am," said the guard. "Next!"

We walked out of the prison into the blistering sunlight. Endless fields stretched around us, the earth made industrial. Monotonous fields of corn and alfalfa. Feed for animals, fertilized by—by what? Some chemical brew from Monsanto. I hated the Midwest. I searched on my phone. "Here," I said, pushing my phone into King's hands. "The Greyhound station is only a ten-minute drive. We can go there and wait for your brother."

King dropped his head into his hands. "Fuck. Fuck!" He kicked a tire.

"It's okay," I said. "Look. We'll go to the bus station. It can't be that big. We'll find Darius. We'll bring him the food we brought. And we'll drive straight home."

King spoke through clenched teeth. "You mean drop him off at the halfway house."

"Yeah. Exactly. And the halfway house is right near my place. So you'll be able to see him . . . whenever." I shook the brown bag we had, which unfortunately sounded like I was shaking treats at a dog. "His food is right here. He'll be really happy to see us."

"This better work, Belle."

How is this my fault? "We don't have another choice."

At the Greyhound station, we waited, we waited, we waited. I stood outside, hoping that sunlight killed Covid, trying not to think of the crowded air of the prison van. And then the van appeared, and I ran inside and grabbed King, and he ran out.

The men filed out of the vehicle wearing nondescript clothes. The clothes they came in with—blue jeans, T-shirts, some of them carrying sweatshirts and winter coats, wearing Timberland boots. They were mixed, some Black, some white, some Hispanic, some looking Middle Eastern. And then King took a step forward, and there was Darius. They hugged, and I glimpsed his face before it disappeared into the warmth of King's shoulder.

The hug lasted too long. King was supporting Darius.

Darius lifted his face, and King spoke. "Darius, this is my friend Belle. She drove with me."

"Hi," I said, waving one hand a little bit.

Darius nodded at me. His face looked like King's, but white and gaunt while King's was olive and filled out. His breathing was shallow, open-mouthed. "I remember you." His neck strained. It took a moment for him to fill his lungs with air to breathe out his words. "You wrote me letters from the tree."

"Um, no," I said. "That wasn't me."

He nodded again, and King steered him toward the car. "Here's some food, man."

Darius looked inside approvingly. "This looks great. Thanks."

But he didn't eat any. He sat in the car and put the bag by his feet, then leaned his head back.

We drove east. Sometimes Darius coughed. There was a strange energy in the car. I had expected to feel love, warmth, closeness, gratitude—something big, something to fill up the space. Instead, the car felt more empty. This was it? This was their reunion?

"Just let me know if you want to stop, man," said King.

"Thanks," said Darius. And then they were silent for another five miles, punctuated only by Darius's coughs.

"We were planning on driving straight through," King said, breaking the silence.

"Sure," said Darius.

From the back seat, I tried to see Darius's breathing. And then I couldn't stand it anymore. "Darius," I asked through my mask, "do you have Covid?"

He shrugged. "I got sick about a month ago. The doctor gave me some cough drops. I didn't take them, though. They contained honey."

"And—you've been sick this whole time?" King was trying to make eye contact with me in the rearview mirror, but I resisted. Darius didn't say anything. "Darius, can you breathe?"

He gave a depressing chuckle.

Now I found King's eyes. "King, maybe we should go to the hospital."

King tightened his grip on the wheel. "No."

"Why?"

Darius spoke. "Belle, it's really nice of you." He paused to breathe. "I don't have health insurance."

"So what," I said. "It's your *life*."

"Hospitals are just there to make money," said King. "They don't do anything except watch you die."

"King, my mom is a doctor."

He paused, then said icily, "Don't you think that proves my point?"

I flinched. "Fuck you."

"You don't know what you're talking about."

"I do about this," I said. "Darius, you need help."

"I'm fine," he mumbled.

"See?" said King. "He's fine."

"He's not fine."

Still the fields swooshed past us. My hands were shaking. "King, he can't breathe. Millions of people are dying from Covid. Okay, maybe not millions. But you've heard the sirens. He needs to see a doctor."

"You think he's going to see a doctor in the hospital, Belle? No. He's going to die in the waiting room just like all those other people."

"Not if we go to the hospital here. If we wait until we get back to the city, yeah, that might happen. But the hospitals here are empty."

"I'm not going to drop my brother off to die somewhere."

Darius shook his head back and forth. "Guys, guys. Let's not fight."

"Fine. Let's stop at a CVS."

"What's a CVS going to do?"

A pulse oximeter, I thought. *A thermometer. A pharmacist who can call an ambulance, and then he'll have no choice but to go.* "I have to puke," I declared, and the car screeched to the shoulder.

Okay. I actually didn't this time. But I walked away from the car toward a field of alfalfa that smelled like burning and leaned down. I waited, hoping that this would work. And eventually it did, because King came out. "You okay, Belle?"

I wiped my face and looked up at him. "Yeah. Are you mad at me?"

"Why do you always think I'm mad at you?" His hand reached for my side; I curved into it. I was watery near him. I leaned into the pressure there, about to apologize, but stopped. We kissed, and I hoped he couldn't taste my lie. "I love you," he whispered.

His hands moved over my waist and hips, and I looped my fingers around the back of his neck, making a net that would keep him near me. "I love you, too," I whispered.

"Listen. I know you're worried about Darius. He's going to be okay."

I looked toward the car as though I could see something there. Of course I couldn't. "King, what if we get to the halfway house and they don't let him in? Then he'll have to go to Woodhull."

"That's not going to happen, Belle." He hooked a finger between my shirt and jeans, let it rest on the bare skin. If I was water, he was lightning, and together we were an ocean made electric. "Trust me."

I sometimes hated King and sometimes loved King, but I always, always wanted to fuck King. I searched his face for the answer to the question I hadn't asked, the question my body was asking. He closed his eyes and kissed me again. Every time we had sex—no, every time we kissed—no, every time he looked at me, I thought it was going to be the last time. I thought there would never be another moment ever again. This time, when we kissed, his hand unbuttoned my pants, and I leaned into him, like a ship opening to salt water. Something breaking, something beautiful, and then a storm.

We walked back to the car together, hip to hip. Darius was sprawled out in the back seat, his head leaning back against the window. "You okay?" I asked him.

He gave a silent thumbs-up.

"Mind if I drive?" I asked King.

"I should probably drive."

I looked at Darius, but his eyes were closed. "What about your brother?"

"What do you mean?"

"I'll drive and you can help him," I said, getting into the front seat before King could stop me.

I pulled out from the shoulder and onto the road. King dozed in the front seat: Like always, I was energized after orgasm, while he was sleepy. There had to be a hospital somewhere. Didn't farmers get injured all the time? Losing fingers, chemical burns, stuff like that? I wished I knew something, anything.

The road unspooled before us, humming and empty. Straight and flat. We were nowhere. I drove ten, fifteen, twenty miles, waiting for a sign for a hospital, and then, when there was no sign, waiting for a sign for an exit. There was only the humming of the road. And then there was more humming because my phone was buzzing. "Hey, Tatiana," I said, pressing the buttons on the car's audio screen. "You're on speakerphone."

King shook himself awake.

"How's it going?" she asked. It was always strange hearing Americanisms in her Russian accent, the same way I felt when I heard my father say "like" in a sentence.

King glanced into the back seat. I watched concern flicker over his face—the first moments of remembering where we were and realizing that things might not be okay. "We got Darius," he said.

"Is it okay for me to post an update for the GoFundMe?" Tatiana asked.

"Sure," said King.

There was an awkward silence. "What do you want it to say?" Tatiana prodded. I could practically see her in her room in Brooklyn, fingers poised over the keyboard.

"We're on our way home with Darius," I said. "Thanks for all your support?"

"Sure," said Tatiana. "Send a picture over, too."

New pictures meant more shares, which meant more posts, which meant more funds. I looked in the rearview mirror. Darius had not stirred. "Darius? Darius, are you awake?"

His shoulders lifted as he tried to breathe: a gasping inhale, then exhale.

"Thanks, Tatiana," King said, then hung up.

"Why'd you hang up?"

"Why'd you try to wake up Darius?"

"He's not even in good enough shape for us to take a picture of him. And I'm supposed to pretend everything is fine?"

"No one is asking you to pretend anything, Belle. Why do you feel like you always have to pretend?"

I kept my hands steady. "Look, I'm getting off at the next exit. Darius needs help."

King turned in the passenger's seat and reached his hand out to Darius. "Darius, how are you doing, man? You okay?"

"Don't bring me—to the hospital—," Darius exhaled.

The fields moved past, monotonous, green, unnamed. "You're

really sick, Darius," I said. "We're trying to help you."

"Don't leave me," he said.

I tore my eyes from the road and met his in the rearview mirror and nearly hit a discarded, shredded-up tire.

"Sorry!" I yelped. Uncertainty spun within me as fast as the car's wheels. "Darius, what about Urgent Care? They won't keep you there."

We passed some white low-slung buildings: egg farming. I tried not to think of the horrors contained within, the birds birthing, over and over again, pushing out almost-life ceaselessly, white moons dropping from their bodies. King spoke. "They can't cure Covid. They won't do anything there."

Straight ahead through the windshield: a brilliant sky, aching with spring. Below: the unceasing green fields that at first glance are beautiful, but, closer, are another factory, industrial corn and alfalfa, poisoned earth, poisoned leaves, poisoned insects, poisoned weeds, poisoned farmers—and us, in the hermetically sealed car, breathing in Darius's poisoned breath. The unnatural landscape, natural disease. Or was it the other way around?

And suddenly, there it was. I was in danger. King was in danger. And—was there—in me—also in danger—

"We have to go to CVS," I said. "I need a pregnancy test."

King leaped up so quickly that the car tilted, his strength unbalancing our metal and rubber ship sailing across the continent. But he said nothing as I took the next exit, pulled to the shoulder, and googled "pharmacy locations" as the corn waved at us in its loneliness.

It turns out you don't pee on the stick. You're supposed to pee in a cup and put the stick in it. Just another way the media has lied to us!

While I waited, I checked my texts. "*Send picture for update when you can,*" Tatiana wrote. There were also Instagram notifications and an email from my professor confirming that my student teaching practicum was submitted. "*I hope this email finds you well. In these trying times . . .*" I scrolled past it.

I took my phone out and took a picture of the pee cup with the stick in it and sent it to Tatiana. "*Not for update. :(,*" I wrote.

She called immediately. "Are you pregnant?"

I was sitting on the bathroom floor of a Starbucks while Darius and King waited in the car. Neither stubborn boy would agree to Urgent Care, but I got them to at least stop at a CVS, where we bought acetaminophen for Darius's fever and a humidifier for his cough. A humidifier that could do absolutely nothing in a car. I scooted my butt closer to the cup and tried to peer in. "Yeah," I said, poking at the stick.

"I see a line." I waited for that feeling to come back, the feeling in the car with the open sky and the knowing, but I didn't feel anything.

"You'll be okay," Tatiana said. "Do they have Plan B there?"

I dumped the pee in the toilet and flushed. "Hold on a sec," I said and took a picture of the stick. The line was really pink—more magenta. Did that mean something? Then I threw that out, too. "Sorry, I couldn't hear you."

"Belle"—I could see her running her hands through her hair, twisting it up, her nervous habit—"whose is it?"

"What do you mean?" I asked, turning on the water. "It's mine."

A Russian curse on the other end of the line, then laughing. And then I was laughing, too, and crying.

"Belle! This is why you do not use dumpstered condoms. No. More. Dumpster. Condoms."

I couldn't tell if I was crying because I was laughing or laughing because I was crying. "Do you really think that King gets his condoms from a dumpster?"

"Probably! From where else would he get them?"

"I don't know. The store?" I wiped my nose on the back of my wrist. "I guess I always figured that he shoplifted them."

"And you're not on birth control."

It was half a question and half a statement. I thought about trying to explain to Tatiana how precarious all of it felt. My relationship with King. If it was even a relationship. Which it was not. How I was afraid that if I took any step toward him, the whole edifice would shatter. And so going on birth control would have come too close to promising myself that it would happen again. That each time wasn't the last time. "I just figured that . . . like, that it wouldn't . . . I don't know. I didn't know he would still. . . ." I swallowed. "Birth control takes like a month to work."

"Mmm," Tatiana murmured. "Well . . . now you're fucked."

"I know!" I said, wiping tears from my face. "What the fuck!"

Tatiana dissolved into riotous laughter.

I smiled at the face I saw in the mirror, blurry with tears. "Hold on. I have to wash my face."

"I'll get Plan B for you at the pharmacy," Tatiana said. "You don't need a prescription."

"Thanks. Yeah, it would be a pain to get it here." Someone knocked on the door. "I have to get going. I miss you."

"Wait," she said. "How many weeks pregnant are you?"

"Umm, I was supposed to get my period yesterday. So that makes me . . . two weeks pregnant?"

"Let me check," she said. "That doesn't sound right." I stared at the door. "Belle, you're four weeks pregnant."

"No, I'm not," I said. I pulled up the calendar on my phone. "I had my period four weeks ago."

"You start counting from the first day of your last period," she said. "I'm reading it on WebMD."

I started laughing again. "I hate this," I said. "Okay. So can I still take Plan B?" I wiped a few more tears from my eyes, and then I started crying a lot.

"Let me look this up. I don't think so. I'll call you back."

"Thanks," I said, wiping the tears away. I wasn't sobbing or anything like that. Just a lot of water everywhere, running down my face into my chest and shirt, snot on my sleeves. And then, even though it was so, so, gross, I slid down until I was lying on my back on the tile floor. I put my thumbs in my belly button and pointed my index fingers down to my legs, and I felt my hands on my body and imagined what was growing inside me.

It's not like I was struggling with a choice. That would mean that I had a decision to make. But there was no decision: I'd have to get rid of it. I just couldn't put it in the words I knew. It didn't feel like reproductive freedom. It didn't feel like control over my own body. It felt, instead, like someone had made the choice for me by ensuring that I wouldn't be eligible for paid time off until I'd worked a certain amount of months. And that day care was too expensive. The world I lived in didn't want me to have a baby, and so I wouldn't have it. I breathed in and felt my low belly rise and fall, and I cried a little more for the poppy seed inside me, splitting and growing and splitting and growing. "I'm sorry," I said to it. It didn't matter if it was alive or not. You can love something that's not alive. You can love your future.

And then I realized that there was still one life I had left to save. One life, that is, besides my own.

I carried some ice water back to the car for King and Darius. "Sorry I took so long," I said. "It's positive."

"Congratulations," said Darius at the same time King said, "Oh, wow," and took his hat off.

"Crazy, huh?" I said, plopping next to King, who was sitting in the driver's seat. "I'll take care of it when we get back."

"Do you need me to do anything?" asked King. He looked worried.

"No, that's okay. Tatiana is going to—" King's expression froze me. "What?"

"Tatiana?"

The car suddenly felt very hot. It was too much to look at King, so I looked at Darius. "Yeah. Um. She called while I was in the bathroom. So . . ."

"You told Tatiana before you told me?"

The pain in King's voice thudded. "I—" The truth was, it hadn't even crossed my mind to tell King first. *"Whose is it?"* Tatiana had asked, not knowing that I was sleeping with King, and my dumbass answer: *"It's mine."*

"I'm sorry. I'm such a dumbass."

"Fucking shit, Belle! I'm not calling you a dumbass."

"It's yours," I said. "Like, it's definitely yours."

"What are you talking about? Of course it's mine. Who else's would it possibly be?"

"We shouldn't be having this conversation," I said, desperate to stay in the parking lot but also desperate to escape. "I'm going to have an abortion as soon as I can."

"You're going to kill it?" King got out of the car and walked away. He wiped his face and stared at the sky as though drinking in the blue.

And then the sirens came. Slow at first, far away. They pulled into the parking lot. I climbed out of the car and waved my arms, directing them over. "Here," I said, when the EMTs came out. "This is Darius Kneiger. He's having trouble breathing."

King followed behind the ambulance while I stayed at the Starbucks, drinking an oat milk latte and drawing. My pen followed the same instructions I'd given my students, that abstract drawing video I'd posted in another lifetime, and for the first time, I listened to my own voice.

Look: Here's a room of bubbles. A room of poppy seeds. A room of triangles, of rectangles, of squares, of hearts.

I call him King; his parents named him Eric Kneiger. Two names for the same life.

Here's a shape that has no name. And another and another.

Here's a map of my pain. Here is my body; here is my phone. Here is the *Communist Manifesto* and Adam Smith. "A Modest Proposal" of tiny bodies. There's my father's green card; there's my mother's asylum application. The seas rise around Belle Harbor. The virus sweeps the streets of New York City until they empty.

This whole time, I had been thinking that I needed a theory to make sense of the world, thinking that I couldn't decide anything. But I'd forgotten that existing was an action. The act of living can be a rebellion.

For a long time, I sat, letting the pen lead my hand. Letting the ink decide what to draw. I wondered if Darius wanted his life saved. If King did. I touched the drawing. But the only answers there were the ones I created. The only place I would be able to find an answer was the place inside myself.

5

UNWELCOMED GUEST

by Jocelyn Bystrom

B efore the first light of dawn, he crept. Seeking warmth and comfort from a mid-December rainstorm he padded along his nightly foraging route in the early hours after midnight. Whiskers alerted him to a pool of warmth coming through an unexpected opening. With poor eyesight he trusted his acute hearing to detect danger. Not wanting to fall prey to the owl who frequented the nearby sycamore or become a hearty meal to something slithering. He listened with prominent, thinly furred ears for any movement in the underbrush. There might be a predator lying in wait, poised and ready to devour. Slimmer than his brown cousin, he'd just started fending for himself after leaving the nest. He was nervous, panicked, and his heart pounded in his chest.

Suspicious by nature, he tentatively explored the gap. Heat pushed outward from the entry, invited curiosity, and offered shelter from the elements.

Might his next meal be found within? The thought of bedding down protected from colder evenings and mornings of a Los Angeles winter was a summons that commanded. He wouldn't let this opportunity pass without at the very least checking it out.

Several intriguing scents piqued his curiosity as the air passed the patch of skin rich with smell receptors on his raised nose. His whiskers detected the aromas of barbecued meat, dog feces, and the finest morsels his kind considered fine dining. Was that fresh fruit? his neural receptors asked. This new location offered the welcoming prospect of a next meal, and additionally, a cozy place to bed down for a creature of the night. Lured through the opening by curiosity and instinct, he made sure to leave fecal droppings along the new route. He wanted to be sure, in the event of an emergency, that his escape route would be remembered.

Ascertaining no further movements, he proceeded with caution. He didn't want to activate any motion sensors, like those he'd set off around the corner earlier, triggering brightness and momentary blindness. Feeling optimistically safe, he scurried inside, an uninvited guest.

What's this? she wondered as she knelt for closer inspection, believing she spotted a crumb or scrap, fallen and unnoticed earlier to the kitchen flooring. She became hypervigilant while trapped at home, like a caged animal, for these past months of the countrywide lockdown. She'd decluttered and learned to play the guitar, but the walls were closing in.

Working from her new remote home office, she missed her daily commute into the heart of Los Angeles each morning behind the wheel of her new Toyota Prius hybrid. She'd usually been lost in thought while driving from the mountainous suburb along the seacoast as she headed downtown.

Who could have predicted a pandemic would cage and silence a fiercely independent, adventurous lover of life who'd been on a clear path to management? She paced within the confines of what once had been her sanctuary and wondered if a vaccine would be found anytime soon and enable a return to her typical day in the life as a laser-focused working gal well on her way to launching a successful career.

She wanted a life that provided escape from quiet suburbia to the energy of a vibrant global metropolis that pulsed with nightlife, theaters, museums, shopping, and attractions on Hollywood Boulevard and was home to baseball's elite at Dodgers Stadium.

Memories of evenings spent in the city with friends, going to clubs and parties, or catching a baseball game from behind home plate were clouded by smoke from forest fires burning with reckless abandon while the sun glowed red and rippled.

Following summer's scorching temperatures, leaves had fallen, Halloween costumes hung unworn in closets, holiday shoppers shopped online, and gift giving was completed by post rather than in person. Only days remained before she'd ring in the New Year.

Luxuriating in the warm embrace of abundance, he couldn't believe his luck. He was able to fill his belly, satisfy his thirst, and find a perfect place to bed down. He could stash a more than adequate food supply. He could rest easy with the knowledge of an amassed fortune of kibble cleverly stored in the shadows behind storage boxes blanketed with a light layer of dust.

Headed downstairs to the basement and chest freezer to retrieve ground beef she needed to make her evening meal, she was reminded when she observed what had been forgotten, the still-opened sliding glass door. She judged herself harshly for her clumsy forgetfulness and, without thought, swore in anger at her stupidity.

She'd been in a hurry and easily distractible of late. Who hadn't been on edge during these strange days of uncertainty as the world held its collective breath amid a global pandemic?

Everyone, it seemed, was taking the time to squeeze in at least one of the many New Year's Eve good luck traditions. She, like many, made resolutions to ring in the New Year with utterly civilized goals, in hope that better fortunes lay ahead in 2021.

Ollie, her cocker spaniel, brought her attention back to the present as he sat scratching at the glass patio door, hoping to go outside and play fetch. Opening the patio door, she'd thought, *I'll be right back.* Then she'd headed out to frolic with the dog and then pulled a few newly sprouted dandelions attempting a hostile takeover. Standing to stretch after crouching, she looked up at her wilted hanging baskets up on the top deck needing to be watered.

Climbing the outside stairs to the sundeck, she reached for and filled the watering can at the outside tap and quenched her winter hanging baskets. *Thank goodness*, she thought. Her prized flowering baskets wouldn't wither and die.

Inclement weather systems had appeared one after another this past summer, without bringing badly needed rain and respite from the ravaging teeth of forest fires on California's West Coast. Global warming, it seemed, was becoming more evidence based each year.

Momentarily, she traveled back in time to her childhood when she'd lived in Mesa, just east of Phoenix. Her daddy had gently scolded her whenever she forgot to close the door behind herself, on her way outside to play. Only grown-ups remembered not to let the air-conditioned, frosty air escape outdoors during the sweltering heat waves.

Now, she was the culprit with no one to blame for the still-opened sliding glass door with an inviting gap. It wasn't the comforting, cool air escaping out as it had in Phoenix, but rather blasts from a heat pump providing warmth in December. Walking across the rec room, she'd closed and locked the door without a second thought before heading back upstairs with the frozen package of ground beef.

Padded feet, keen night vision, and sensitive whiskers enabled silent movement throughout the darkened amusement park and proverbial wonderland of good fortune. Were there humans here? He didn't think so. He remembered learning about humans from others in the nest who'd conversed by means of pheromones and ultrasonic vocalizations. He had been warned about humans. Contact ought to be avoided at all costs. Interacting with humans could exact a heavy toll.

As he climbed, he heard something unusual in the distance. A noise that got louder as he crept up a carpeted ladder and discovered a jaw-dropping treasure of breadcrumbs and dried-out, grated cheese. He was grateful for his flexible body and squeezed beneath a gigantic stainless steel cube that he sensed was still hot but cooling. Underneath, he found the perfect place to sharpen his constantly growing teeth. This would certainly help get rid of his nagging toothache. Instinctually, he knew to be on the lookout for insulation, wires, straw, cardboard, paper, and other materials to build a nest.

He was especially lucky when he found dishes full of water and an assortment of delicious bits and pieces. He nibbled without worry although his ears perked up constantly on alert; his nose told him a canine was nearby.

Feeling the sinews under her skin tighten, imagined whiskers bristled. A tiny black pellet previously believed to be a fallen crumb was indisputable evidence of an unwanted intruder. With a bolt of clarity, lightning struck, and she remembered the sliding glass door.

Called to action, the feces retriggered instinctive impulses and compulsive behaviors emerged. She needed to clean and sanitize now, right now: everything, everywhere. Tears ran down cheeks as she headed to where she kept antiseptic chemicals and the vacuum. Her ears became bionic hearing receptors.

Like a wildcat on the prowl, she summoned her inner agility and nocturnal instincts; something unwelcome was in the walls. She'd find its hiding place and show no mercy. Her controlled lifestyle, cramped by this dreaded virus, was now exacerbated by a villainous intruder.

She built a strong fortress to protect what was hers before stopping to groom her face and ears.

Bolder now, he stood erect on hind legs and searched each nook and crevice for even richer rewards. After chewing through insulated wiring that had caused sparks to shoot skyward, like fireworks, he vocalized his pleasure with squeaks and steepled his hands like a guilty villain, having done a wicked deed.

Through sleepless nights, she lay, forced to share her tormented mind and dwelling place with a visitor who actively filled her thoughts with disgust.

Each day, she woke to additional evidence of nocturnal destruction. With exacerbated angst, she scrutinized, checked, and rechecked the house for evidence. Fear demanded she remove any daytime reminders of his nightly crimes, like one of her coworkers who'd routinely covered a bruised and battered face with double wear, stay-in-place foundation to conceal abuse.

Like a murderer, she schemed and plotted without remorse, knowing she could scrub residual blood from beneath her fingernails and eliminate evidence of strategic planning. It was time for the intruder to know who the alpha member in this matriarchal pack was. There would be no further encroachment permitted to her territorial expectations for cleanliness. Conjuring pointed incisors and a barbed tongue, she dug debris left behind out of the cracks between boards of her refurbished, antique kitchen table. Every closet, nook, and storage container were searched by the determined huntress.

As if a vaccinologist motivated by exponentially increasing death tolls, a result of the Covid virus, and with unlimited financial resources, she would find an antigen and eradicate transmission of his crimes. Like learning another galaxy had been discovered four billion light-years from earth, she couldn't quite get her head wrapped around the news that over one million Americans were dead. She was becoming numb to the destruction of the virus and how it had affected humanity.

She moved mountains, collected, and tossed treasured memorabilia destroyed by his incessant chewing and prevalent urine stains and feces. Countless garbage bags went to the landfill as she decluttered without Marie Kondo's life-changing magic. She had a more potent weapon than hatred, an instinctual need to hunt and kill, like a lioness on the prowl for prey.

Each pile of rubble, ravaged item in her pantry, and newly discovered chewed wire inspired nocturnal plots to knock off her quarry.

Days passed, baited traps lay untouched, and uncontrollable anger acknowledged that he was a clever fiend.

His unrelenting threats left jagged psychological scars and added agitation during an already trying period of caged solitary confinement.

Cherished documents lay shredded into ribboned waste, as if confidential recycling. Family photographs collected and stored for grandchildren in decorative photo storage boxes now held images blurred and redacted by incisors. Each photo now created a foggy past rather than joyful family history.

Inhaling shallow ragged breaths, she exhaled discouragement. Nighttime scurrying meant a dawn of wreckage and sunrise featuring destruction. The enemy had moved in and hadn't minded leaving testament of his skills. He'd found her jewelry box and apparently crowned himself with a bejeweled halo much to his liking.

She became fixated on the whereabouts of this thief in the night, who'd intruded into her sanctuary. Fear threatened her body, like a virus infecting an unvaccinated host. She questioned her security, invested in motion sensors and additional lighting, and cleaned the house from top to bottom without regard for pandemic rations on cleaning supplies. Antiseptic wipes she deemed essential on her weekly shopping list and hoarded in her pantry alongside the toilet paper, cleaning supplies, masks, hand sanitizer, surgical gloves, and bucket of dog food.

Once, twice, thrice she vacuumed each day as if powered by ever ready, fully charged batteries and a feline with nine lives. Vacuum cleaning till well past guests who were unable to visit might question her sanity. Like a maniacal robotic vacuum spinning and spiraling, she squealed a final robotic meow.

Imagining his death hadn't restored her sense of peace or calm. He needed to be dethroned and eliminated.

By dawn he was curled into his nest after refueling from his hoarded treasure trove of possibilities. He spent hours running back and forth from the pantry—where he'd located baking supplies, the dog's kibbles, and other tasty treats—to his lair. Time and time again, he returned to his palatial nest amid the buttress of springs, insulation, and cushioning, where he created a velvety bed fit for rodent royalty from her chesterfield's upholstery and stuffing.

He chewed easily through the soft leather and created a cozy bedchamber inside this castle fortress. He couldn't wait to celebrate with friends and spread the news of his recent windfall.

He'd won the lottery and had ample stores of food for an extended stay. With his crib secured, he needed only to avoid entrapment. Increasingly cocky, he strutted about in his now shiny black fur coat, like an aristocrat. He was well-groomed and ever ready for a night on the town. He left smear marks of urine and droppings to ensure his safe passage home after his nightly carousing.

He could scurry, climb, and forget the perilousness of cougars, weasels, owls, and snakes. In the dead of night, he stole through rooms, between joists and beams and behind the plaster. After chewing through several ceiling tiles, he discovered what he considered a blue-blooded playground from where he now crept and peered through the openings to reveal a bird's-eye view of the dining room.

Had humans created this unbelievable feast for his pleasure? Maybe humans weren't so bad. Perhaps he'd been mistaken after hearing incriminating tales as a wee pinkie, furless and with pink skin back in the family's nest.

The table below was set with fork, knife, and a hearty helping of the finest flavor profiles human hands could prepare. He was dressed for dinner and ready to dine.

Awakening before sunrise, she lifted covers that had become blankets of heaviness. Waking from nightmares became the less desirable option as it was during daylight hours she obsessed over cleaning and was unable to relax. At daybreak, something had crept and now clouded the sunrise like blackout curtains. His shadow still lurked after first light and told tales of his nightly shenanigans and destruction. Devastation in the aftermath of nightmares caused her a perpetually clenched jaw as she attempted to eat her morning bagel. He'd infected every cell and fiber of her being, like a runaway virus without a protective vaccine.

She padded down the hallway, away from the temporary comfort of her down-filled duvet after waking, then remembered.

Arriving in the kitchen, she ran tap water, filled the kettle, and placed it on the stove top before dialing the heat to max. While waiting, she listened for the tell-tale whistle that would signal a full rolling boil and the spout venting a cloud of steam. She unloaded the dishwasher, obsessively cleaned the countertop and sills, and then groomed while anticipating the scented warmth of cinnamon, garam masala, ginger, and cardamon from her favorite cup and saucer. Who could relax when a houseguest had overstayed their welcome?

Wait a minute. She wondered: Why wasn't the kettle whistling? Why wasn't the burner on the stove top glowing bright orange?

His coat was now a lustrous midnight black and showed telltale signs of months of clean living and good fortune. He hadn't found a way out or been able to tell the others yet about his new life. The other pups from his mischief would be wide-eyed and full of envy when they learned about his marvelous new residence. He needed to find an escape route soon and tell the tale.

She discovered the chewed wiring after the burner had neither sparked or glowed. Holes had been gnawed in the dropped ceiling tiles and remnants of tile and insulation lay strewn below on the floor. Small mountains of splintered scraps lay in not one but three separate areas of her home. This new evidence evaporated any calm or hope of a glorious summer sunrise with more typical soft pink clouds streaking across the sky. A day, when prepandemic, she would have been inspired and able to head out for a morning wander in the forest or along the beach with friends. Instead, caged at home and under house arrest by the new realities during the pandemic, she'd wanted to meet up with friends but didn't dare. She couldn't without risking infection.

She feared catching the deadly virus, which had spread through her neighborhood and across the nation leaving hospitals filled with patients struggling to breathe, on ventilators fighting for their lives, and far too many dead.

Instead, with fierce determination, she imagined countless ways to rid her home of the known enemy she believed she could defeat. She playfully plotted his execution with murderous thoughts as she drooled in anticipation and prepared to pounce. She even called in the exterminator.

What was happening? His stomach hurt and his poop was green. He rested a little longer and decided to rely on his stash, but his pantry stores were getting low. He'd become accustomed to relying on wide-open access to unlocked treasure chests and effortless availability to anything he wanted. He'd become lazy living on easy street.

Today, he knew, he would need to venture out again and this time in broad daylight. He'd protect and camouflage himself from this new predatorial enemy. Just thinking about it made his tummy ache and caused him to experience shortness of breath. He began suffering wicked headaches and, earlier in the day, loose stools.

He headed to where he knew food was kept to locate something, anything, to help his aching belly. Food had become scarce recently, but more importantly, he needed water. He had an aggressive thirst after his bowels had howled without warning. He knew this time it could be a more costly hunt. He listened for movement, perked up his ears, but heard nothing.

Called to action after making the lasagna she planned for dinner, she set the table and put the still-warmed pan of baked lasagna on the table to rest and set. She would enjoy it when she returned. First, she needed to walk her dog.

She couldn't wait to delight in her favorite flavors melted together: Parmigiano-Reggiano, beef, and a special sauce in among the ribbon-shaped pasta. A side of garlic toast and a stemmed glass filled with her favorite pinot noir had her mouth watering in anticipation. She'd tried a new recipe with a flavor twist she thought she might enjoy that included crab and shrimp with béchamel, rather than a ragù sauce. She had a yearning for seafood recently. Taking a quick walk around the block, she'd arrive home to a feast.

It was getting harder and harder to motivate herself to cook full meals since the beginning of the pandemic when she could no longer dine in the company of family or friends, entertain, or host dinner parties.

She'd walked the dog and returned home to find feces on the kitchen table. He'd been out and about and during daylight hours. How dare he? He must be desperate, as desperate as she, to brush up against friends and purr again, though it still wasn't recommended.

The broadcast news for the past five months left her fretting and fearful of the delta variant, and she limited her outings to shopping once each week for essentials only and to walk her fur baby. At least that was allowed.

The humans must not be home. It wasn't fun to leave his nest to locate food when the light hurt his eyes and he was feeling ill. But he was hungry, and his belly grumbled with displeasure. He missed his littermates. Enticed by hunger and distracted by illness, he crept across the top of the stairway.

Surrendering his fears, he trusted time-tested, proven-safe passageways and crept within the walls. He needed to return to the human's storehouse of delicious morsels. He made a quick stop and ensured there were no sounds or movements. Then crept up and onto the kitchen table. He'd found scraps there before and on occasion an abandoned plate or pizza box. Then he sensed it—his olfactory neurons, tipped with hairlike cilia, smelled something that made his heart race with excitement: cheese. With elevated hopes, he approached warily. It smelled fishy and appeared heaven-sent.

Right before his eyes was a whole meal, prepared and ready, as if they were expecting him.

She waited by the door watchful for the exterminator, who'd called to recheck their trapline set weeks earlier. She hadn't heard the telltale *snap* but hoped.

Surrendering his fears, he sat to dine. Then fattened by delicious morsels lovingly prepared and plated by his host, he zipped back along those same foolproof paths toward the safety of his nest.

"We got him!" Had she heard correctly?

Ahh . . . finally.
She exhaled angst and breathed in sweetness. The masked and gloved pest control agent held up her reward and exclaimed, "This is one shiny-coated, well-fed black rat."
Home alone, at long last. The want-to-be executioner without remorse hadn't sanitized her hands before nesting her shiny black prize on the mantel. Unlike an Oscar that Hollywood's elite actors might either secret away or add to a trophy case, she'd had her prized rat stuffed.

6

STOPPORTUNITY

by Jessica Jiji

"I would begin with 'ladies and gentlemen,' but that excludes folks in the nonbinary community," said the Master of Ceremonies. "So let me just say, 'Dear friends.'"

Watching the awards ceremony on her laptop, Delancey appreciated this deft welcome by the MC, who knew how to read a room, even if it was only a virtual one.

Hearts popped across the screen, replacing the usual rumblings of applause in the traditional banquet ballrooms where waiters circulated among self-congratulatory guests basking under soft lights. No one would have wished a pandemic on the world, but at least it killed charity dinners where sumptuous meals were served to the rich in the name of ending blight and suffering for the poor.

The MC, dressed in a smart suit at least from the waist up, continued the run of show. "Today we honor this year's International Relief Aid Champion, a gift to our world: Bekah Finney, who we honor for her lifesaving campaign, Stopportunism."

Lifesaving? Delancey smirked. On-screen Bekah smiled with a blend of confidence and humility. Their relief aid nonprofit prevented many deaths, but its communications department could claim none of the credit for that.

Delancey double-checked the slash through her video icon and the tape over her laptop's camera. "Speechwriters should be heard and not seen," Bekah had said back when Delancey came up with a name for the award-winning campaign.

Before the pandemic gave her purpose, Bekah bristled at wasting her strategic mind on approving vacation days, signing budget requests, and managing a team that did work so necessary and routine it would never win accolades and therefore bored her.

Delancey fervently wished Bekah had a challenge to keep her from complaining and solicited ideas from whoever would listen: the donor committee members milling around the Nespresso machine, fellow thwarted creatives working in speechwriting, and even Nasir, the political analyst who looked more like an athlete.

"Bekah needs a project to really shine," Delancey had suggested to him, hoping for a conversation that might carry past that one elevator ride.

". . . A spotlight on herself?" he asked, black eyes flashing.

That pissed off Delancey, who felt Nasir should have realized the value of a charismatic humanitarian director. Instead of a dull bureaucrat imposed by a donor country, in had waltzed this confident American former war correspondent. "We must be compassionate and communicative, empathetic and emphatic," she sang on her first day, aggressively forming sound bites.

The Zoom ceremony switched over to a video showcasing Bekah's accomplishments, which sparkled in a parade of praise across the main screen, culminating in an emotional scene on the front lines of the pandemic. Delancey had organized the production, and even though she knew every frame, she turned up the volume.

Bekah stands in the middle of a medical facility, a pained-yet-determined look in her eyes. "To those who truly help, I say 'thank you.' And to those who would exploit, I say 'watch out!'" she warns dramatically.

The overwhelmed clinic let them film there after Delancey pleaded for an exception on the grounds that the Stopportunism campaign was "making a difference in the lives of people."

As a speechwriter, she knew that was a lazy phrase, but like "no more critical time," "a role to play," and "for our children's children," it was hard to avoid. And effective, serving to convince the exhausted urgent care staff to allow the team to set up lights, mics, and cameras in front of the beds of sick people who served as the backdrop for Bekah's promo.

Delancey glanced at the long list of speakers cued up to burnish their own image by praising Bekah, successfully branded as the embodiment of caring and integrity.

"URGENT" Delancey's phone screen glowed with a text from the humanitarian director herself.

Looking up at her bedroom/kitchen/living room, Delancey felt a stab of loneliness. It had gotten so bad since New Yorkers went indoors, she was grateful for any contact, even a text from her boss. Thank goodness for the fire escape, where banging pots in appreciation of frontline workers served as a nightly reminder that she wasn't completely alone.

"A corporate rep for refugee assistance joined the call," Bekah wrote. *"Need to press their points for more $. Add three lines ASAP."*

Delancey had a good hour to find, process, and incorporate messaging for the humanitarian director to divert another donor's funds to Stopportunism.

"Sure."

A quick edit didn't stress Delancey, who was experienced enough to dance up to deadlines and meet them with a kiss.

She briefly considered inventing the numbers. Bekah wouldn't care—but no. Delancey smiled and dialed her crush.

"Hey, Nasir."

"Delancey! What's up?"

The city was quieter from the pandemic but still had some roar left. "You're outside?"

"Sorry, can you hear me?" He wanted to help. She wished it could be for anything more valuable than another Bekah show.

"Awards time."

He was silent, so Delancey explained: "International Relief Aid Champion of the Year. Sorry to bother you—"

"It's the middle of the speech; now she wants a change?"

"We have a good hour, so . . . it happens, you know."

"She's crazy," he said, "but I can help."

"You in the office?" Delancey was already pulling on a dress and trying to coax a spritz from her long-neglected perfume.

"Down by West Fourth."

"I'm so close! Wanna . . . ?" she began.

"We can meet?" he asked.

"Give me ten."

A coat of lipstick and quick dash across the empty avenue later, she saw Nasir on a bench with his phone tuned to the award ceremony and his laptop cued with reports.

Sidewalk stickers marking six feet apart ticked a path to Nasir.

He slid to make a space for Delancey, and she slipped into it. The slacks he used to wear to the office had been switched out to jeans, soft at the knees, relaxed at the waist.

Like all New Yorkers, they were far enough along to have social distance fatigue but not close enough to a vaccine to relax. Still, she leaned in, mask on, and gathered the facts from his documents.

"You ready for the transfer?" he asked.

A sleek black puppy bounded close and then zipped away.

She updated the speech, glancing at the time on her laptop to keep track of when she'd have to run it live for the acceptance. "Hmmm?"

Delancey typed: "A girl named Awira who I met in a refugee camp" and then checked the numbers on Nasir's report. "Fine to use a Kurdish example?" she asked.

He nodded. The puppy yelped. Delancey looked up. And time spun back a bit.

"Transfer?" she asked.

Nasir looked properly sorry. "But they told you, right?"

Delancey waited.

"She's bringing her speechwriter from the other agency," he said quietly.

On the phone screen's Zoom, Bekah beamed as another official praised Stopportunism for exposing those seeking to mine the pandemic for profit.

Thwack. Delancey shut her laptop. From years in the trade, she knew there was still a good half hour before Bekah's big finale.

Thirty minutes to decide: follow orders to revise the speech, or refuse and get fired?

"And where'm I gonna go?" She fixed her eyes on Nasir.

"Writing press releases." He knew this was two steps down and three years back; he just hadn't thought he'd be the one to share the bad news. "You okay?"

"Sure. Yeah. Great." She looked down, allowing the tears to fall. He put a gentle hand on her leg.

"Stopportunism is siphoning funds from operations," Delancey said bitterly, no longer seeing the bounding puppy as her vision blurred.

"I know." He caught her eyes and his came into focus: clear and sincere. "The new speechwriter gets a big raise, plus Bekah's hiring a team to beef up her YouTube channel, and she's signed with an agent to book speaking engagements."

"Paid?"

Nasir rolled his eyes to confirm—*of course.* "Huge fees in her pocket. But she'll be too popular to criticize."

Pandemic times had shifted the norms of distance so far that as soon as Delancey leaned on Nasir's shoulder and he put an arm around her, it was five-alarm hot. And when he lightly kissed her face, she knew.

Delancey typed. The words flowed so easily, she and Nasir had time to go back to her studio apartment before Bekah read them off the teleprompter.

"During these difficult and painful times, we see a light of hope. It shines on the faces of essential workers who are finally appreciated for their previously invisible efforts to help us access basic goods and services," Bekah preached with all the emotion of a minister on a hot Sunday at church. "This light shines on the sense that we are all united in our pain and sorrow but also our joy and dreams. And it illuminates right and wrong in a stark truth that I'd like us all to remember: No one is above opportunism. No one . . ."

Delancey's futon was folded into a couch where she and Nasir shared a view of her laptop.

". . . can say they've never been tempted. With millions of dollars and so much at stake, individuals around the world need to be reminded that yes, there will be heroes, but those are the people who step up without a thought of reward—not the ones who take, take, take only for their own glory. And that's why I am so proud to announce . . ."

"She'll take a beat here, because I wrote 'pause dramatically,'" Delancey said. "Plus, she's a natural."

She temporarily stopped the scroll, sensing that her boss wanted a moment to freestyle.

Bekah went off script with well-rehearsed spontaneity. "I wish I could shake each of your hands, but I'm looking into all of your eyes on this screen that is helping us prove that nothing can stop our solidarity," she said. And then, disarmingly down-to-earth: "Of course, I can't see y'all who have cameras off."

Bekah punctuated this with "ha ha ha"—which Delancey mimicked in real time—"but even if I can only read your names, I'm feeling your hearts, finding the common cause we need to get through this, together!"

"And go," said Delancey, resuming the scroll on the teleprompter app that controlled the text of Bekah's speech.

"I stand here as a proud example of the kind of Stopportunism that shows the way with intelligence, empathy, and integrity . . ."

Nasir's hand brushed Delancey's. And before they could bother to disinfect, they grasped each other tightly.

". . . without wasting money on selfish interests at a time when the world needs selfless acts."

Their grip relaxed. It was the most natural, sweet, sexy touch Delancey had ever experienced.

"And so," Bekah said with flourish, before processing with her mind what, commanded by the scrolling text, flew automatically out of her mouth, "we are ready to return the two point seven million dollars that has been wasted on a despicable self-aggrandizement which never should have happened: my own . . . office?"

"You fucking did it!" Nasir hugged Delancey. The scent of shaving cream on his skin mixed with the spritz of sweet fragrance in her hair.

"No, no, I'm sorry, that was a mistake," Bekah backpedaled. "I am not abolishing my office. I'm donating my time here. A lot of overtime hours, and hey, you need a PR team to sell a good idea. How is this opportunism? Just because I want to receive awards to make us all look good? Find a better spokesmodel than me and I'll step aside, dammit! We raised more than two million dollars. I'd like to double that. Who's with me?"

Bekah's mouth continued moving, but no one could hear a word she said, in the manner that inspired 2020's most commonly uttered phrase: "You're on mute." Only she wasn't the one who had turned off her mic.

"PLEASE STAND BY" took over the screen. "THE INTERNATIONAL RELIEF AID CHAMPION OF THE YEAR CEREMONY WILL RESUME IN A MOMENT."

Bzzzz . . . Delancey's phone.

"THE BIG BOSS" flashed across its screen.

Nasir sat up straight.

"Hello?"

"Delancey?"

"Yes."

"This is the office of the executive president. We're told you wrote the Relief Aid Champion of the Year speech for Bekah Finney?"

"Yeah . . ."

"Please hold for the EP."

Delancey expected the Big Boss to demand answers, but instead he asked for advice.

"You can always say you're launching an investigation to buy time," she suggested. "Announce a blue-ribbon panel. And if—"

Her eyes met Nasir's.

"And if you really want to fix this, ditch the campaign. Otherwise, honestly? They'll laugh us out of town."

The president hung up.

The Zoom resumed.

But Delancey and Nasir were too busy celebrating to watch what happened next.

7

FULL MOON FEVER

by Thomas Walsh

<u>AUDIO JOURNAL</u>

L unar date 15 September 2022, 1700 hours.

  This is extraordinary. What a welcome back. A total lunar eclipse smears its way onto the blue-black canvas of nearby space. It's a light show like no other.

  Every 2.5 years, give or take, we get a version of this beauty. The fact that it's happening on my first day back in the lab after my five-week forced sabbatical—and that I've got this brand-new beast of a scope to myself today—is especially great.

  Rust red, harvest apple red, salamander red . . . the lunar blotch comes in many shades as it evolves through eclipse stages, incredible contrasts to its everyday look. And even though Earth's shadow is literally putting the moon in the shade, the resulting clarity of the lunar surface, in a soft scarlet spotlight, brings us imagery like we'll rarely see again.

  This telescope, tilted on its rakish forty-five-degree angle, is the width and length of an adult maple, as heavy as a bulldozer. The thing is stupendous. It's also new to me.

  During those five weeks of sick leave from the observatory—a week of feeling just plain shitty; then the positive test, a stunner for me

75

and my seemingly invincible health perception; then two weeks in isolation, the boulder-covered road of treatment, staying inert, hating the way slow recovery feels but enduring; and almost two more weeks of slow bounce back—this monster device, long rumored as a huge upgrade to our facility if the budget got approved, had been green-lit and then installed.

Colleagues were enthralled, me too. This was my first crack at using it. The scope's name, in fact, expresses its enormity just right: Mega-View. Nickname: the Mega.

15 September, Entry 2, 1720 hours.

Poof! A meteor or some TBD object just swooped into the picture, upper-right quadrant of the surface. A pinkish-red splash, a tiny moment of impact; it stood out so incredibly because of the "cinematography" from this scarlet atmosphere, combined with the front-row seat courtesy of the Mega. Meteors and other space debris are common up there, of course, but during an eclipse, under Mega's eye, they look smashing.

I shake my head in wonder. As I turn, my eye catches the blue-framed etching that hangs above my work space—one of my favorite quotes, from Yeats: ". . . And pluck till time and times are done/The silver apples of the moon/The golden apples of the sun."

Anyway . . . meteors and space flotsam slamming into moons around the solar system is all in a day's work. But seeing one live and in close-up on our moon is exhilarating.

Entry 3, 1735 hours.

I turn away from the telescope, back toward the lab. The room is always too warm. Right now, hot. Or maybe it's just my body temperature shooting upward, based on . . . what I'm seeing.

I wipe real sweat from my face. Which conjures, darkly, Covid memories. My bed at home was a perspiration chamber for weeks. Never experienced anything like it. But now—is this stress sweat on my face?

What is this optical beast showing me?

I roll my chair away from the eyepiece, the diameter of a coffee cup. There are five of them sprouting from the scope's base, like jumbo mushrooms. The chair slams into the overcrowded desk behind me.

The jolt shakes loose another thought. In my heart, if not head,

No way I saw what I think I just saw. Rationally, scientifically, I tell myself it's a glitch, an oddball tremor in the monster telescope's DNA.

I've never used a device of this scale before, so . . .

I lower my head and gaze in.

The lunar surface, centered so gigantically in this frame, looks faked, artificial, like a drawn reproduction. But it's real. Most of the expressions on the moon face—the pockmarks, acne, birthmarks—are fantastically visible, in a rich red hue.

Gazing back at me, uniquely illuminated by this deepest expression of the moon, are some "rock stars" of the lunar band—the Sea of Tranquility, the Sea of Cold, of Serenity, the craters Plato and Kepler.

And crater Copernicus. Where I just saw . . . it.

On the barren floor of Copernicus, framed in Mega's Technicolor clarity . . . I saw *movement*. An object, cylindrical, impressively big, crawling, gliding, doing *something* inside Copernicus's peak-enclosed surface. Inching across, heading west.

Now . . . it's quiet and still. Then—there it goes again. A moving object. Forging along inside Copernicus's "arena" setting. The same pace and trajectory, same direction as before.

And it stops. Right at the crater's center.

I have to tear myself away. This is too bizarre to be true. And the bone-deep fatigue from my bedridden weeks is making a comeback. I've gotta lie down.

Entry 4, 1750 hours.

After a twelve-minute attempt at a cat nap on a cot down the hall . . . tossing, muttering to myself . . . I drag myself back to the scope. Halfway fearful, half exhilarated, I bring my face in to see.

That unnameable object is still there. In the same dead-center spot where it "parked."

Now there's something protruding from its barely discernible stern. It's oblong, sticklike. Despite the incredibly tight close-up view that Mega provides Copernicus crater . . . some features of the object are hard to pinpoint. I'm remembering that despite Mega's stupendous power, it's gazing 240,000 miles into the distance.

Anyway, whatever is jutting out from the object wasn't there twenty minutes ago. And the way it's angled . . . on a forty-five-degree tilt . . . somehow reminds me of this very scope I'm using. That kind of angle just works best. What I'm seeing up there weirdly mirrors this device that I'm using to see it.

Then . . . something, ever so slowly, is emerging. As near as I can discern, it brings to mind the way a flower begins sprouting petals from its stamen. Something . . . is blooming out of the object.

Entry 5, 1800 hours.

Movement stopped. The object parked on the floor of Copernicus and the scope-like thing sticking out from it are paused. And now what?

The scene conjures possibilities in my head: It looks like a submarine with a periscope spread open and weirdly tilted . . . and a satellite dish blossoming from a steel frame . . . and maybe some kind of battle vehicle, like a tank, with its weaponized snout pointing.

Straight at us?

Entry 6 1816 hours.

I'm hot. This is fever—I'm so used to its rising spread from the head through the body, but this one is a deeper heat, more raw, like a burn pit just beginning. No delirium—but the syndrome throughout the time on my back was that the hallway of fever inevitably led to the chamber of head-spinning heebie-jeebies. What some bizarre pseudoscientists nicknamed "pink spiders" and "jimjams." Meaning, delirium would follow.

I thought I was past all this shit! Like cured!

Is it not done with me yet?

Entry 7 1824.

The lunar surface is being pelted by objects. That is what I am seeing.

Almost identical to that first presumed meteor that whizzed in and thudded silently on the red-tinged mountains-and-craters landscape, there have been more. A lot more. Separated by just a few lunar miles from one another. There's a precision to them that looks intentional. Or is that just my fever-laced perspective? Still not feeling delirium—am I? This is a clear-eyed observation, even as I'm possibly heading toward sick again.

Entry 8, 1835.

The strikes on the moon surface have stopped. The eclipse's scarlet glow is fading fast, the primary tones now silver-white-pink. But sharpness of detail from Mega's gaze and the eclipse effect remains spectacular.

I'm poised to reach out to my colleagues, the other staffers, even the multi-Ph.D. chiefs, those imperious souls to whom nothing seems dramatic or wonderful because . . . it's just science? But I stop myself. For some eerie, nonscientific reason, I'm savoring the solitude of this discovery or breakthrough or . . . vision.

Entry 9, 1852.

I use the bathroom, swallow some pills, have a few bites of yogurt.

Back at the scope: What I see now *cannot be.*

The object that glided across Copernicus an hour ago is still in its spot—surrounded by a dozen others, all identical. Most have sprouted the bloom-like shape from out of their forty-five-degree-angle protrusions. The rest are *in the process of blooming, the same way, right now.*

Cannot be.

My body is simmering with fever, my forehead scalding to the touch. No other symptoms, no delirium.

I'm terrified.

◆

Patient Patrick Madsen was brought by ambulance to the Wildbrook Emergency Room on 15 September. Patient had a fracture in his right foot, deep contusions on both hands, a forehead gash that required nine stitches. Patient was incoherent, flailing.

◆

Waking up in such a dismal, disinfected place . . . surrounded by white curtains, and though they're light, they feel confining to the point of menace. I'm trapped here.

Last night . . . the woman who allowed me this little device strictly for the purpose of my audio recollections—they're watching me, I know it; she wouldn't admit it, but she sure didn't deny it—was sterile and coolly helpful for a little while. Until I guess I crossed a line, asked too many questions. Then she clammed up.

She filled in just a few details.

I was found on the ground below the second-floor window of the lab's observatory. Window was open. Did I jump? A flimsy try at suicide?

Or an escape attempt?

The last thing I remember . . . is from when I was staring through the colossal telescope's viewfinder at the moon. In spectacular close-up. Pinkish-red hues all around from the eclipse's closing illuminations. My fever had boldly gone where it had never gone before—burning me up.

And I knew, in my scientist brain and in my heart of hearts, that severe danger was coming right at us. From the lunar surface.

All else is a blank. No other memory.

◆

From the *Journal of Disease Study*:

There's growing evidence that Covid and new psychotic episodes are connected. In July 2020, researchers reported that a fifty-five-year-old woman in the United Kingdom, with no history of mental illness, arrived at a hospital days after recovering from a severe case of Covid with delusions and hallucinations, convinced that the nurses were devils in disguise and that monkeys were jumping out of the doctors' medical bags. In March 2021, a fifty-seven-year-old man turned up at Columbia University's New York-Presbyterian Hospital insisting that his wife was poisoning him, that cameras had been planted throughout his apartment, and that the patients in the hospital's emergency department were being secretly murdered.

"Covid's potential for long-reaching effects," said Jared McClintock, a lead epidemiologist at Stanford University, "is very high. We don't know how high, because we've never been here. But these compelling stories of deep delusion are strong indicators that this disease can leave hieroglyphs on the walls of victims' psyches."

◆

From SolarSystem.com:

For nearly an hour last night, our moon became ground zero for a dramatic and essentially unexplained celestial event.

An apparent meteor shower that had not been visible on lunar-monitoring radar pelted the moon's surface with an almost rhythmic regularity. All of the estimated thirty-five space-debris objects crash-landed within two miles of one another inside crater Copernicus, the fifty-mile-wide "Monarch of the Moon," just northwest of the body's center.

The objects' impacts were concentrated in such tight proximity that astronomers were dumbfounded.

As one pointed out, "This precise grouping of the objects felt almost choreographed, like they were acting in unison. Add another new space marvel for us to study."

♦

Patient log from Wildbrook Health Center:

Subject began screaming at medical and hospital staff that "the pods on the moon" were in place and taking dead aim at Earth. At one point, he shrieked, "They're preparing to fire!"

8

I CALLED HIM MOZART

by Susana Aikin

During the pandemic I fell in love with a cat.
I called him Mozart, because the first time I saw his round eyes through the window I was listening to the overture of the *Marriage of Figaro* for the tenth time that morning. It was something I'd taken to with desperate frenzy since the beginning of lockdown. I couldn't stand waking up to the silence and stillness around me. Silence in the streets, silence in the building, in the apartments around me, everywhere, like a strange deafness, a feeling of floating inside a blind tank, heavy and wet—and all of it in solitude. So I'd jump out of bed, turn on Spotify, and yank up the volume to the max, secretly hoping someone would come banging on my door, and I would have to open, see a human face even if red with rage or livid with frustration at my transgression of residential building noise laws. But that craving was also laced with some degree of terror—any encounter could instantly trigger my fear of being exposed to the virus, catching that infamous nano invisible entity always ready to strike at any chance of contact. No, it's better if no one stands outside my door—so why the provocation? I think I'm losing my mind going back and forth between fear and desire for human contact. Anyway, despite increasing levels of volume, not a soul ever showed up. Maybe they also feared my manic state; or even enjoyed Mozart themselves; or maybe they were not

there, having fled the city, or were already dead from boredom, loneliness, lockdown—

Just like me.

But back to Mozart. For the first time since the beginning of my solitary confinement, something, someone, was looking in on me, attentively, unflinchingly, possibly trying to assess my degree of madness or my abnormal melomania. We stared at each other—he with round green eyes on a black and white yin-yang medallion-like face, and me with my bed hair and my oversized, overwashed pajama T-shirt. We stood there mesmerized for a beat, but the moment Figaro and Susanna finished their first duet, this feline onlooker pulled his gaze away from mine and lifted his lithe elegant body in preparation to— walk. No, no, no—I ran to the window, opened it, and begged. Don't leave, please. Please. I was astonished when he actually turned around and looked at me again. Then it dawned on me—the music, of course. Who could stand this ridiculous volume? I ran back to my tablet and banged on the minus button. I returned to the window and opened it— please do come in.

And I couldn't believe that he did.

He walked around my living room for a bit and then, with a supple weightless movement, jumped on the couch and sat, expectant. I positioned myself at a demure distance, hoping not to scare him away. We locked eyes again for an instant, and I saw a flash, like a blazing pulse of light inside his vertical pupils. I felt my heart glow. Then he lay down and curled up and didn't move when my hand, tentative and shy, worried at any possibility of rejection, approached his furry neck and caressed it softly with one finger. We stayed like that for a while, listening to Figaro's cascading, and I felt in my gut that this cat was drinking the music with as much glee as I. So I named him Mozart.

Well, that was it—our love was cemented. I ran to the kitchen and ransacked my shelves in search of some delicacy, some cat manna, something to ensure his gastronomical pleasure, convince him he had arrived at a good place, a great place, and that this could be, at least for the moment, his final destination. I went into the kitchen cupboard and reached for the collection of emergency foods I had hoarded among other supplies at the beginning of lockdown—and there behind a tower of toilet paper, hand sanitizing gel, boxes of masks, bags of pasta and rice, tomato sauce, and all the rest, I was relieved to find a good stack of tuna cans pushed all the way back on the upmost shelf. I pulled out one of my mother's fancy floral bone china plates and laid out half a tin of chunky tuna for him, right there at my feet, together with fresh filtered water inside a matching teacup.

Although the stink of the canned fish wafted instantly into the whole of my mini-apartment, Mozart didn't come around immediately. He took a few minutes to show his face at the door before he gingerly approached the succulent offering, sniffed it, dipped his tiny tongue inside the water, and finally, delicately, began to tackle his feast.

Thus, Mozart and I lived together in lockdown bliss for two heavenly weeks. We would wake up together, have breakfast together, listen to music lying on the couch side by side— Everything was perfect, but for one small detail. Mozart began to lose interest in his mono diet, and the tuna chunks were left intact on his plate time after time. I began to worry, eager as I was not just to keep him healthy, but also happy, satisfied, and thoroughly convinced that there was no better place in the world for him to be. Then it struck me for the first time that I just had to do much better in the food department. So, I put on my coat, hat, clunky boots and ran out to C-Town.

I don't know about anyone else's corner of the world, but the supermarket in my neighborhood has practically become a disco during these lockdown times of pandemic. Loud music, people sweeping up and down with carts, checking each other out while pretending to browse increasingly empty shelves or reading microscopic lettered ingredients on packages and cans. Here was the only justified place where we might spy on others, throw furtive glances into their carts, figure out what they're eating in solitude, what secret snacks have become their comfort foods. In any case, just for oneself, it is the ultimate place for something to do that makes sense: think about food, plan to eat something, salivate at the anticipation of something coming out of the forbidden outside world that can sit in your mouth, on top of your tongue, waiting to be triturated and ingested in a moment of total oblivion about viruses, contagion, infected surfaces, neighbors, and snotty children. In short, a public space where one might forget oneself.

But of course, it's not totally like that. I walk in tightening my mask, dousing myself with an overgenerous glob of hand sanitizer, putting on my social distance get-the-f*ck-out-of-my-face stare, determined to get to my business and return to the safety of my apartment as soon as I'm able.

I make a beeline for the pet section and stare blankly at the shelves while all sorts of names, images, logos, and fanciful designs jump at me, pour in through my startled eyes and flood my cerebral cortex. Friskies, Meow Mix, Tiny Tigers, 9 Lives—they all swirl before my field of vision—salmon, turkey, chicken, beef, you name it. Then I see it among the rabble—a box of Felix Soup Tender Strips with the picture of Felix the cat looking just like Mozart. Black and white head in equal balanced patches, wide green eyes staring out in relish at the exquisite tidbits about to be guzzled. This was it. I felt a rush and piled up my cart with a bounteous quantity of Felix products. Then I decided to visit the cat bed and bathroom department where I also picked out a fluffy cat house, a new litter tray, and even a cat tree.

I was heading for the till, quite engorged with the obscenity of my spending splurge, when I saw him. Walking through the glass doors, sweeping into the shop with his usual swagger, muscular legs bulging under loose gray chino pants, long shaggy brown hair and dark shades, although the day outside had turned quite sunless. He's followed by a friend, much in the same flair, although a few notches down in hubris. I've seen them together before—they always walk in maskless, fail to use the hand sanitizer, sneer at any poor clerk who dares point to the rules. And when the supervisor is called in, they snigger as they pull up bandannas over their mouths, only to lower them again when the guy turns his back.

I'm talking about my upstairs neighbor. Although I've never been formally presented to such individual, I know him by sight and endure his frequent slamming in the building lobby, his grazing past me with not even a side glance, in flagrant disdain of my corporeal scope or even my existence. That, paired with his recent antisocial behavior at the supermarket, has put him on my blacklist of least favorable neighborhood schmucks—my particular catalog of PSAs—or pandemic sociopathic assholes—a category that has exploded in large numbers around me like radioactive mushrooms since the beginning of lockdown. But this one is definitively PSA number one.

And why have I even noticed his over-muscular, bullyragging legs? I have to confess that before I discovered what a jackass he is, I thought him attractive. When, about a year and a half ago, I first saw him huff and puff up the stairs carrying his furniture and boxes as he moved in, I had the fantasy we might be friends, or at least good friendly neighbors. He looked different from all the stuck-up occupants of this apartment tower, where stares turn blank and robotic in the elevator whenever any nearby life unit is detected, and basement laundry rooms are always quiet and empty, plastered with threatening rules and caveats. Scruffy-sexy; long, loose strands of hair; slim chino pants—it all sounded like a window into a different human paradigm. And male to boot.

But no, he just turned out to be the antithesis of the other residential chilled snobs. Rude, crude, and plain brutish.

I usually see him and his crony grab a cart and ransack the beer and snack department. I'm certain they're the type of people who, despite lockdown rules, still get together to drink and watch sports or whatever other crap they're into these days. It makes me snort with rage, because it's irreverent morons like these who are drawing out our state of imprisonment, instead of helping contain this fateful epidemic.

Despite all this, I find myself directing my cart toward the beer section, parking it a few feet from the offending neighbor and his friend, and pretending to browse the shelves while I listen in to their conversation.

"He's gone," I hear PSA number one say. "He's been missing for two weeks now—I don't think he's coming back."

"But they do that kind of thing, don't they? I mean, go a-hunting, have affairs, hang out—but always return to their owner," his friend replies.

"Nah—he's never been away for more than a day or two. I think something bad might've happened," PSA number one insists.

"Well, there are people stealing pets right now, you know? All these desperate suckers going nuts while sealed inside their apartments. . . ."

"Yeah, I heard the neighbor's dog went missing—"

"That might have happened to Buster."

Then it hits me. They are talking about Mozart! And his given name is Buster—what an ugly, undignified name for a cat!

A flood of confused thoughts rushes into my mind, and I feel slightly faint. I haven't given a thought to where Mozart might be coming from or where he belonged before he stepped in through my window—it just very naturally felt like a magical gift from the universe that was otherwise punishing me in so many ways. Mozart was the recompense for losing my job, breaking up with my friend, feeling stuck and imprisoned in my tiny apartment—the whole gamut of calamities that have befallen me since the beginning of the pandemic. It was as if Mozart had spontaneously manifested into being to mollify my loneliness and cure my permanent state of panic and paranoia.

But back to the supermarket aisle— I've heard enough and I have to get out of here. I race my cart back to the cash register and quickly place all items on the conveyor belt, pushing away all thoughts coming from that part of my mind, which is beginning to question whether these purchases are a good idea. I stomp back to my apartment. I have no intention of returning anything.

Back home, Mozart is still snoozing away on the couch in the same position I left him in. I swell with happiness as I approach him, and he allows me to caress one of his paws with a finger. To come home and find someone lying around, waiting for me—what better earthly joy could I hope for? He opens his eyes lazily and flashes me one of his dazzling green stares. A cascade of words erupts from my lips, and I tell him about all the things I bought for him at the supermarket. But the list seems to bore him. Until I bring out the cat house, and he jumps down to sniff it. He circles around and finally steps cautiously inside. I rush to open a can of salmon and put it in his bowl, and he's instantly behind me—now this will be his real feast.

Later we sit together on the couch and Mozart jumps into my lap. We watch *Stranger Things*, but Mozart is not into horror thrillers—the screaming and baleful music upset him—so I change to *SpongeBob*, which I perceive he tolerates better. I hardly dare move for fear he will leave my lap. He feels so warm and cozy. But as I continue to watch the adventures of SpongeBob and his crowd, a thought about the upstairs PSA worms into my mind. Here I am, happily settled in with Mozart, but one floor up his true owner is missing him. And that's not the worst of it. What about if Mozart decides to return to him? All this emotional and hard goods investment for nothing? I shift in my seat as anxiety gushes into me. Can I keep Mozart prisoner in my apartment? Never open windows or doors for fear of him escaping? That, I decide, would be the best line of action. But is that fair to him, to me, even to the moron upstairs? Mozart might have ended at my place as the next best spot when, for whatever reason, he couldn't make it back home. And what if that moron spots Mozart through the window or through the sliver of my open door? Finds out I am keeping him. Finds out I have stolen his cat. Would he storm into my place, threaten me, ram his body up against mine, grab my jaw with rough hands and threaten to report me to the police?

My mood is spoiled with all these worries, and by the time I get to bed, I'm close to a basket case. Mozart follows after me, and I soon find him next to me on my pillow, purring away right into my ear—how extraordinary can this cat be? I snuggle closer to him as tears of happiness well up in my eyes and I finally plunge into sleep.

But I toss and turn all night long with dreams of Mozart being kidnapped by another neighbor and PSA number one taking me to court to strip me of custody. I wake up bleary-eyed and feeling nauseous. I need to pull myself together and make this decision. Mozart must return home. I feed him another can of salmon and watch him dejectedly as he eats. Then I take him in my arms, wrap him in a big clean towel, and head out the door. Mozart doesn't resist, but when we approach the upstairs door, he meows. I take it as a sign, and swallowing my regret, I knock at the door.

At first no one comes. I knock again. Then loudly and

insistently. Mozart meows again, this time in a disgruntled tone. Am I making a mistake? Maybe Mozart is done with his previous life and consciously made the choice to find a new home. Temptation to turn away assails me when the door opens with a swing. PSA number one stands at the threshold in pajama bottoms and no shirt, his hair tangled over his bare, well-toned shoulders. And he's wearing no shades. It's the first time I see his eyes. I'm aghast to realize they're as green as Mozart's.

"What the hell—?" he starts, but then he sees Mozart in my arms. "Oh, boy!"

"Your cat came to my window, and I let him in, and I fed him and he spent the night, and I was truly convinced he was a stray, although had no intention of keeping him, I just wanted to make sure he was all right, and—" A torrent of words rushes out of my mouth as I realize I've forgotten to put on my mask, and here I am naked face to naked face with this man whose expression of annoyance is changing into a wide grin. I hand over Mozart. "Hello, Buster," he chortles, "you fugitive little shit." But Mozart jumps out of his arms with the loudest bawling meow and disappears into the dark background behind him.

"Well, thank you very much," says PSA number one, returning to me. "And now if you will excuse me, I'm off back to bed." And grabs the door to slam it shut.

I stand there in shock. Of losing Mozart, of having handed him over to this brute, to this true pandemic sociopathic asshole. I struggle to harness this glut of emotions. I reckon I'm just stunned at this scene of miserly gratitude. Tears swell in my eyes.

PSA number one freezes in mid-movement of door shutting. "Are you okay?"

"I— Yes, I'm totally fine—it's just that Covid seems to affect my eyes and they tear up all the time," I lie.

"I guess it affects us all differently," he lies back.

He watches me for a moment. Then, "All right, thank you very much once again. I owe you one. And will see you soon at the supermarket—yeah?" He smirks and his eyes flash a last green sparkle before he closes the door. Gently this time.

I stay frozen in place. I'm having a hard time digesting this final turn of events, this neighbor's change of attitude. Or I'm just bewildered at one fact that just hit me. PSA number one and Mozart have very similar ways of squeezing their pupils as they look at you while a most peculiar ray of light glistens out of their green eyes. Can this be true of cat and owner, that they might share certain physical traits, gestures? Are pets extensions of their owners or even the other way around, owners extensions of their pets? I shake away these crazy speculations and head downstairs.

By the time I return to my apartment, all these thoughts have vanished into one grim realization. Here I am, alone again in an empty, tiny apartment sealed away from the world. I flop on my couch. And then I spot my cell phone on the coffee table, extend one finger, and punch on Spotify—back to drowning my overall emptiness in the *Marriage of Figaro*. The overture music fills the room at an ungodly volume, but underneath it all, I sense a small tapping, like a quiet scratching on a slippery surface. I turn my face to the window, and I see him.

Mozart is back.

9

PLAYING DEAD

by Brittany Sirlin

The mountain was used to solitude. Aside from the few months during the height of ski season, all was relatively quiet. That didn't mean that life came to a complete standstill throughout the remainder of the year. At night, black bears could be spotted rummaging through the garbage cans of cabins scattered alongside the slopes. The locals who enjoyed hunting still scoured the forest; if not for the kill, then at least to kill some time now that the virus kept everyone home. Overall, quarantine hadn't impacted everyday life all that much. Certainly not in the way that it had for Sloane, who was struggling to catch her breath as she walked uphill with her two young boys.

They took this same walk every day since their arrival, and just like at the start of each of those fourteen climbs, Sloane was beginning to shake. She never did quite understand the appeal of quiet, wide-open spaces, but this was more than a lack of appreciation. The endless terrain ahead of her spurred the earliest sign of a panic attack—the only sound for miles the click of her teeth as they began to chatter. It wasn't the unexpected spring chill of the mountain; it was the adrenaline that coursed through her as she watched her son race into the distance.

"That's too far, Caleb!" Sloane shouted. Her words escaped as a cloud against the cold and echoed back. She clenched her jaw, trying to stop the shaking. But when it made its way to her hands, she brought her wrist to her mouth and sank her teeth into the taut skin.

"Calm the fuck down," she hissed, glaring at the purple ring that blossomed on the side of her hand. She had always been an anxious person, nothing a little Xanax and her weekly yoga classes couldn't cure. With neither of those available to her now that she was living in Middle of Nowhere, New York, her daily mantra would have to suffice.

"An attitude of gratitude," she repeated aloud with each step. Sloane looked down at the ten-pound stranger tethered to her chest. Otto was making soft suckling sounds, his mouth ready for his next feed.

"I am grateful for my family," she cooed into the top of Otto's head before trudging on. The grass beneath her feet was dead and brown. She sidestepped the patches that were still covered by small white mounds of whatever March had left over, but the wetness managed to seep into the sides of her leather boots.

"I am grateful for . . ." She kicked at a rock and watched it ricochet against the larger boulders leading down to their temporary home. The sides of her mouth turned down at the sight of the squat house. She cursed its chipped paint and fumed over the logs piled haphazardly out front before sighing and refocusing her mantra. "I am grateful for a safe space."

It wasn't easy to find an available house to quarantine in. Sloane's husband, James, had spent days researching their options. When James opened Google Maps and typed "New York, New York" in the search bar, Sloane chewed on her bottom lip while she waited to see how far they would be living from her beloved city. In her thirty-five years, she had only ever left Manhattan on summer stints to the Hamptons and the occasional family trip to Europe.

The screen lit up with the blue of the Hudson, the beige boxes of over four hundred neighborhoods, and the yellow of intersecting highways. Sloane gazed lovingly at those little yellow lines, each one a vein pumping life into the heart of her city. She held her smile with effort as James began to zoom out, eager to show where their new home would be. At least for the next few weeks. At least until life returned to normal—whatever that might mean.

James reassured her that it wasn't even that far from the city, but then he scrolled away from the charming river towns and past the popular ski destinations of the Catskills. When he did finally zoom in on what he had been looking for, the screen quickly turned to green. Just green. Nothing more than a single yellow line leading into the town of West Kill, New York.

They had settled on a two-bedroom farmhouse-style chalet after a discouraging search on Airbnb. Most homes that suited their preferences had already been scooped up by the rest of the Upper East Side—at least by those who didn't already own a second home. The description included "cozy" and "tranquil," which Sloane understood as small and secluded. The *small* part wasn't the problem; it was the *secluded* that sent sharp pangs to her forehead. She had pressed her fingers to her temples, and James rubbed her back in silent acknowledgment.

If it were up to James, they would have left sooner, but the idea of uprooting with a one-month-old left Sloane paralyzed. She would run the list in her head: crib, stroller, bottles, diapers. Even their current postapocalyptic lifestyle paled in comparison to the idea of moving into the unknown with a new baby.

But that's what they did.

Sloane tried to make the best of it by spending their afternoons outside and allowing her older son to explore different trails. Each pathway was relatively clear, aside from some rocks and the occasional boulder.

"Mommy, catch me!" Caleb cried out as he ran, his legs pumping with all his strength. He was drifting to where a darkened mass of trees bordered the mountain.

"Slow down, honey!"

She quickened her pace, trying to close the gap between them, but could only move so fast with Otto bobbing along in the baby-blue silk of his sling.

"Caleb! Slow down!"

Her three-year-old finally stopped to examine a chipmunk that had skittered across his path. When it ran into the wooded area to the right, he skipped after it.

"Caleb! Stop! Slow d—"

Sloane was silenced by a loud, authoritative command.

"Listen to your mom!" a deep voice barked from up ahead.

Caleb scurried out of the woods and back to his mother with his head down, a puppy with his tail between his legs. He began to cough, struggling to catch his breath from the combination of the uphill run and the iciness in the air.

Sloane put her left hand in her pocket and quickly spun her diamond ring toward the palm of her hand, a nervous gesture she had acquired from her mother. She scoured the area until she noticed the amber glow of a cigarette. A man dressed in full camo was standing in the thicket. Behind him was a clearing with a small pond and a dilapidated cabin to the right of the water. Even after their eyes locked, neither of them said a word.

"Are you a soldier?" Caleb asked innocently, his voice raspy from his brief fit.

There was a click of the man's rifle. Instead of answering Caleb, his eyes remained steadily on Sloane.

"What's he, about five?"

"Three actually." Sloane placed a hand on Caleb's shoulder and moved her body slightly in front of his.

The man cleared his throat. "This pond has tadpoles. Should have frogs in another week."

Caleb tugged excitedly at his mom's arm. "When will it be a week?" He looked up at her with furrowed blond brows, still trying to work out the concept of time.

"Soon," Sloane choked out, unable to find the words while this man pelted her with his dark eyes. He brought the cigarette to his lips with calloused, dirt-caked hands and then scratched at the thickness of his beard.

"They can lay two hundred eggs!" Caleb proudly declared.

Sloane smiled down at Caleb. The man peered at Sloane. When she allowed herself a quick glance, their eyes met before she quickly turned away.

"You shouldn't let him run off, you know."

Sloane was stung by the unsolicited advice. "Yes, well, he loves to explore and—"

"That pond is deep."

He took a final, greedy drag and began to cough. Little bursts at first that quickly turned into a loud, rattling rhythm. Sloane brought a hand to her naked face, feeling vulnerable without her mask. She took a step back and pulled Caleb along with her. The man watched with watery eyes and pressed his lips together, trying to stifle the hacking that kept threatening his throat. When that didn't work, he turned around and started to walk toward the black pickup truck parked next to the cabin.

Caleb bounced from one foot to the other. "Mom, can we look for tadpoles now?"

Sloane pressed her lips to the top of Otto's head and kept her eyes cast down. If this man was watching them, she didn't want to be caught looking back. The engine started, and she began to relax as she listened to the crackle of gravel beneath tires.

Caleb stomped his feet. "Mom!"

She shuddered for a moment and then focused on Caleb, "Okay, let's look for some tadpoles."

She grabbed his hand with a newly ignited force and tightened her grip with thoughts of deep ponds and strange men. They walked hand in hand until they stood at the perimeter of the murky water where their feet sunk into the wet earth. A fleet of tadpoles quickly squirmed from their hiding place. Caleb threw himself onto his knees and thrust his arm elbow deep into the sludge.

"Baby, no!" Sloane screamed and grabbed the elastic waist of his pants. Otto began to wail having been startled by the jerky movement.

"Dammit." She seethed through gritted teeth. "Caleb, let's go home and wash up."

His face was pinched. "No! I'm not going," he said with his fists balled at his sides. Sloane remained quiet, and after a moment, he glanced up and said, "Fine, but he's coming too."

Caleb unfurled his tiny fist and revealed a single, slimy tadpole.

"Please! He's my pet and he can live with my frogs!"

Sloane began to sway as Otto's cry became deafening and desperate.

"Sweetheart, this tadpole needs to live in the pond so that he can grow into a big, strong frog one day."

Caleb examined the delicate being in his palm. ". . . And so the virus can't get him, right, Mom?"

Sloane gave her son a sad smile. "Exactly."

They both turned their heads toward the cabin at the soft thud of a window being closed. Caleb moved closer to his mother as they realized they were not alone. On the back deck, there were no chairs, no plants, nothing placed as decoration. Certainly nothing that implied an invitation. A curtain fluttered in the single window. On the other side of the window, an elderly woman stood very still while she examined the strangers on her property. James had told her about the neighbor, the woman who lived in the woods of West Kill for most of her eighty-seven years. He had heard that her name was Carol and that she was always greeted warmly at the local farmers market and the post office. Carol must have liked where she lived very much. What she did not like, Sloane imagined, were the tourists during ski season and the rumors about a recent influx of city dwellers.

Sloane offered a smile and a small wave. When Carol frowned in response, Sloane recoiled as if the gesture was a personal attack.

"What is her deal?" Sloane mused steadily, keeping her lips from moving.

Caleb's head was dropped to his chest while he continued to admire his catch. Sloane knelt with Otto as best she could, still feeling the sting of Carol's disapproving gaze.

"Caleb?" She picked up his chin and leaned in. "Drop it. Now."

For the ten minutes it took to get back down the steep hill, Sloane could feel the mountain at her back, mocking her—the deafening silence suggesting *you don't belong here.* The fearful child in her could swear that somewhere in the distance, she heard the cackle of that strange old woman. Sloane let out a cackle herself, a low, bitter sound as she remembered her favorite defense for living in New York City: *You can make a big city feel smaller, but you can't make a small town feel bigger.* Sloane wrapped her arms around herself, nervous that this small town may very well swallow her whole.

As the ground leveled beneath their feet, they could see the light from inside the house as it blazed bright against the 5:00 p.m. darkness. Caleb stomped his way to the front door, decorating the wooden steps with little, muddy footprints.

"Shoes off!" Sloane called after him, but Caleb squealed and ran full speed toward the sound of James in the kitchen and the soothing aroma of sizzling onions and garlic.

Starting in the early days of their marriage, he frequently welcomed Sloane with this sauteed combination. It didn't matter what the nightly recipe was or when the bulk of the cooking would even take place, he always set to this task first. This signature scent would fill their apartment on most evenings, and there were days when it would reach Sloane in the elevator on the way up to their floor. It always melted away the hardest of days, and she hoped her husband's magic trick would work the same here as it had always done at home.

"How was your day?" Sloane shouted down the short hallway toward the kitchen.

"Oh, you know," he called back and gave the frying pan a quick shake, "all work and no play." James's laptop sat open on the countertop, multiple documents scattered across the screen. Steam rose from the scalding pan and disappeared as it hit the microwave just above the stove.

Sloane walked to the small bassinet next to the couch where she detached Otto from her body. The brown wisps of hair on the side of Otto's head were matted with sweat. She gently placed him down, moved toward James, and kissed him on the cheek before pushing past. Sloane's eyes were focused on the open window above the sink. It was the only window with a view up the mountain.

She slammed the window shut with surprising force.

"What are you doing? I just opened that!" James protested.

Sloane whipped around, her loose chestnut hair catching in her lashes. "When *you're* the one out there with the boys all day, *you* can control the temperature."

James stood wide-eyed holding the spatula midair.

Sloane winced. "I'm sorry." She came up behind him and pressed her cheek to his back. She wrapped her arms around his waist and added, "Long day."

"Oh yeah?" he asked gently.

Sloane paused for a moment. "Kind of strange, actually. I met the locals. . . ."

James turned toward his wife, still in her embrace, and raised his eyebrows.

Sloane shook her head. "I don't know; something just felt off about this guy we met today."

"Well." He paused. "You must have met Carol's son. Everything feels a little off right now. No one knows how to interact anymore."

Sloane lowered her voice to a whisper. "James, he had a gun."

"Yeah, Sloane." He sighed impatiently and moved from her grasp. "People have those out here."

"Well, maybe you're used to that kind of thing, but you know how much I hate it."

James grew up in Milton, Pennsylvania. It was a small town where the only excitement was the overflow from Penn State football games. It was also a place where the local rifle sales at Walmart were consistently in high demand. When the time came for James to choose a college, most of his peers donned their Penn State sweatshirts, but he found that he was yearning for something different.

James applied to New York University where he met Sloane midway through senior year. She captivated him with her quick wit and street-smart attitude. Sloane knew where to get the best of everything the city had to offer. She took him to places where the employees greeted her by name. At a time when James felt like a fish out of water, he was mesmerized by the way Sloane moved through her world with grace and confidence.

He watched his wife now, standing with her arms folded tightly over her chest, a deep line embedded across her forehead. She wondered if he was starting to realize that what had once seemed like a city girl's ferocity was, in fact, a deep mistrust of the unknown.

Silence filled the space between them, and they turned their attention to Caleb, setting up his collection of plastic frogs along the edge of the dining table. They leaned back against the countertop, but Sloane kept her eyes fixed on her son.

"What do you want from me, James?" she asked softly. "I want to be at home with my new baby, not here, wandering around this place with these *people*."

James pulled Sloane toward him, spinning her so that they were face-to-face.

"Look, this is hard on all of us. All I'm asking is that you at least try to make an effort."

"I don't think I can," she said before swallowing the tightness in her throat.

James moved away from her and shifted his attention to the cutting board where he went back to slicing onions.

Sloane disappeared into the bathroom, locking the door and grabbing the nearest towel to fill with fiery tears. Her cry seeped through the cracks of the old house and drifted into the darkness.

The night was a restless one, filled with strange noises and even stranger dreams. Sloane dreamed of calloused fingers and brooding eyes. He stayed with her through breakfast, a silent distraction while she and James sipped their coffee, an unnerving presence as she fed Otto and dressed Caleb. After pulling Caleb's pajama top up over his head, she sat cross-legged on the floor. She blinked hard, trying to quiet her thoughts. Caleb was standing in front of her with a rapidly moving mouth and bouncing body. His hazel eyes shone brightly into hers.

"Please, Mom, can we go now?" Caleb whined.

Sloane stared back, her eyes stinging from last night's mascara. "Go?"

"To the pond!" Caleb tugged with sticky fingers at the neck of her oversized T-shirt. "Come. On. Come. On."

She reached for the baby wipes and began cleaning his hands. "I don't think so, kiddo."

James shot her a quick, sharp glance and placed his mug on the counter with a heavy hand.

"I'll take you later."

Sloane rubbed at the black specks on her cheeks and bore into James.

"You're busy. I can take him."

"Sloane," he began with raised eyebrows, "I'll move some things around."

His attention moved away from her, and his expression lightened. "I'll take you to the pond after lunch, buddy."

"Don't be ridiculous." Sloane tossed the wipes to the side and rose to her knees. "It's fine."

She leaned closer to Caleb to where the tops of their foreheads almost touched.

"We can go back to the pond, but we stick together." She put a single warning finger between them. "No running off."

James opened his laptop and began stabbing his fingers against the keys.

"And," Sloane admonished, "no talking to strangers."

Caleb hugged his mother, and the entire family set into motion for the day ahead.

By 8:00 a.m., Sloane was in uniform: a backpack filled with Otto's pacifiers, multiple snacks, and several diapers. She had a baby wrapped and strapped to her chest and a toddler fused to her side.

Sloane opened the front door and shielded her face with one hand as she squinted at the partly covered sun. "I am grateful for . . ."

A rustle of leaves sent a wave of panic down her spine. Another day of empty space and empty time to fill. Of avoiding potential dangers and unforeseen injuries. Of keeping her distance from other people, people who might have the virus or other harmful intentions. She stiffened and squeezed Caleb's hand, unable to move from that first step.

"Mommy"—Caleb placed his other hand on top of hers— "there's nothing to be afraid of."

She smiled down at him and nodded before they both descended the stairs and started the upward climb.

The pond was still and the morning quiet. The house across the way appeared to be empty. The deck remained bare except for a red fishing net that rested on the splintered deck. The paint on the handle was chipped, and the net appeared to be ripped in more than one place. Caleb ran straight to the house and turned toward his mom before reaching the deck.

"Can I?" he asked with hopeful eyes.

Sloane bounced Otto as he began to fuss and stared at the closed curtains. She half expected them to move, and when they didn't, she gave Caleb permission with a quick nod.

Caleb grabbed the net and skipped back toward the pond. Otto's fussing turned to shrill demands for something soothing. Sloane patted at the side pockets of the backpack in search of a pacifier.

"I want to catch a tadpole, or a froglet, or even a frog!"

"Well, wait one second. I can help. Just don't—don't move." Sloane bounced and searched while Otto cried.

"Mo-om?" Caleb sang.

"Fine!"

Sloane paused her search and inched toward the water. She

pressed her toe into the soft patch of grass before retreating from the edge with Otto. Once again, the tadpoles dashed out from their hiding places. Caleb didn't hesitate. He took one giant step forward and plunged the net into the water. Sloane positioned the pacifier into Otto's mouth just as the wet soil beneath Caleb's feet gave way. Caleb was waist-deep and slipping farther beneath the surface. His boots and jacket added to his struggle as he clawed at the muddy perimeter.

Sloane hesitated, unsure if she should detach Otto before throwing herself toward the water. What had been a split-second hesitation felt like a lifetime before she dashed toward Caleb and fell to her knees. She grabbed at Caleb's arms and felt the tug of his waterlogged body. Three cries, each unique in their desperation, shattered the morning calm. Sloane positioned herself on her side to protect Otto. She held onto Caleb's jacket and pulled, her muscles burning with the effort. A shadow fell over them, and a pair of rough hands swept under Caleb's arms. With one swift movement, he was removed from the water and placed back on solid ground. Caleb sucked in air as he cried and instantly coughed it back out. His neck was strained and his eyes wide with shock as he looked up at the man. The man placed his hands on Caleb's shoulders and modeled breathing deeply through his nose before pushing the air from his mouth.

"You're okay. You're safe," he reassured Caleb in a steady tone.

Caleb tried to copy the breathing but kept glancing at his mother.

"Don't look at her," the man said with firm kindness. "Look at me."

Once again, he took an exaggerated breath through his nose and exhaled slowly through pursed lips. Caleb followed his lead, and by the third round, his breathing had steadied and the panic had subsided.

The stranger reached for the red net floating farther away from them. His eyes crinkled with a smile as he wrapped his hand around the handle.

"This was mine when I was about your age."

Sloane put an arm around Caleb and gently pulled him to her and away from the man.

She cleared her throat. "Thank you for—"

He held a finger to his lips, and without making a sound, he dipped the net into the water and scooped it back out. In the net was a small greenish-brown mound. The man picked up the frog, closing his fingers around it before gingerly placing it into Caleb's cupped palms. The frog jumped and startled Caleb who tried to grab hold of its legs before tossing it back into the pond. The frog landed with a splash and then bobbed, belly up, to the surface.

Caleb stared ahead, the sides of his mouth turned down, and began to quiver.

"I killed it," he said in a small voice.

He looked to his mother, who retreated even farther from the water, stroking Otto while muttering between quick gasps, "Grateful. I am grateful."

The man turned toward Sloane, registering her shaking hands, and moved back toward the pond where the frog, motionless, circled with one of its legs bent at an awkward angle.

Caleb shivered as cold droplets seeped down the back of his neck. He released a high-pitched whimper, and Sloane winced at the sound. She ran a hand over the back of Caleb's damp head and searched for words of comfort, but there were none, only the terrifying bombardment of *what if*. What if this stranger, this man she feared, hadn't shown up and the pond claimed her firstborn? What if by saving Caleb, he now transmitted the virus, putting her entire family at risk? Nothing could be trusted anymore. The stability of her life in the city had given way as quickly as the ground beneath Caleb's feet. Every concrete, curated aspect of their routine had lost its shape since they decided to leave. She wanted to run, to get away from this place, but while the adrenaline pulsing through her screamed those demands, she neither took a step nor uttered a single word.

The man removed a fresh Marlboro from a vest pocket. "He ain't dead yet, just scared."

Suddenly, there was a splash of water.

The frog flipped over and disappeared beneath the surface.

10

TASTE THE FRUIT

by Heather Siegel

"And . . . exhale," David said, opening his eyes to the cloudless blue sky. His body rested in a corpse pose atop the wild grass of his backyard, his fingers lovingly petting its pesticide-free blades, the sun washing over his dark curls and sunscreen-free chest—the way everyone should take in the rays, he thought, to give their bodies a chance to activate natural vitamin D, instead slathering on sunscreen all the time.

"Then slowly . . . ," he called, curling upward to sit, ". . . taking your time, come to a lotus position." He perched like a Buddha in black nylon shorts, enjoying his broad shoulders, thick legs, and general vitality—confirmed by a recent bio age test he'd taken online, estimating that while his chronological age was thirty-five, his true biological age was eighteen, thanks to all his healthy lifestyle choices. "And in this final moment of your practice," he continued, "remember to be present and mindful of your intentions. . . ." He imagined himself a dandelion sprouting up from the dirt as he pushed off his ankles and rose from the grass. He strutted to the glass patio table, where his open laptop rested. Leaning forward to the red-lit camera, he palmed his hands together with sincerity.

"Namaste," he offered.

"Namaste," a handful of voices chorused back, and David ducked beneath the awning to better see the faces of his online students, nine of them, bowing back from their Zoom boxes. Some showed backgrounds of similar suburban New York backyards, though judging from their lush greenery, they were padded with the monospecies of Pennington Kentucky 31 or Zenith Zoysia grasses. David knew this not only challenged the neighborhood ecosystem but also harmed it with the use of heavy fertilizers—something he was still petitioning the village about. Others' backgrounds portrayed office spaces, garages, and closets: understandable escapes, David thought, from their families on this Thursday morning, five months into the pandemic.

"Thank you, David!" Beth, a sixty-year-old grandmother, called, and David bowed again. Before lockdown, via eight weeks of spinal gyrations, he'd single-handedly weaned her off pain meds, healed her back, and undoubtedly preserved the long-term health of her liver.

"Great class as always, bud!" Sylvester called, and David nodded. With a recent homemade elderberry concoction alchemized on his own stove, David had bolstered Sylvester's immune system—evident by how Sylvester had managed to dodge Covid for the second time, though his entire family had gotten it.

"So, David, are we definitely on for class in the schoolyard Saturday?" Lucita asked, tugging down her Athleta top over her menopausal middle, vastly shrunken, David knew, thanks to his remedy of evening primrose oil, probiotics, and red ginseng.

"That's the plan," David said.

"Yay! I'm so excited to finally have an in-person class!" Lucita clapped her hands, and David smiled, feeling the benevolence of his teachership, as he knew she'd joined his studio over a year ago hoping to socialize. She lived alone and, unlike David, was not enjoying the incredible isolation of lockdown.

"But don't worry, I will keep us socially distanced," David offered for those dubious about meeting up against the advice of the Centers for Disease Control and Prevention, like Marlene, who was muttering goodbye through her mask, though she was in her own home, alone. David suppressed an eye roll as he said goodbyes, trying to summon sympathy for her—as he had for everyone afraid of getting the virus. Covid was real; he would give Dr. Fauci that. But he couldn't understand why no one trusted enough in the ancient wisdom and strength of the human body to fight the virus off— At least those whose bodies were in balance.

Years of down-dogging and inhaling essential oils had taught him, years of resisting conventional Western medicine and saying no to Big Pharma, years of hiking the Appalachian trails and the Blue Ridge Mountains, years of polar ocean dips and communing with the earth and its abundance of messages: Yes, nature could kill, but she could also heal. What researchers needed to do was get out of the artificial laboratory and into nature, where every part had its counterpart, every disease, its cure.

"Even the disease of restlessness," he said to himself, running his hand over a potted shrub of Saint-John's-wort as he headed for the back door to his kitchen. He plucked a fuzzy red and white fruit and munched as he stepped inside, recalling how the world had panicked over lockdown orders, when meanwhile, he'd rejoiced like a schoolkid on a snow day. Of course, he'd fretted about the bills, especially on the heels of his wife Jenny losing her substitute teaching income, but with his students agreeing to remote courses and a little help from Uncle Sam, he'd been able to not only keep the quinoa and organic chicken on the table, but also literally, for the first time in his adult life, begin to live his dream.

Eating, sleeping, resting, loving, spending time outside: *This* was the way of the wise, the way everyone should be afforded the luxury to enjoy without the pressures of the daily grind. David had always preached this to his classes, often citing a favorite line from Thoreau's *Walden*: "Live in each season as it passes; breathe the air, drink the drink, taste the fruit, and resign yourself to the influence of the earth." But to be able to fully embody this lifestyle was nothing short of a gift.

Obviously, not everyone shared his opinion—his own kids Edie and Max, nine and thirteen years old, fought him on hiking the nature preserve or taking their boxer Lonny for yet another a walk— Truth be told, even she'd begun ducking under the table at the jingle of the leash. Jenny, too.

"How about you guys 'resign' yourselves to the influence of the earth, and I'll 'resign' myself to watching *Hoarders*," his wife offered while kneading dough for the latest loaf of zucchini bread, trying to break the monotony of having zero plans.

Meanwhile, the times Jenny got out of her own way and joined them—walking beneath the canopies of trees, breathing in the medicinal air, grounding their bodies to the natural electrical energy of the earth— David noticed how her cynicism often melted away. Or how his kids' creativity seemed to spark beyond making mind-numbing TikToks. Recently, Edie had even picked up her sketch pad, and Max had gone back to building towers of Legos.

He stepped past their current masterpieces and shuffled into the small wooden kitchen of their 1950s Cape-style home. Not the rural Montana or North Carolina cabin he'd once envisioned for his life. But soon after they'd married, Jenny confessed she couldn't bear moving far from her aging parents. David suspected she also couldn't bear being too far from urban pleasures, but he loved her deeply, not the least of which for her cynicism and wit, and so he'd relented, doing what he could for the time being to create an oasis with sage-green walls, honey wood floors, collages of the kids' drawings, and David's nature photographs.

A pot rattled on the stove, and he moved to lift the cover, inhaling cumin and pepper as he dipped his finger in to taste the chili. Jenny was showering down the hall, so he stole another sample, then stepped outside to the front yard to pick fresh cilantro, the missing ingredient.

His garden was flourishing. Alight with the song of bees, the rows and boxes and pots were lush with varying species of vegetables, herbs, and edibles—all of which had once peeved his neighbors. But that was before supermarket scarcity and flatten-the-curve charts prompted a few of them to solicit David's help with their own gardens.

He brushed past sprigs of dandelion and bushels of romaine and passed a potted shrub of mint, stopping to nibble on a sweet and peppery leaf of dead nettle. As he chewed, appreciating the small dose of natural vitamins C, A, and K entering his system, he ran his hands lovingly along the inflammatory-fighting heart-shaped rosettes of garlic mustard with their white, sweet-looking flowers he knew were really horseradishy. He continued past the small, dusty-looking leaves of the lamb's-quarters, rich in protein and calcium—though better cooked than raw, to remove their natural, toxic oxalic acid—and found the cilantro. He broke off a few sprigs, sniffed their soapiness, and turned back to the house, when a small cluster of mushrooms caught his eye.

Parasols, he recognized instantly from their telltale umbrellalike tops. He kneeled to examine this incredible, spontaneous gift from his garden—sprouted likely on account of the organic manure he'd imported. Yes, parasols, for sure, he confirmed, stroking their tan scales and examining the distinct separation of their gills from their stems— thin, dense, and firm under his fingers.

Alongside this cluster of five mature mushrooms were smaller, whiter, ellipsoidal spores, which David knew would eventually round and flatten when they matured. Remembering this, David was suddenly aware of the synchronicity of finding these shrooms, as he'd come across an article about these edible beauties just last week in an organic gardening blog. Parasols were known for their abundant protein, B vitamins, and fiber—their extract was even known to ward off cancer cells and fight microbial and viral infections.

"A little extra Covid precaution," he mused, bowing down in thanks to the invisible garden gods, as he plucked one up from the soil and sniffed it.

It smelled starchy and nutty and maple syrup–like, and he
instinctively licked it. It was tasty—so tasty, he couldn't help but nibble
the tip, then chomp some more. In a salad, it would make a nice
accompaniment to the chili, he decided, and plucked three from the
cluster and carried them inside to the kitchen. There, he rinsed them in a
strainer, dried them, and set them on the counter. The mushroom had
activated his appetite, and he paused to confirm the sound of the blow-
dryer running, then smuggled a bowl of chili, heaping on organic sour
cream, and dropping the cilantro on top. The tomato was tart—he
estimated the pot needed another thirty minutes or so to cook—but he
wolfed it down. The pepper stung his tongue, and he dug in the
refrigerator for a coconut Bai, which he downed in one long swig.

He spent the next twenty minutes catching up on emails, then
another half hour taking Lonny for a walk. When he returned, his
stomach murmured and he once again sorted through the refrigerator,
this time finding a container of homemade vanilla almond yogurt. The
sweetness was refreshing after the spicy chili, and he sprinkled blueberries
and sliced almonds on top.

"I was just about to make the kids some cauliflower pizza," Jenny
said, walking in. She wore her favorite, holey Nirvana T-shirt, with one
tuck into the buttonhole of her stretchy, curvy jean shorts. New, David
noted, but he knew better than to remark upon it.

"You want?" She turned her head, her freshly diffused brown lob
hairdo scenting the room with coconut musk and something chemical
David suspected was not on the paraben-free shelves of Whole Foods.

His stomach gurgled again. Between this morning's session and
the walk, he was suddenly ravenous. "Sure, I'll have one or two slices—"

Edie skipped in, her bare feet squeaking on the wood floor.
"Dad? After lunch, can we watch *Avatar* and make ice cream sundaes?"

David turned to his little girl and snagged her just as she tried
making a run for it. She squealed with delight flailing her bony limbs.
"Ice cream sundaes. Someone's acting like it's Friday night!" His son
caught wind of the fun and ran in from the adjoining room to pounce on
his dad. David maneuvered to the living room where he let them pin him
to the ground. It was a Thursday at 1:00 p.m., he thought, but why not
enjoy a creamy indulgence—especially some of that delicious artisanal
five-ingredient mint cashew chip from the plant-based Brooklyn
Creamery.

He broke from their tackles with the ease of a bull, and as the
kids continued leaping on him, he shucked them off and snorted for
effect. His daughter tried wrapping her skinny arms around his shoulders
while his son pulled at David's wrists, trying to undo his dad's balance.

David freed himself, whirling on his hands and knees to face off again, just as the room began to spin. He fell back on his feet, feeling light-headed, an icy cold sweat rippling along his skin.

"Tackle his legs, Edie!" Max cried, pummeling into his father's chest.

David lost his breath and tumbled onto his side. The room seemed to spin faster.

"Dad?" Edie leaned down, her brown hair smelling of violets and Barbie dolls. "Dad, try to get me off!" She leaped onto David's waist.

"Edie, Max, stop!" David roared, but somehow the words left his mouth in a hoarse whisper.

Jenny called from somewhere high above him. "What's going on?"

Edie stood. "We were just playing."

David moaned, curling tighter into himself.

"David? Is your back hurt?"

Another rumble formed in David's belly, and this time he knew it wasn't hunger. He pushed off his wrists, heaving himself up—his thick arms and legs, suddenly thicker than a bull's, as thick as an elephant's limbs, he thought, feeling very much like the mammoth beast as he staggered and lumbered.

The toilet.

He had to get to the toilet.

"What did you guys do to him?"

"We didn't do anything!"

"Does this mean we can't watch a movie?"

David slapped the hallway walls for balance. "I'm fine." He thrust himself forward. A few more steps to the powder room were all he needed. His bare foot landed on a Lego. "Goddammit——"

The chili was coming. He didn't know which way first.

He gripped the bathroom doorframe, threw himself inside, and swung the door closed. As he flipped up the lid, the contents of his stomach projected into the water, filling the bowl. He slapped the handle, flushing it down, but the chili kept coming. So did the almond yogurt and fruit, the coconut Bai, the granola he'd had for breakfast, perhaps the vegetarian stew from the night before. He puked and flushed. Puked and flushed. Wave after wave. His skin felt aflame; his body shivered. A sharp pain twisted his gut, and he heaved himself up, undid the drawstring of his cotton pants, and emptied his colon until he couldn't imagine anything was left inside of him.

"Can I get you anything?" Jenny called from outside the door.

"I'm good," he eked out.

"David," Jenny whispered. "Do you think it's Covid?"

"It's not Covid." He moaned.

"Gastrointestinal distress is one of the early signs," she continued.

A surge of annoyance pulsed through him as he registered she'd been at it again: watching the news and falling for the fearmongering.

"You're going to have to quarantine—"

"—Relax," he yelled through the door. "It's not Covid! And even if it is, my body will handle it."

"Maybe you can but the kids. Oh my god, I saw my mother yesterday. David. She's seventy-five."

"Jenny, please. You need to calm . . ." He trailed off as the reality of the last two hours sank in. His head whipped up.

The mushrooms.

He had to get them off the counter.

Jenny?!" His voice was weak. It would not carry. "Jenny!"

She was no longer at the door; he heard her in the kitchen. The plates coming down from the cabinets. He could not leave the toilet. Another wave overcame him, this time in tandem. His bottom evacuated while he vomited into the trash can. "Jenny!" Why wouldn't she listen to him?

"You guys want onion and garlic on your pizza?" he heard his wife calling. What if she saw the mushrooms? What if she decided to shred them? He was a bullish elephant, but she was constitutionally weaker; Edie, a featherlight ballerina; his son, a scrawny computer engineer.

He lifted his ass from the porcelain and opened the door. "Jennyyy!"

"What is it?" She came running.

"Jenny, don't eat the mushrooms."

Her face peered through the crack. "What mushrooms?"

"The ones on the counter. Bag them up. Hurry."

"David? What did you do? . . . Oh my god, do I need to call an ambulance?"

"Just do it!"

Another round overcame him, this time with only spasms and spittle. There was nothing left, thankfully. He pulled himself upward and went to the sink. Washed his face with cold water and rinsed out his mouth. Sweat poured over his skin. His bones shook. The room would not stop moving.

He opened the door and stumbled a few feet to the master bedroom, where he collapsed on the bed, a searing pain stabbing his gut.

"David, I'm calling 911."

"Noooo!" he called. "It will pass. . . ."

"David! You ate a poisonous mushroom."

"Calm down. It wasn't poisonous," he mumbled, even as an uneasy feeling overcame him. "I'll show you . . . get the laptop." He climbed beneath the covers.

Jenny brought it over and sat next to him, bolstering a pillow beneath her back.

"Look up the parasol mushroom," he instructed.

She did, scanning the article, then gasped. At the bottom of the page was a small highlighted box, the title of which read, "Beware of Parasol Look-alikes."

"Was it one of these?"

David squinted at the screen. He had not heard of the look-alikes, and it surprised him. At a glance, the mushrooms were identical to the parasol, except many had greenish tints to their gills and light green spores. David thought about the mushrooms on the counter. The spores had been white . . . hadn't they?

Jenny clicked on a link: "The false parasol . . . aka, the vomiter, David. . . . David you could get bloody stools."

His teeth chattered. The stabbing pain would not subside, and the light of the screen hurt his retinas. He turned from it and lay his head back on the pillow. "What's the remedy?" he asked.

"There is no treatment, David. . . . You're supposed to vomit it out."

"Well, there you go," David said. "Done. The earth made an offending compound and its remedy all in one."

" . . . And seek medical care if the symptoms worsen. . . . David, you need to see a doctor."

"It's already out of my system." David pawed the laptop closed. "Relax, I know what I need. . . . And it's not some drug-pushing emergency room. . . . Can you shut the shades?"

Jenny rose from the bed. "Fine. But if you get worse, we are going in." Motherhood had long since preempted Jenny's naturalism phase, David knew. But he also knew he needed to step aside and let his body work its homeostatic magic.

He spent the next several hours returning to the bathroom. He was shivering and sweating, but his stomach had all but emptied, and he could only spit dribbles of saliva into the toilet water. "Rest and hydration," he murmured to himself, though he had trouble drifting off and keeping down the requested coconut water or bone broth.

Around midnight when the house was asleep, he returned to the laptop. This time, he googled about the other possible parasol look-alikes, not because he thought he might have ingested them, but to learn about antidotes, which, despite Jenny's insistence that there weren't any, he knew he could find in his garden.

To be more precise in his remedies, he took the baggie down from the top of the refrigerator, where she'd tucked them, and held it to the computer screen, comparing the mushroom's shape to the picture of another fungi displayed: the death cap.

He did not read the details about kidney and liver failure. He would not entertain the thought he might have mistaken a benign mushroom for a fatal one. Nor could his mind bend to such a mushroom growing in his suburban garden, even as he remembered choosing the soil for its South African origin. His focus was on the cure for even the worst of the look-alike offenders, for he understood that in natural healing one always needed to stay a step ahead of symptoms and that the body would excrete any excess remedies it did not find useful. So he perused the botanical sites that had always served him well, then walked outside to his garden.

He found the suggested plants in the silvery moonlight: oregano, basil, thyme, ginger, and the most important, garlic bulbs. He plucked them with care and returned to the kitchen where he boiled water and steeped the green leaves of the plants and gingerroot, mixing in honey and cardamom. This would settle his stomach. The garlic would act as the antifungal.

He sipped the tea while he chopped two cloves and set them on a roasting pan in the toaster oven, lightly drizzling them with olive oil. The smell churned his stomach, but he noticed the tea was staying down, so when the garlic was ready, he forced himself to spoon the roasted cloves into his mouth. He waited for a reaction, and when there wasn't one, he climbed back into bed to let his body continue fighting. His skin hurt to the touch as he slid between the sheets, and he closed his eyes and wished for sleep.

Before he knew it, he was awake again, only the light streaming in from the half-shaded window signaled morning had come.

He smelled cinnamon and coffee and could hear Jenny clanging plates and glassware. He reached over and sipped more of his herbal tea, which was now lukewarm. His skin felt less painful, he thought, and with that, he decided not to join them in the kitchen. Fasting was helping to restore balance.

He slept some more, and when he woke, the sun was near setting. He studied the golden slant, the way it rippled over the tree leaves swaying by the windowpanes. He felt immense gratitude for his home and his bed—and even more for his body's ability to have carried him through.

The door opened and Jenny peeked in. "You're up," she said. "How are you feeling?"

David shimmied up, checking himself. His skin had completely revived; his stomach had settled; the cold sweat had dissipated. Even his muscles felt strong again. He reached for his tea and drank the last dregs of his healing concoction.

"The worst has passed," he said, hoping to discourage a discussion about yesterday's events.

"You got lucky," she said, changing from her day sweatpants into her night sweatpants.

He left it at that and curled up again, knowing sleep would only further restore his systems. He dozed peacefully through the night, and at 8:00 a.m., when his phone alarm sounded with Coldplay's "Viva La Vida," reminding him of the schoolyard class and his livelihood, he rose, feeling more invigorated than he had since nibbling the mushroom.

He shuffled to the kitchen and prepared a pot of fair-trade bulletproof coffee. The smell of the oily, acidic liquid brewing, however, turned his stomach, so he forewent making his usual cup and instead filled his water bottle with more of his herbal tea, squeezing in fresh lemon juice. The garlic, still about three teaspoons worth, sat in a small ceramic bowl, floating in the olive oil. He grabbed a spoon, and despite the nauseous wave moving toward his throat, he quickly glopped the healing mixture onto his tongue and swallowed.

The nausea subsided, and he scribbled a note to Jenny and tacked it to the fridge. *Back in an hour and a half.* Then he rinsed his mouth with Tom's of Maine and dressed in drawstring pants and a loose black T-shirt inscripted with *Just Breathe.*

As he pulled his curls into a low bun, he hiccuped—the mouthwash splashing back up to his tongue, a mix of herbs, garlic, mint, and acids. He spit into the sink, then went to the garage and got his mountain bike. His hands felt sweaty, and he told himself it was the summer heat, even as he leaned down to the side mirror of Jenny's truck and caught a glance of his bloodshot eyes, their underneath purpled.

"Residual effects," he said as he mounted the bike and pedaled the three blocks, feeling a bit as though he were cycling underwater. The sun was hot, and it seemed almost to burn his skin that had begun to grow wet with sweat. *Not surprising*, he told himself, considering all he had gone through in the last forty-eight hours. Nor was he concerned as he hopped off and said hello to the group, already assembled beneath a wide oak tree, and his heart fluttered in a new way.

I have been bedridden, he thought. *And hardly eaten.*

His students called and waved from their mats spaced six feet apart. "Hi, David. . . . Good morning! . . . 'Sup, buddy. . . ."

"Morning, everyone." David forced a smile as he leaned the bike against the tree, grasping the bark for balance. "Let's begin right away," he said, eager for them to avert their gazes, as his heart once again flitted inside his rib cage. After class, he consoled himself, he would make triple the dose of garlic—maybe not even roast it; instead, he'd take it raw with honey for a double antifungal whammy.

"We will start by closing our eyes and paying attention to our breathing. . . ." His own breath was labored, but the words flowed from his mouth on automatic pilot, so that he didn't notice. "Vinyasa is about the intimacy of our breath to our body, the knowledge the body wants to impart to you in its natural state." He pushed down the knowledge his own breath and body was trying to impart and focused on the series of poses he would walk them through, each with a handful of moves.

". . . Continuing Sun Salutations," he said, gripping the ridges of the bark, as though trying to extract something it could not yield. "Move from child's pose to down-dog, holding for eight breaths. . . ." This time, his heart jerked in his chest, and he looked to the sky, which also seemed indifferent to helping him, its vast smooth and blue dome shrinking his existence.

Water. He needed some immediately.

Of course, he told himself; he was dehydrated after all he had been through. But he'd forgotten his bottle of herbal lemon tea on the countertop. He reached into the pocket of his drawstring pants and pulled out his phone. "Now, walk your hands backward to your feet, and slowly roll up one vertebra at a time. . . ." He texted Max. *"Bring me my water bottle."*

His son arrived at the end of the sixth series. By then, David had taken to sitting beneath the oak tree, resting his back against it, his legs in lotus position, so as still to assume a sense of sage authority.

"Thanks, kiddo," David said, trying to sound cheery as his son handed him the BPA-free bottle; he knew that by then, his students expected him to be halfway deep into the crow pose with them.

"Dad, you okay?" Max whispered. "You look a little yellow."

"I'm good buddy, go on home. . . . Excellent, and now we move into the warrior poses series. . . ." He undid the cap. He was aware that his fingertips hurt as though freezer burned. "Excellent . . . and now warrior two pose. . . ." He walked his students through the cobra pose, the cow pose, and the happy baby pose, gulping swigs of tart water, even as the water did not want to stay down.

He tried breathing through the urge to purge, tried mind over matter; but as the class nestled into shavasana, David instructed them to close their eyes and quiet their minds, then crawled around the base of the tree and, as quietly as he could, retched the water over its gnarled roots.

The water ran clear, as he no longer had food in his system, but it soon appeared rust colored; and when he finally caught his breath, he saw that color was his blood, glistening under the shaded leaves. His body was exorcising tissue damage the mushroom may have done, he told himself, as he rolled to his side, clawed the bark, and pulled himself to a stand. *After all, it was only a few nibbles*, he continued in his mind. *Primitive people must have eaten worse, and they survived.*

He reached for the other remedies in his garden he would employ to assist his body in healing. Turmeric . . . pau d'arco . . . onions. *Of course*, why hadn't he eaten them from the start? He would also eat them raw, with the garlic, he decided: Bite them like apples, and let the antibacterial allicin kill whatever bacteria was infecting him.

He wobbled around the tree, brought class out of session with a namaste, and heaved himself onto the bike.

His legs were feathers by then, his heart a small fish flopping in his chest. He brought the empty bottle to his lips and tried depositing the remaining droplets onto his tongue. His body would not have it. "Electrolytes," he muttered. "More coconut water." And with that, one house from his own, he fell onto the Turners' perfect, newly fertilized sod and vomited again, his face becoming one with the plastic-like green blades. When he brought his hand to his mouth to wipe the excess, he saw what Max had seen: the yellow tint to his skin. A sign of jaundice, a sign that his organs were being tested. He needed to get to his kitchen.

He dug deep, summoning the last of his bullish reserves, and crawled to his front porch, where he tapped on the bottom of the door, the white metal of the screen burning his hand.

"David? . . . Oh my god," Jenny said. And he lay his head on the concrete as the siren sounded in the background.

Mushrooms, he heard next as the EMTs brought him back with oxygen. "Wife said it was out of his yard." The ambulance was moving; shapes of buildings and trees blew past. A hand held up the plastic baggie to the window.

The mushrooms illuminated in the clarity of the sunlight, but David's mind would not concede to the sight of the light green–tinted caps, the striated stalk rings, and the white veils of the death cap. Nor would he succumb to poisoning himself with who knows what concoctions were in the EMTs' bag of tricks, which is why as the technicians pricked a needle into his arm, he flailed and cried out, "Do not put that garbage in my veins!"

They strapped him down then, so that he lay flat upon the white, starched cot, his palms facing upward.

"Going into organ failure," someone said.

"Jenny," David mouthed with so much he wanted to tell her: that it was time for the kids to walk Lonny; that the parabens in her hair products were what were likely exacerbating her elbow eczema . . .

Beeping sounded, and he closed his ears and concentrated on his cures, walking his mind back to his garden. The bees were buzzing as he moved among the healing vegetables and herbs. The garlic and onions were just within reach.

11

AN IOTA OF HARM

by Taylor Days

For fifteen years, Ella's father said just one thing when she left the house each morning for school. It wasn't "I love you" or "Have a good day." He said, "Be alert," and locked the door behind her. She supposed he wouldn't be pleased to find her this way now, three gin and tonics past sober on a vinyl bench affixed to the wall in a dark bar uptown. Her lashes were lowered behind the fragrant curtain of Eli's long black locks, and the neon lights behind the bar threw columns of shadows along her face. His right arm, draped across her shoulders, was so heavy with bone and muscle that she could barely breathe under its weight. She considered asking him to remove it, but instead she gripped his other arm with both of her hands like an inexperienced swimmer being slowly escorted into deep water.

They walked here from the sushi place she chose in Midtown, but at some point, he led her down a street she had never been on, and now—even as a native New Yorker—she wouldn't be able to retrace her steps if she tried. She was only vaguely aware of the hour—late—if time was even still a thing. Once in Amsterdam, she had gotten so high, so daffy and displaced, that she tried to open a bathroom door in a hotel lobby with her room key—it was already open—and it wasn't even her hotel. The wispy memory floated alongside her on the vinyl uptown bench and dissipated before she understood why. So she hadn't kept her wits about her as her father had so often cautioned her to. He would be chagrined to find her so drunk and addled in this dive bar. But he wasn't here, she was. And though she felt a bit foggy—she knew that the answers and maybe even the questions were here, too, on Eli's soft, firm lips, pulling at hers like the dizzying, unrelenting, electrifying tide.

"Why do you feel like this?" she whispered.

"Like what?" He asked it into her mouth, still kissing.

She giggled. He stopped and pulled away.

"Come to Brooklyn," he commanded and then searched her face, trying to read her thoughts.

Her thoughts were that Eli was magnificent. It was the only word for him and a word she never used in any context other than to describe him. They met back in October at a party on the Lower East Side she'd gone to with her friend Joy. They'd stood outside, huddled together and shivering in short flared skirts and tank tops until the bouncer checked their IDs and let them up a small set of metal steps with black industrial pipes for bannisters. At the top of the steps, Ella and Joy filed into a foyer with twelve other twentysomething girls, all glitter eyeshadow and dry shampoo. They squished into the hot, overcrowded freight elevator, where their perfumes combined and became one communal scent, cloying and chaotic.

The doors closed and they arrived on the second floor just thirty seconds later—then grew nervous waiting behind the unyielding doors for another thirty until they finally opened. When they did, the girls spilled out, relieved, into a giant dark loft space with a stage and navy lights. And there was Eli, his beautiful face obscured slightly by the microphone, nothing but a tunnel of darkness between them. And the light at the end of it, Eli's smile and deep dark skin. He was singing a slow one, though she would come to know that he didn't really have that many of those. You could dance to most of his stuff, but when she walked in, he was singing one filled with longing and minor chords; one that built slowly, a funicular headed toward some steep precipice. He played the guitar effortlessly, as though it was someone else's fingers accompanying him. And when he sang, he didn't open his mouth and push sound out—instead it bounced and hummed against the flaps in his throat and resonated up and out, gifted with its own agency.

Three months later, after they'd met at the loft party, Ella agreed to go home with him. They left the uptown vinyl bench for the January bitterness, running down the subway steps to catch the D they took to his apartment. Inside the train, Eli leaned against the door between the cars and held open his coat—an invitation. Ella stepped inside and he closed the flaps behind her. She was a hummingbird in a vertical nest, hurtling through space toward Brooklyn.

Ella's father was an architect by trade, so perhaps his watchfulness began as an occupational hazard. His job had been to create spaces where people could work or learn or play. He had to anticipate what their needs might be while using those spaces, and he had to keep them safe while they did it. He was driven by that charge and even more vigilant regarding her safety than the public's. She often chose the term *vigilant* to discuss how he raised her. It was objective and maybe even generous. She imagined the adjectives she could have chosen instead on a spectrum: *vigilant, protective, cautious, careful, paranoid.* Her mother had chosen the last of these and left them.

It was true that he was attentive, but it came from a place of love. And is it paranoia if you're right? He was quick to anticipate anything going wrong, but the trait her mother viewed as negativity had done a pretty good job keeping Ella safe and healthy. There was the time he told her not to eat the chicken at that restaurant on Orchard, and everyone else who ate it got sick. Or the time he showed up at her sleepaway camp to take her home right before a massive storm hit Montauk. To Ella, it was loving, if overzealous, parenting. But for Ella's mother, the restrictions felt unnecessary. She could only see the times when he was negative and nothing happened at all: Don't get in that cab; the driver's a nut. She acquiesced but resented it while she waited twenty minutes for the next one. To her mom, he had been controlling, and she had escaped.

For most of her life, Ella wasn't like her father. She was reckless, spacey, trusting. And it wasn't until he died that she became anything else. One month after his burial she was twenty-six and abroad: Her friend Idgee invited her to a resort in the Caribbean, all expenses paid, to celebrate Idgee's upcoming marriage. Ella, Idgee, and Joy landed in the Bahamas and stripped down to their bathing suits immediately—starved by the city for sun and salt air. By that afternoon, they were at the beach, floating in the warm ocean. This water was warmer than any ocean she'd ever been in, and they treaded atop the gentle waves until the sun set and they could only see stars.

The next day Ella woke up on the wrong side of the hotel bed with a bad feeling about paradise. Even with fresh-squeezed guava juice and pancakes at breakfast, she couldn't shake it. That afternoon they went for a walk around the property, down winding pathways and across footbridges suspended over ponds filled with koi, but Ella's extremities had become lead and she had a hard time keeping up. Idgee, an emetophobe, examined Ella and leaned away, wrinkling her nose.

"Um, you okay?" She raised her right eyebrow.

Ella nodded reassuringly, but despite the warm, soft breeze, she felt as one does before a fall, suspended in space with her uneasy stomach caught in her throat. By the time they arrived at the lazy river, she really did think she would lose her guava juice. And then it happened: a sharp, white, searing pain in her head, and then water rushing, subsuming her mind, the sound of it filling her ears, filling her eyes until the water formed shapes, and the shapes formed images, and the images created a story so clear she knew what would happen. They could not get on this lazy river. Idgee would have an accident.

There were some boys on the ride; maybe they were thirteen or fourteen. Ella couldn't see them yet, but she knew they were there. They were clogging up the man-made stream with their bodies and inner tubes on the slow-moving current for fun, in an attempt to create a more rollicking body of water. The narrow opening they left between themselves and the wall were now shallow rapids, and the boys would bump Idgee right off her tube as she passed because she was pretty and they wanted to watch her fall in. But Idgee wouldn't expect it. She'd go flying into the currents and get swept downward with a speed she wouldn't have anticipated in a lazy river. She wouldn't have time to do the geometry, and she'd hit her head—hard. Ella and Joy would ride back to JFK in stunned silence. There wouldn't be a wedding.

Ella watched Idgee's face as she tried to explain what she'd seen. Idgee was confused, then incredulous, then concerned, and finally angry. Ella could see why. They were in paradise, about to meander down a lazy river as a group of single girls for the last time, and Ella seemed to be breaking girlfriend rule number one: Don't make your friend's bridal thing about you. Ella knew how this looked. But what was she supposed to do? Not say anything? Let Idgee get hurt? Idgee finally agreed not to get in the water and to go back to the hotel—she wrapped her towel around her waist and shoved her freshly manicured feet back into her water shoes. She gave Ella her best, most photogenic angry face, dark eyes flashing with betrayal, then turned and began to tromp back toward the hotel—walking just ahead of Ella the whole way. Ella followed through the landscaped foliage and cacti, kicking herself. Was this Ella's inheritance? This insight? What good was it if it caused her to lose everything piece by piece as her father had? He had lost his career, his friendships, and even his spouse. For this—gift? A gift he didn't have to use?

As Idgee stormed the steps to the hotel lobby, Ella followed behind and began to understand how her mother could feel imprisoned. Don't go to the drugstore right now. Wait ten more seconds before we cross the street. The demands probably added up, felt excessive. Ella watched Idgee avoid making eye contact by studying the fire map above the elevator button so closely you'd have thought there'd be an exam. Ella understood why her mother didn't stay.

Two days after they returned to New York, Ella was leaving Walgreens when she got the call she knew she would.

"I don't think you should be a bridesmaid, Ella."

"Fine. Right. Of course. No problem."

"And"—Idgee took a deep breath and said the last part fast, like she was pulling off a word Band-Aid—"I'm going to ask you not to come to the wedding."

"What?"

"Sorry, Ella."

Ella spotted a bench outside of a playground and swung her packages onto the seat. "But, Idgee, why? I don't understand. Because I asked you not to get on some ride?"

"It's not about the ride."

"It sounds like it is. It sounds like you're disinviting me from your wedding because I wouldn't let you get on a lazy river. A Cyclone, I'd understand. . . .

"Ella." Idgee ignored her joke. "It's really not. I just— I don't trust you."

"You've gotta be kidding me," Ella retorted. "We've been friends for what, a decade, and you don't trust me? I know all of your— You don't trust me?"

"Not like that. . . . Look, El— I've got a lot of mental illness in my family—you know that. And I know you have a lot in yours, too."

Ella opened her mouth to respond but couldn't decide what to say so she closed it again. She joined her packages on the bench.

"I think you need some therapy. And I'm willing to help you get it. I'll call psychiatrists; I'll go with you to Bellevue or Urgent Care. Whatever it takes. But I'm betting you don't think you need any of that."

"Idge, let me explain—"

"Do you?" Idgee demanded. "Do you agree that you need help?"

She could agree. Do a little therapy. Insurance would probably take care of most of it. She and Idgee could probably be back on track in few months. But even though she didn't feel prepared to lose anyone else so soon after her father died, she wasn't crazy. She wouldn't let Idgee think she was. She had only been trying to help her.

"No, Idge." Ella shook her head slowly. "I'm really okay."

On Idgee's side of the phone, it was quiet, so for a moment, they both listened to the trucks and sirens and horns on Ella's.

"Fine." Idgee ended the break. "But I can't watch you have a breakdown and not do anything about it. And I don't want to risk this life that I'm building by having you in it when you are clearly unwell."

A loud guffaw escaped from Ella's belly, not only because it was a ridiculous assertion, which it was, but also because she was embarrassed. A small, prune-like woman with a cane and a fresh roller set passed by and wearily glanced up at her.

Idgee paused, perplexed by Ella's reaction, then continued, "I have a lot going on right now, and I just don't have space for it, El."

"Idgee. I understand about the wedding, truly. But don't you think we could move past this eventually? I mean, you're my friend. I love you."

"Love you, too, El. Gimme a call when you get some help."

At Eli's apartment, she took off her jacket, draped it on his chair, and sat at his desk. Above it, mounted on cork, were pictures of his mom and little sister, his EMT certificate, and images of him onstage with his band. There were handwritten song lyrics, articles for nursing school, and a series of her smiling outside his show at Joe's Pub a couple of months ago. And then on the desk itself: matches, sage ash on a porcelain dish, a silver hamza dangling from a black string.

Ella admired Eli's spirituality. Her father was godless, and her mother was Catholic and traumatized. There had been no religion in her home at all.

"Can brunch be a religion?" she'd asked Joy one Sunday, rooting around in the pastry basket for a chocolate croissant and sticking it next to her yogurt parfait. Joy smooshed her pancake in between her two clasped hands and bowed her head.

Perhaps he would believe her if she told him what she could do? Maybe he would see it as a gift from god. Eli sat on the edge of his bed, watching Ella gaze at his desk for a few minutes and then asked, "Did you want to do my work or . . . ?"

"Ha," snipped Ella.

"Why don't you come and sit next to me?" he suggested.

"Nah, I'm good."

"Oh yeah?"

"Yeah, I don't sit next to snarky people." She shrugged as if to say "Rules are rules."

"I apologize, my good lady." He had a fantastic British accent for some reason, and he liked to employ it in moments like these to make her laugh. "Would you be good enough to join me on the bed?"

Ella stood, did a pique turn, and plopped down next to him. For a moment, they sat there, rocking gently in the waves from her drop.

"You okay?" he asked her. "You seem, like, a little in your head."

"Yeah. I'm okay." She paused, thinking about how much she admired him and then, realizing what a fine line it was between admiration and jealousy, added, "Sometimes I just really wish I had what you have."

"A tiny apartment?"

She shook her head no.

"Crushing student debt?"

She smiled. Shook her head again.

"What do I have?" he asked.

"Faith."

Eli considered this a moment and then spoke. "You know what you need?" His face lit up with an idea.

"What do I need?" *Please tell me*, Ella thought.

"A massage."

"That is exactly what I need!" Ella exclaimed. She leaped across his bed and nestled her head into his pillows, ready to enjoy a nice, long full-body massage, but she fell asleep so quickly that she was only briefly aware of Eli's determined thumbs working the muscles on either side of her spine.

The next morning Ella opened her eyes and found Eli kneeling on the floor, his face a few inches from hers.

"You're beautiful," he said.

She rubbed her eyes, then rolled them.

"Would you want to marry me?" He grasped her hand.

"Could I get some coffee first?" Ella smiled but Eli did not. She blinked at him. She sat up in bed. "This has turned into a conversation I need to be upright for."

Eli laughed. "Say you'll marry me, and I'll order pancakes."

"So this is a pancakes-for-marriage kind of a deal? Aren't I worth bacon?"

"I don't fuck with bacon, but I'll throw in some eggs."

Ella slid down and wrapped her legs around him.

"You're crazy," she murmured. "It's been three months."

"I don't care. I love you."

"I know what you love. I don't think it's me, per se."

Eli bit the side of her lavender undershirt and pulled like a puppy. "It is you."

Ella considered for a moment.

"It's you," Eli repeated, deadly serious, looking up at her face.

"It's a little fast, E."

"But would you?"

Ella thought for a moment. Eli was incredible. His timing was wonky, but she could see marriage in their future. And if she could see it in their future, what was the difference between a few months and a few years?

"Can I—" Ella took a deep breath. "Can I think about it?"

"Take all the time you need. I'm not going anywhere."

"'Kay." She smiled. Nodded. Then he was next to her, on top of her, in less than a moment. She inhaled his scent and tried to stop time.

"But you don't need these clothes to think about it, right?" He slipped a warm hand beneath her undershirt and drew his fingertips along her side.

"I do—they're my thinking clothes."

"No, no, Newton did his best thinking . . ."

And then they were laughing and kissing, and when Ella fell asleep again in the warm, sunny studio, she imagined that she could never be happier than this.

When she woke up that afternoon, Eli was playing play a song she'd never heard before. She couldn't tell if he'd written it or not. It sounded both old and new: an arresting, haunting lament. And though it was beautiful, Ella felt frightened—the first time she'd ever felt that way with Eli—but she didn't dare stop him, even though the notes he sang wove a fabric that both warmed and trapped her. As Ella lay there, warm tears fell from the outside corners of her eyes, slid along her cheekbones, and came to rest near her hairline. She felt clear, sharp, and focused, as though everything that had ever happened to her had only left wisdom and no fog. In fact, she had everyone's wisdom. The wisdom of the past and the wisdom of the future. My word, she had been so intoxicated by him she couldn't see it before, but now she perceived everything with perfect clarity. She opened her eyes.

Less than a year from now, Eli would become a nurse. It would suit him, and he'd love it. The women in his study group would fuss over him, and because he'd be one of the only men in the class, they'd be completely enamored. They'd make him cookies, and he'd bring them home for Ella to munch on while she quizzed him for the nursing exam. He'd crush it, and by January, he'd have a good job at a hospital in the city. They'd walk out of the door together in the morning and take the train to work—she'd get off at Fourteenth Street, kiss him goodbye, tell him to be alert. He'd smile and crumple up his face, still confused by her inside joke with herself, and then nod, like usual: "Yeah, yeah, yeah . . ." They'd be in such a groove—texting, takeout, gigs on the weekends—that they'd be gobsmacked by how suddenly a virus would evict them from their blissful mundanity.

Ella could see it all in less than a minute: how Eli's cousin who was studying biology at the University of Washington would call Eli and tell him to be careful, make sure to order extra masks and wear them—this thing was no joke. A week later, Eli would begin to see people come into his ER with symptoms . . . all kinds of symptoms. It was a respiratory virus. But some people had GI symptoms, too. And others tested positive with no symptoms at all—it was nowhere and everywhere at once. By the end of March, it would have a name. And it would change everything.

Eli would be at work constantly. The doctors and the staff would all be catching it, and soon the hospital would be overwhelmed and bursting at the seams. They would have to hire independent doctors and nurses and respiratory therapists from all over the country to replace the ones who were out sick—so many that sometimes Eli would only recognize a few of the people he worked with on a shift. Mostly his coworkers would recover and come back, but sometimes they wouldn't.

Eli would be exacting and meticulous. When he would come home, he'd open the door with the gardening gloves she left by the flowerpot outside the first door. He'd take off his scrubs and mask and shove them in the trash bag she would leave for him in the downstairs foyer; flip up the blue plastic clasps on either side of the clear Rubbermaid bin they'd slide under the mail table in the downstairs hall; then take out new clothes and put those on. In her mind's eye, she could see him there, switching his shoes and dousing his hands in antibac. For a while, they'd be fine.

Ella's full-time job would become finding groceries. The supermarkets would be empty, save for the lone dented orange or mangled romaine head. The shelves would be barren. No meat, no beans, no coffee, no milk. No milk! She'd never seen that before. Joy would send her a text from the market close to her house: *"I found rice! Want some?"* Ella would say yes, and Joy would leave it at the building's front door, wordlessly wave up at Ella from the street, and then hop back in her car. Everything would be quiet. Now and again, the silence would be broken by sirens. Some were in the distance, and some were close by. And every night at seven, Ella would sit on a chair by the window and ring her bell for the health care workers—for Eli.

The guy who ran the soul food spot on the corner would give her the information for the food vendor he used—they'd have a bunch of stuff still since a lot of the restaurants they supplied were shutting down. By April, it would officially be a pandemic. Joy would send links for off-brand bulk sites that might still have toilet paper. Whatever Ella could get to arrive would get dragged into hallway purgatory. They wouldn't take anything into the apartment until it had been cleaned or untouched for three days. She would stand in the stairwell in her socks and step between bags and boxes looking for pasta. Find it. Wipe down the box. Wash her hands.

People would die. She could see all the news she would watch that year in an instant—Anderson Cooper's face above a death count that would roll up to a number that would stop being sad when it became incomprehensible. And then Eli would test positive.

He would get sick on a Tuesday in August of 2020. She could see the date on her phone as she watched herself answer a text from Joy asking how Eli was feeling. Eli wouldn't want to come home even though Ella would say she could use Joy's car to pick him up. Instead, he would walk uptown to his sister's house because she'd had the virus already and would think she would probably be safe for a bit. Ella could see him walking uptown and then the rest as a flash—Eli FaceTiming from his sister's couch, then back in his hospital as a patient this time, then everyone's shock when he doesn't recover. There will be contributory factors—including some sort of undiagnosed heart condition that he didn't know about. And even in the blur of it, Ella learned what the world would feel like without Eli. It would be cold, bleak. Pointless. Ella would feel his absence in her core.

It wouldn't be safe to have a service and so they'd do a Zoom thing. Afterward, Ella would have to figure out what to do with the groceries in the hall, all the dirty scrubs and the clothes in the Rubbermaid bin. The porcelain dish and sage ash. The dangling hamza.

She was paralyzed as the visions unfolded, rushing toward her with the speed and inevitability of a brakeless vehicle. When she could finally move again, she erupted out of bed, reinflating her lungs, sucking in huge gulps of air.

Eli stopped playing and turned to look at her, first with excitement—she was awake! And then concern when he saw the wild terror in her eyes. Eli took her face in his hands and searched it for answers the way he had last night at the bar.

"What's wrong?" he asked. It was such a small question, so disproportionate to the answer, so she began to giggle and couldn't stop. She laughed until she couldn't breathe, and her sides split and tears ran down her cheeks. Then something inside her shifted, and in the next moment, she was crying instead—so hard it hurt.

What kind of paternal inheritance was this?

Unruffled by her emotional slideshow, Eli waited.

She didn't want it. But there hadn't been anything else from her dad, not a house or a car—this was all she had of him, this power she had seen ruin all his relationships, this "gift" that brought him nothing but loneliness. No, after what had happened with Idgee, Ella had promised herself she would never say anything to anyone about what she knew.

Ever.

But it wasn't that simple; she could see that now. She understood her father perfectly: He had done what he set out to do. He'd kept her safe. She'd never met an iota of harm—had fewer accidents or illnesses than all her friends combined. She followed his rules and obeyed his commands, and things had turned out fine.

Safety couldn't be all there was to life, could it? Her life was a stagnant puddle of precaution.

What kind of life was that?

12

DANCE OF THE BIRDS

by Laura Castro

I'm sitting on my sofa watching sunlight move across my living room walls and onto the floor. I stare at my walls a lot lately, so it's a good thing I like the way they're painted. A scenic painter, who used to work on movies, taught me how to give them a cloudy, indefinite look, as if you could walk right through them—which, of course, you can't.

I'm trying to take a positive approach to this Covid "self-isolation"—see it as a kind of retreat. I'm eight days into it and conscious of my good fortune to have such a pleasant place in which to isolate. Yet, much as I value solitude when I can't have it, I have a countervailing need to be the midst of the crowd, held in its embrace—part of a tribe. Maybe I'll finish up some correspondence—that letter I was writing to a young political prisoner. Ramon.

Instead, I open a beer and a can of sardines and sit down to a David Attenborough documentary on rain-forest birds. There are these birds called manakins, which have elaborate mating rituals in which they perform complex dances, either solo or with assistants. They are tiny birds in bright jewel-like colors, and each variety has a unique dance. Sometimes the dance is successful, and the tiny bird ends up with a mate to carry on its species, sometimes not. I feel for the manakins whose dances don't pan out—though I suppose there's always a next time. And, oh, those dances are beautiful!

As one of the creatures that failed to find the appropriate mate to propagate its species when the time was right, I value my friendships with younger generations—for example, women in their forties, fellow artists or activists, who could be my daughters and have brought their own children into the world. I love that two such women, who live nearby and come to meetings in my home, know exactly where the knife-and-fork drawer is in my kitchen, and how to buzz in other people at my front door—the way one's daughters would. I suppose I won't be seeing them for a while.

Restlessness is getting the better of me, and I'm curious about the mail, hoping for a letter from Ramon. I wonder if he received my latest package of books. His supporters, of whom I am one, consider him a political prisoner; police say he's a common criminal. His cellphone video of a cop killing his African American older friend—a kind of father figure to him—was published in the *Daily News* and seen around the world. Police surveilled him, and we believe he most likely was framed. As a retired teacher, I can't help taking pleasure in Ramon's curiosity, resilience, and forays into self-improvement, coming as he has from rough beginnings. He requests books on topics ranging from Angela Davis to pre-Columbian voyages.

"I learned a lot about oceans, currents, and trade winds I never knew existed," he wrote, after receiving the volume on ancient voyages. "It's a great book, very knowledgeable."

I return to my secluded apartment after my first exercise outing in a week, eyes adjusting to the dim entryway after their unaccustomed dazzlement from sunlight pirouetting off building facades. I am twenty-one days into isolation. How I'd love to chat casually with some neighbor in the hall. I've read that positive social interactions cause oxytocin to head straight for our hearts, calming them, removing stress, lighting us up with feelings of well-being—even extending our lives. I try to imagine what life is like in "the box," as Ramon calls solitary confinement.

I start picturing him as he has appeared in photos, thin-faced, surprisingly slight of build, haunted eyes. Guards resent his testimony against the police officer who killed his friend, so he frequently "catches tickets," as he puts it, for trivial infractions, like wearing his hair in braids. As a result, he has spent a good deal of time in solitary. Adding to his troubles is a gang war at the prison.

"Someone tried to cut me for points," he wrote in his most recent letter, pondering whether it might not be safest to "catch another ticket" and remain in solitary for the rest of his sentence. Talk about self-isolation!

I empty a bottle of antidepressant/anti-anxiety pills onto a clean white piece of paper on my dining table. I am thirty-six days into isolation. I count the pills: thirty altogether, and they are scored down the middle, so that makes sixty if you cut them in half. I find this a satisfying number. I've taken to counting things: cans of soup on my shelf, rolls of toilet paper, number of deaths in my zip code.

Four days ago, I learned of the suicide of an old friend, alone in a new town, far from friends and former work. His wife, a friend of mine for fifty-two years, had died of cancer—on Valentine's Day, of all dates—just weeks before the virus hit. Isolated in the dream home near the ocean—they had built it for their retirement but lived there together only a few weeks—he was unable, it seems, to bear the loss of the love of his life.

"I never loved anyone so much," he said in one of our last phone conversations. *At least they had a great love*, I thought, looking for consultation. Yet, to end his life . . .

"I feel so guilty," I kept repeating to the woman who called with the news. I should have called him more often, I thought; perhaps that would have tipped the balance.

As I turn the pill container over in my hand, ambulance sirens on Ocean Parkway seem particularly persistent. A few days ago, an ambulance pulled up across from a neighbor's house, but a woman the paramedics came to collect died of her Covid before they could take her. A friend in Queens says a refrigerator truck is parked on the next block, because there's no room left for bodies in the hospital morgue. Up to now, I've been able to withstand this kind of news, but the suicide has knocked me off my stride.

After a pause, I tap the tiny pills back into the bottle without taking any and replace them at the rear of a pantry shelf, where they have sat untouched for more than a year. While I think of myself as a hopeful person, I requested them after hitting a wall of uncharacteristic despondency. Following frequent trips to court as part of a support community for undocumented immigrants—some fleeing gangs in their home countries, others detained after living here twenty years, a few as young as sixteen brought to court in orange jumpsuits, then taken away while their mothers wept—an unrelated incident, the mass shooting at a Pittsburgh synagogue, pushed me over the edge into momentary despair over my paltry ability to change anything. I rallied without touching the pills, but knowing they were at the back of my cupboard had helped me regain my fighting equilibrium. *And so it will be again*, I tell myself.

Slipping off my shoes, I stretch out on my loveseat and let

sunlight slanting beneath partially unraised blinds warm me. I like that the loveseat is just the right length for me to sit longways with my feet up. It was the first brand-new sofa of any kind I ever bought, and for a long time I used it sparingly, thinking to keep it pristine. I see things differently now. If we are all going to die of this plague, I want to have fully enjoyed my sofa. Perhaps I will raise the blinds just a little more. Prolonged grief, I have read, can physically change the shape of the human heart.

After a spell, I check the day's emails. The virus is ripping through prisons, and Ramon is in the prison infirmary with a fever. Perhaps worse still, prison guards, angry that his sentence will be up within the year, are proclaiming that he won't live to see his release. One threatened to infect him with the virus, and Ramon's cleaning products, such as they are, have been confiscated. Another guard reportedly said, "You aren't going to make it home, 'cause you want to snitch on us! Suck my cock, you bitch!" Ramon's girlfriend, Desiree, says he's afraid to eat the prison food.

While I can't yet shake off the shadow of my friend's suicide—the emptiness left behind by his slamming the book shut on his life—I am drawn to Ramon's thirst to live and Desiree's to have him safely home. I close my eyes and project my will that Ramon survive. I do not have a habit of prayer or believe in a godlike entity who changes things for the better if we ask nicely enough. I believe the word "god" originates in the concept of "good," however, and I have a habit of sending out strong thoughts for "the good." I want Ramon to live, heal, know love in his life. Desiree too. As I focus my mind on breathing out thoughts for these goods, the ambulance sirens sound more distant in my ears.

I am sipping grappa from a shot glass and letting the liquid warm my throat. Over the past few weeks, I have become part of an online tribe, working remotely from one another for Ramon's release. I am in cheerful spirits and feeling *engagé*, as the French would say. I do not know how big the tribe of Ramon's supporters is, or even what others are doing exactly, but knowing they're out there warms me like the grappa. I believe they include members of a "cop watch" group, some African American anti-police-brutality activists, and others like my journalist friend who got me started writing to Ramon in the first place. My computer is open before me. I view with a feeling of satisfaction the emails I've been writing.

"Dear Office of Special Investigations . . ."

"Dear Acting Commissioner for New York State Prisons . . ."

"Dear Acting Executive Deputy Commissioner . . ."

" . . . I have not yet heard back from your office. . . . I am deeply concerned for the life and safety of . . .”

I will wear these people down. I have time on my hands. No social distractions, not even a pet to feed, unless you count the houseplants I'm coddling in my kitchen. I pause to relish a favorite line:

“I am a retired New York City high school teacher. . . .”

I love writing that. The teaching career I arrived at late in life, after hodgepodge work in the arts, was the most respectable I could imagine for myself. At times like the present, I relish wearing its respectability like a badge. I know my emails go on file somewhere—like my letters to Ramon and his parole board. Well, I laugh to myself, perhaps feeling a mild effect from the grappa, if they bring back McCarthyism or COINTELPRO, they'll know where to find me—provided they don't have bigger fish to fry and the virus doesn't find me first! At any rate, I feel rich in respectability. Why hoard it like capital when it can be out in the world doing some good?

I close the computer. Perhaps one more tiny smidge of grappa? I haven't been to a liquor store since February, and I've made the single bottle last, measuring out fractional amounts, days apart. I go to where the bottle is sitting among my enormous houseplants, which refuse to thrive anywhere but in the singular slant of light that comes through my kitchen window. Plants are notional that way. Like all spoiled pets, mine are indulged, taking over counter space, displacing kitchen gadgets.

Carefully pouring out the extra drop of grappa, I remind myself not to get my hopes up too high. Chances of success in cases like this can be slim. But you never know. Seventeen years ago, a judge read a letter of mine aloud in court in defense of his decision to release a Muslim man I knew, swept up in the post-9/11 dragnet. I let the grappa slide across my tongue. If we don't try, what chance is there? Maybe it's time for another victory.

It's almost 7:00 p.m., the hour that, in the best of times, can feel lonely when you're alone. Tomorrow I'll try to help set up direct communication between Desiree and a state senator's office, but there's nothing more to do this evening. The building is eerily quiet. The apartment next door mirrors mine, but opens onto a separate hallway, so I almost never see the night nurse who lives there with her husband and child. Occasionally, I see her stride down the front walk, a petite, straight-backed figure with short-cropped raven-colored hair. The building's thick walls muffle most sound, but sometimes I think I hear a high, silvery laugh I imagine is hers. I like to think it's a sign her husband wants to make love to her or that she's playing with her child.

I start laying out utensils on what remains of my counter: my mother's old Revere Ware pan lids in different sizes, metal serving spoons, wooden ones, a deep spaghetti pot. It's time to bang these utensils to thank the frontline workers.

"Excuse me," I say aloud to my houseplants, elbowing my way past them to open the kitchen window.

The nurse next door will have already left for her night shift. I like that her husband is usually home to hear the noisemaking in her honor; but to be honest, I also do this for myself. I am hoping that one evening a vaguely musical individual will be attracted to the timbres of my utensils and respond to rhythms I produce, perhaps enticed by my own response to theirs—a kitchen-utensil call-and-response. There is someone in a house catty-corner from my building who plays an interesting-sounding "instrument," and I have hoped to strike something up. It never quite takes. Maybe one evening it will dawn on them what I'm trying to do. That "musician" isn't out tonight. I send my diminuendos and crescendos into the evening air anyhow.

I am basking in the remote glow of Ramon's release. It has happened swiftly and with little fanfare, only days after the murder of George Floyd. Just a brief announcement on Facebook and a plea from Desiree for privacy. It is late May.

This morning I could have sworn I heard a crow out my kitchen window. I looked it up on the internet and, yes, there are crows in Brooklyn. In fact, more than there used to be. Crows are not as spectacular as David Attenborough's dazzlingly feathered dancing manakins; but they are said to be smart, persistent birds, with a sense of humor. I read in *Scientific American* that, like the crow in Aesop's fable, one has been observed dropping pebble after pebble into a vessel of water, to get something it wanted floating on the water's surface to come within reach.

Warm spring air drifts through my open windows. I am holding the last letter Ramon wrote to me from prison. I read it one more time.

" . . . I want to thank you for going out of your way to try to send me that book. I appreciate it but I rather you hold off till this crisis is done and over with. I'd hate to hear you've gotten sick behind it. I'd rather our friendship than a book. Take good care of yourself and stay off those streets."

Though I cannot see him, the man next door whose wife is a night nurse shouts from a window:

"I love my wife!"

13

FOG

by Rebecca Baum

The waves broke from the clouds, boiling whitecaps emerging from thin air. Maxine stumbled in the wet sand, her balance thrown off by the luminous illusion created by the early-spring fog. Her roller bag saved her. Clutching the handle, she turned and fixed her gaze on the dark form advancing through the mist, her husband, Martin.

He was slow, still recovering from the bout of Covid he'd suffered six months ago, or beset with the "long" version. Who knew? The doctor's convoluted prognosis at last week's appointment had left them unsure.

When they'd last been on this Fire Island beach, for their honeymoon in 2002, Martin's physique had drawn glances from men and women alike. Now, his broad shoulders sagged. The barrel chest he'd enjoyed since his college football days had caved. She knew that beneath the murmurs of the ocean, a delicate wheeze sounded with each of his exhales, like a kettle soon to boil.

She regretted the giddy impatience that had prompted her to suggest they "take a stroll" instead of waiting for the next ferry at the pier where they'd prematurely disembarked. A quarter mile in moist sand was more schlep than stroll.

Maxine released the luggage handle, letting the bag plop into the sand. She lowered her small frame onto the soft nylon and waited for Martin to catch up. A little breather and they'd finish the last leg of the journey to the vacation rental.

Hugging herself against the wet chill, she stared at the incoming waves. After each lick of the sand, a silvery film sparkled, then disappeared. In the frothing curl of receding waters, a helmet-shaped object emerged. She pegged it as litter until a spiky tail shot up, as if declaring the existence of life.

"Horseshoe crab!" she yelled to Martin, who'd almost reached her. She'd seen many of the prehistoric-looking creatures on East Coast beaches over the years, usually overturned carcasses tangled with long tapers of seaweed. But this was her first live sighting.

The thing was a monster, about a foot and a half long, much larger than the dead ones she'd seen. The front section of the wide, glistening shell bore three evenly spaced ridges, front to back. The feet were hidden, creating the effect of an armored Roomba trundling along the beach.

By the time Martin tucked his bag against hers, the sea had drawn the horseshoe crab back into the depths. "What did you say, Max?" he asked. His mask bunched around his neck like a poorly worn cravat.

"A huge horseshoe crab. Freaking bizarre-looking."

"Sorry I missed it." Martin brushed long quarterback fingers across the plane of his crew cut, then hiked up his too-loose chinos.

"Why didn't you wear the new 34s I got you?" she asked.

He shrugged and plopped down next to her. "Superstition? Afraid my body will get the wrong message if I give in and wear the 34s."

She unzipped her fleece and pushed back the hood. By now, the humidity would have transformed her dark shoulder-length hair from soft curls to an electrified frizz. She covered her husband's hand with her own, still graceful and strong, but with thickening knuckles. Martin stared ahead. She wondered if his quiet signaled contemplation of the cold Atlantic. Or one of the little lapses he'd been having since the virus. He squeezed her fingers. "Seems like anything could come out of that fog, doesn't it?"

The last few meters of beach were clean-swept, as if they were the first people in all eternity to mar this pristine stretch. They climbed the stairs to a wooden walkway that led to the small community of beach houses where they'd be staying. The walkway soon branched into a series of crosswalks, each continuing to a conclave of two or three houses. Most of the houses were of a similar style—simple, modern lines built with muted, gray-washed wood that blended into the island's natural environment.

Martin paused to look at his phone. "It's a couple of streets over."

Streets wasn't quite accurate, Maxine thought. Vehicles were mostly prohibited on the island, and the houses were situated along wide pedestrian pathways of cement or wood planks.

At last they arrived at the beachfront address. A gated partition, the size of a small door, preceded the walkway to the yard. And while the two neighboring structures mirrored the style typical of most of the island's homes, this two-story house was distinctly different. The wood was dark-stained. The gabled roof was trimmed with fretwork flourishes. A stained-glass nautical window overlooked the screened-in front porch. A shingled turret disappeared into the thick branches of a towering pine tree.

"What was the host's name?" Martin asked, pausing before the gate.

"Julius." She wrestled her tongue into submission so that she would not add "Remember?" Who was she to raise the alarm about forgetfulness? Names, book titles, the reason she stood before an open refrigerator—she'd struggled with such things lately. Whether this was caused by menopause, early dementia, stress, her own bout with Covid, or some evil combination of all of the above, she could not say. Nor was she especially interested to find out.

She'd once read that even as the aging brain dulled, it developed new capabilities, including resourcing other brains to fill in the blanks. Maybe between her and Martin, they'd be lucky enough to limp through the final phase of life with the equivalent of one functioning brain.

Martin nudged the gate open, then consulted his phone. "It says here the key is hidden within Kali's crown." Sure enough, a small statue of the deity sat on the first of the porch steps. Six arms flared from the voluptuous torso. A long red tongue unfurled between sharp teeth. Maxine dipped her fingers inside the ceramic hollow. "Got it."

The interior was more typical of a beach house. A worn, comfy couch took up one end of the living room, a rocking chair and big-screen TV the other. A braided oval rug was centered on the wood floor. A faint, sweet odor filled the air, at odds with the damp, piney environment. Maxine circumnavigated the room, chasing the scent. A memory of Howie Deckler, her first kiss beside the pool of the country club to which their families belonged, flashed through her mind. The scent grew fainter, then disappeared.

"Oh!" Martin said, stopping at the foot of the stairs leading to the second floor. A rope was slung waist-high between the newel posts, with a hand-painted sign: *Ahoy Matey! Please enjoy the downstairs only.*

"Hmm. I thought the house looked bigger than a two-bedroom," Maxine remarked.

"Max," Martin said, a gentle shot across the bow. "We're here. Let's enjoy ourselves."

"What? I'm not complaining. We have all the room we need. It's just weird that it wasn't mentioned in the listing."

Maxine felt a pebble of resentment growing. The scathing review already started to compose itself in her mind. She resisted the urge, well aware that she was a chronic grudge holder, prone to mistrust and a compulsive pettiness that had plagued her since childhood.

She'd thrown lots of expensive therapy at it, but finally decided to relate to it as a manageable lifelong condition. She'd never be rid of it, but she could choose not to act on it. And the surprising forms her pettiness took were often a source of amusement for her and Martin.

Maxine slid her arms around her husband's waist and pressed her face against his broad back. The steady lope of his heart soothed her. "The place is awesome, honey. I'm glad to be here." And she meant it.

Her good cheer even withstood the disappointment of the downstairs bathroom. She'd planned to chase the chill from her bones with a hot bath once they'd settled in. But there was only a tiny shower. The washing of nether parts would be a yogic endeavor.

"No big deal," she remarked, after investigating the deck overlooking the ocean. "There's an awesome outdoor shower."

They put away the luggage, then prepared cold steak sandwiches from the small reserve of groceries they'd packed. Later, they'd stock up at the island's lone, overpriced market. They lunched at a small teak table on the deck while reviewing meals for the next week.

"Think we should shop now?" she called to Martin. He'd disappeared into the house with the remains of their sandwiches. A moist breeze wended across the deck and crept beneath her clothes. She shivered, and called again, "Martin?"

When there was no answer, she rose from the table and went inside. Martin was on the couch, his phone clutched in one hand, head thrown back, snoring softly. Through the kitchen doorway, their sandwich plates were visible, freshly washed and drying on the rack.

Unexpectedly, grief knotted her throat. A desolate loneliness swept through her. She felt the urge to shake Martin awake or run up the wooden walkway knocking on the doors of the empty houses. Instead, she undressed, wrapped herself in a towel, grabbed soap and shampoo. She hung the towels inside the outdoor shower and latched the splintery door behind her. A slip of soap moldered on the toiletry shelf. She flicked the bar to the ground, replacing it with her own fragrant square.

She moaned with pleasure as the shower rained blessed hot water onto her chilled skin. Soon the little space filled with steam. She cranked the knob farther, to near-scalding, and lathered her body, still trim and strong after fifty-one years of life. Though she'd been markedly less active during the pandemic—online workouts just didn't do it for her.

"I'll get back to biking," she sputtered into the warm torrent. Perhaps even persuade Martin to try pickleball. After a final rinse, she wrapped herself in a towel and unlatched the door. As she stepped out, her gaze drifted toward the far side of the deck and the ocean beyond. She let out a shriek.

A tall, thin man with copper-hued skin had materialized before her. Dark eyes smoldered above a KN95 mask that covered the rest of his long face. The mask bore a strange resemblance, in size and shape, to his white bikini briefs.

"Fuck off!" Maxine shouted. She hurled her shampoo bottle and jerked backward.

"Wait!" The man splayed his slender fingers in self-defense. "I'm Julius!"

The screen door flew open and Martin stormed out. His teeth were bared, his face flushed. He positioned himself in front of Maxine's towel-clad body and lowered his shoulders, ready to bodycheck the defense.

"Please! I'm a Premium Host!" Julius said, tugging his mask up the narrow bridge of his nose. "You must be Martin."

Maxine stepped from behind Martin, whose wheeze had escalated to a whistle. "What are you doing here?" she asked, her voice quivering with fear and anger.

Julius raised his thin arm and pointed to the second story. "I live here."

Maxine snorted. "We didn't pay this exorbitant rate to share a house."

"I apologize for the misunderstanding. But the living configuration is precisely described in the listing. Precisely."

Maxine whipped her head around to stare at Martin. She was piqued that the red flush was already receding from his face. His thick, silvering eyebrows were regaining their usual gentle set, like a dog, briefly disturbed, taht returns happily to the hearth rug.

"Yep," Martin said after a minute of staring at his phone. "That's what it says."

"Did you not read the listing thoroughly? Hon?" Maxine felt her nose bunch. The muscles of her mouth gathered, poised to launch her deep irritation at Martin. Instead she widened her eyes, trying to pack volumes of ire and disappointment into her gaze.

Martin cupped his fist to his chin and pulled at the beard he once had. "Could have sworn the listing said 'entire residence.' But maybe I'm confusing it with the Prudence Island cottage. Or the bungalow in Cape Cod."

"Or maybe the listing was 'updated' after you booked."

"No, ma'am. No, ma'am, it was not," Julius said softly. "My family has hosted guests for generations in our beach home. Never have we faced such an accusation." He bowed his head and folded his arms into his narrow chest. "And generally guests never see me. I use a separate entrance. But I thought you might need this." He brandished a small rectangle of plastic, the long nail of his index finger covering the awful photo she'd taken after squabbling with the surly DMV representative. "I found your driver's license next to Kali."

She moved to take the license, but paused, gesturing to her unmasked face. "Apologies. Wasn't expecting visitors." He nodded and she stepped forward, plucking the ID from his fingers. The sweet odor she'd detected earlier enveloped her, now clearly identifiable as old-school suntan oil, the kind used to fry skin to a crisp. "And sorry for my reaction. I was scared."

"Let's just hit the reset button. I'm going to bid you a wonderful stay. It's unlikely we'll see each other again. Unless you need something. In that case, just message me on the app." He unhinged a section of the railing and disappeared around the side of the house. After a few seconds, a door creaked open and slammed shut, followed by the hiss of a bolt sliding into place.

Maxine felt her shoulders encircled. Martin's warm breath tickled her ear. "I'm sorry, Max. I should have been more diligent with my research."

"No," she said, brightly. "This was last-minute. We were moving fast. You booked a place and seven hours later we're here. It's a win, Martin."

"You are lying through your beautiful teeth," he replied.

And of course, she was. Her whole body was stiffening, her awareness expanding to penetrate the walls and ceilings of the house, tracking the unwanted life-form that lurked upstairs.

She dropped her head to Martin's chest, perturbed by the loss of what she'd imagined would be a few days of freedom from the shuttered claustrophobia of their lives in the city. From the months-long intrusion of her work life into their home. From her own catastrophic thoughts.

Her conscience clamored, chiding her—*what about the health care workers, the disadvantaged, the sick, the dying, the dead . . .*

Yes. Yes. Yes.

And still, her underserving spirit ached and roiled.

Outside the bedroom window, the pine trees wept with condensation, a ceaseless patter that egged on Maxine's insomnia. She spent hours tossing and turning, her ears attuned, batlike, to the floor above. The lightest footfall, the faintest gurgle of plumbing, caused her to relive the day's unpleasant surprise. Several times she was convinced she caught the faint scent of suntan oil. Martin's ragged snoring from his side of the overly firm queen-size bed did not help.

Finally, she abandoned the effort to sleep. Slipping from the bedroom, she padded to the kitchen in search of a snack. As she passed the roped-off staircase, she indulged the petty impulse to assert her presence, stomping heavily across the wood floor, tongue thrust out to a degree worthy of Kali.

She flicked on the kitchen light and searched the fridge. True to form, Martin had squirreled away the remaining fragment of steak sandwich. She popped the bite into her mouth, then ventured into the freezer. "Lord," she intoned. A thick layer of frost coated the perimeter, leaving barely enough room for the pint of chocolate gelato that some other guest had probably left behind. She withdrew the container and was pleased to discover an unbroken seal. Inside, the hard, dark sludge was free of crystals.

Grabbing a spoon, she settled at the kitchen table with her laptop. She Googled "horseshoe crab," curious about the strange creature she'd sighted. As chill coco flowed across her tongue, she watched video after video, learning the species had hardly changed for hundreds of millions of years. She grinned at the sight of a broad female cruising through wet sand with two males latched to her backside. The males were much smaller, with an arch at the front of their shells, the better to dock onto their moving paramour.

As the female dropped clutches of eggs in the sand, the first hitchhiking male drizzled his sperm across the deposit. A second and sometimes a third male splashed his offering over that of his predecessor, hoping to get lucky with any remaining unfertilized eggs.

She paused to study a close-up photo of a horseshoe crab in profile, a white frill of foaming ocean nearby. Its primitive features were rugged and spare. One funny little eye shone from the glistening carapace, seeming to radiate an ancient, amused knowing.

What was it about these weird beasties that charmed her so? Perhaps their dogged persistence, staving off the pressures of evolution for an unfathomable amount of time, staying true to their goofy morphology as a whole planet transformed around them.

And the idea of such unchanging endurance, over millions of years, comforted her, especially now, when the seismic disruptions of the pandemic had rattled her to the core. She'd never felt more vulnerable, more mortal, or more inadequate.

Her spoon hit bottom and she was shocked to realize she'd polished off the whole pint. She was about to close her laptop when another photo caught her eye, thumbnail to a 2020 article in a scientific journal: "Horseshoe Crabs Critical to the Fight Against Covid."

She clicked.

White-coated attendants beneath fluorescent lights peered at a long row of horseshoe crabs bolted to a metal frame. The animals canted downward, spiked tails frozen at attention, a thick band of rubber securing them to the rack. A hollow needle was jammed into each crab. Blue liquid drained from the animals through the needles and into glass bottles.

Incredibly, the horseshoe crab was the source of the only FDA-approved substance for detecting bacterial and fungal contaminants for medical devices and injectables. The entire US medical industry relied upon the blue blood of the squirming bit of prehistory she'd spotted earlier—to ensure something that was meant to heal didn't inadvertently harm or even kill. This included a vaccine for Covid-19.

After bleeding, the horseshoe crabs were returned to the ocean. As many as thirty percent died from the process. Since first being tapped for this special role, their numbers had decreased drastically.

Maxine slammed the laptop shut, her cozy curiosity replaced by the familiar taut anxiety that had haunted her for much of the pandemic.

She fled to the bedroom and curled against Martin's slumbering form. As she hovered in and out of sleep, ghoulish images paraded through her consciousness: rows and rows of horseshoe crabs, racked and bleeding, each gazing at her with that knowing expression.

The next day, the island was again shrouded by fog. After an early-morning grocery run, Maxine and Martin settled on the deck loungers, a pile of books and magazines between them. The fog had shrunk their beach vista to a seventy-yard stretch and enclosed the ocean in a cottony dome.

After twenty minutes, Martin stood and stretched, ribs surfacing through the soft gray fur of his chest and belly. "Want anything from the house? I need the loo."

She patted his rump affectionately. "Have you been doing your Kegels?"

"Of course. I've done five as I stand here speaking to you." His face softened. "You look tired."

"Not appreciated," she said, pressing her fingertips against her eyelids. Her head bobbed gently as Martin kneaded her shoulders. "I'll nap in a bit," she said breathily and patted his hands before shrugging them off. From upstairs, the sound of an industrial-grade blender roared to life. She scowled, then muttered, "Provided Orange Julius doesn't joyride that Vitamix all morning."

Martin's eyes swelled with mirth and alarm. Finger against his lips, he cocked his head, then disappeared into the house.

Maxine rose from the lounger, smoothed her yellow sarong across her abdomen, and strode to the deck railing. She gazed at the incoming waves, hoping for another visitation from the horseshoe crab, as if the sight would reassure her. Or lift the uneasiness that seemed to have settled in her bones. She wasn't sure why the Covid article had upset her so. She liked animals, but she also happily consumed meat. Philosophically, she felt that some animal testing was a necessary evil to sustain human health and control disease. At least until a more humane option was discovered.

But she'd been so taken with the sight of the odd little animal and then amazed by the details she'd learned online, especially its extraordinary endurance as a species. For a moment, she'd felt lifted above the mess of Covid and these uncertain times. The article had slammed her right back down.

She turned her back to the ocean just as Martin emerged from the sliding door, seltzer in hand. Snatching a tattered magazine from the pile of reading material, she plopped back down on the lounger as he brandished the can. At the tip of his thumb, a bright drop of red swirled, expanded, then cascaded down the front of the aluminum cylinder.

"You're bleeding," she said, tracing the rivulet across the soft connective webbing of his thumb, across his hand, to the source of the flow, a deep gash on the pale underside of his forearm. "Jesus! What happened?"

"Huh. I have no idea how I did that. Didn't feel anything." He rotated his forearm to study the wound. Blood spurted across Maxine's yellow sarong.

"Martin! You need stitches."

"Naw. But I should head to the grocery for peroxide. And Band-Aids."

Her husband's habitual calm was normally a welcome counter to her reactivity. But now, as she registered his bemused expression, his equanimity felt somehow threatening. She wanted to shake him into an appropriate state of alarm, to rattle him into an awareness of his fragility. And her own.

Suddenly, she was shouting, "How can you not know the origins of a giant fucking cut, Martin? How is that possible?"

Concern shaded her husband's blue eyes. "Honey, I'm okay. Really." Again, he surveyed the underside of his arm, as if to reassure her. A thin stream rushed from the wound to his elbow and flowed in a single long drip to the ground. Martin blanched, then swayed on his feet.

Maxine cursed and leaped up, guiding Martin to take her place on the lounger. "Julius!" she yelled up to the window. She ripped the sarong from her waist and bound the gushing wound.

A minute passed with no sign of their Premium Host. Again Maxine roared, "Julius! Come down to the deck! Please!"

Her husband cracked open one eye and muttered, "Honey, you might need to message him through the app."

"Are you fucking kidding me?" she barked. Continuing to grip Martin's forearm, she plucked his phone from his pocket.

"But you really shouldn't bother him," Martin said. "It's just the sight of blood. I'm getting wimpy in my old age."

Maxine opened the app and typed, *Emergency. Please come down to the deck.* Within seconds, a rapid clomping resounded from upstairs, then the slamming of the side door. Julius appeared, sinewy and sheened with oil, his white bikini briefs exchanged for sky-blue. He clutched a small bag marked with a red cross. As he hurried across the deck, his slender fingers affixed the KN95 in place. "Oh, my," he said, catching sight of Martin's arm and the blossoming crimson on the yellow wrap.

Martin's eyes fluttered open. "Max. Masks."

Panicked, she looked down at her own hand, cupped around her husband's injury, for all she knew staunching some crucial artery or vein. She glanced at the sliding doors, imagining their masks buried in the unpacked luggage or lost in some nook of the unfamiliar space.

"Allow me," Julius said. He reached into the first-aid bag, withdrew latex gloves, and snapped them into place. "And you'll want to grab shoes. And your purse."

She glanced uncertainly from her husband's pale face to Julius's, dimly noting the man's thick eyelashes, a detail unmarked by her before. Her skin erupted in icy pinpricks. She stared at her own red-tinged fingers, which refused to budge. She would not relinquish her husband's safety to the care of this eccentric, last (she imagined) of the slender, solemn ancestors who rented out the property.

"Maxine!" Julius boomed.

Martin's body shifted slightly. He'd fainted.

A water taxi sped them to the island's walk-in clinic, where the sole physician pronounced Martin's wound deep, but within the clinic's scope of care. Martin had revived from his faint by then, but the doctor insisted on treating him for dehydration. Julius offered to stay, but Maxine would not hear of it—though she did gratefully accept his offer to reserve a water taxi for their return to the rental.

The boat arrived two hours later, as scheduled. As they glided through the mild chop, Maxine slumped against the metal bench, overcome by a peaceful exhaustion. Next to her, flush with IV fluids, Martin surveyed the early-evening sky. His forearm bore fifteen stitches and was neatly bandaged in a waterproof sheath. Maxine planned to retrace his steps from the deck to the refrigerator in search of the edge or shard that had mutilated him. Grateful though she was, Julius might incur her wrath yet. Or at least a measured dressing-down.

Martin's breath warmed her neck. "No more fog," he said, voice raised above the drone of the water taxi's motor. She lifted her eyes. The change had escaped her. In the wake of the pervasive, cloying mist, the sky seemed blown wide open, empty save for a low, gossamer full moon.

As the water taxi docked alongside the pier, the captain glanced toward the beach and whistled in amazement. Maxine followed his gaze. Her breath caught.

An undulating ribbon of horseshoe crabs stretched the length of two football fields along the frothing water's edge.

"Mating season," the captain said. "If you follow that path behind the dune, you'll walk right up to 'em."

Minutes later, husband and wife were barefoot in the chill sand, struck dumb and delighted by the writhing, glistening tumult of thousands of horseshoe crabs on the beach, hellbent on procreation. The animals plowed through, over, and under each other with an intensity that seemed at odds with their quirky anatomy: the shallow helmet of a body; the clumsy spiked tail; the compound eyes, two bits of coal engineered by a child. Maxine could not help but laugh.

In places, the gray and khaki shells of the teeming aggregation bloomed with pale pink or green moss. Clusters of barnacles and tiny mollusks adorned the carapaces of others, corsages and boutonnieres for the arthropods' ball.

Huge female crabs crashed through a wall of males with the relentlessness of tanks, drawing themselves up the beach beyond the tide to deposit their eggs in safety. The males pursued, latching on to the shells of their beloveds and forming ungainly rafts of two, three, or even four creatures.

The incoming tide sluiced through and over the shining creatures, intensifying the melee. When a wave toppled a big female headlong into the sand, Maxine gingerly gripped the edges of the shell and flipped the animal upright. Her triumphant squeal caused Martin to guffaw.

It was sheer, joyful madness, an unfathomably ancient process unfolding toward who knew what end. Maxine lowered herself onto the sand, then offered Martin a hand as he did the same. Once he was settled, she lightly kissed the bandaged site of his injury. Her eyes welled as she ticked off the various medical supplies involved in his healing: needle, stitches, tetanus shot, all blessedly sterile because of the horseshoe crabs.

As darkness gathered, and stars confettied the sky, she thunked her head softly against her husband's, brain to brain. She sensed something intimate and enduring, wise and strong. Something that would carry them through.

14

LOCKDOWN WITH VAMPIRES

by Ross Dreiblatt

On March 15, 2020, I was walking home from work freaked out like everyone else in New York City, or the world, for that matter. I had just been furloughed from my job as a buyer in the Macy's corporate office, because New York City was about to shut down. The CDC guidance was to avoid contact with people, which was why I was walking the twenty-two blocks home instead of taking the subway.

The city was eerily empty and quiet, and I was haunted by movies. *Escape from New York, I Am Legend, The Day After Tomorrow*—God, so many movies, each featuring the death and destruction of the city by aliens, zombies, monsters, gangsters, and by the future itself. And now it all seemed like foreshadowing.

People, buildings, and stuff . . . the reasons everyone loved New York. New York had the best stuff, right? Jewelry, fashion, food, all kinds of stuff. Suddenly people and stuff were off-limits. Now it's just people hiding in buildings with their stuff. I liked people, I liked being around so many of them, but I was a bit of a loner too; it wasn't easy for me to make friends, so I was working on it, trying to reach out to people. Which was why I was a little anxious about being stuck in my apartment by myself for however long this thing would go on. Tomorrow was the big shutdown—bars, schools, entertainment . . . everything. But it was the bars shutting down that had me worried.

Why? Because there were thousands of bars and there were always people in those bars, even at 3:30 a.m. on a random Tuesday. I was a New York barfly. It was how I connected to the city, to the people. It was how I tried to reach beyond myself. There was always an array of interesting drinking establishments to blow off steam, have an intriguing new drink, or have a compelling conversation with a stranger. There was always the secret hope that some stranger may become a friend.

Some of my more notable collection of barfly conversations with strangers: There was the head librarian from the New York Public Library, who was an encyclopedia of amazing book recs (I kept in touch); the former City Council member who could read minds (yep, read mine almost word for word); the Russian who claimed to be Vladimir Putin's love child and showed me a pic of him and Vlad at a birthday party; the pilot who lived through an actual highjacking . . . there's more, plenty more. These were the people and stories you could collect only in the bars of a densely populated place like the city.

People told me their stories because I did something that no one did anymore: I listened, and I listened carefully. I asked questions, which was an acquired skill. I acquired it because I myself had no such stories to tell. I was an empty vessel. In my forty-one years of life, I have had nothing interesting to offer. Nada. I felt I was the very definition of average white guy, so I collected these stories to give my life a little bling. Like a Bedazzler for the soul.

I made it home to my third-floor walk-up on Bedford Street. My West Village neighborhood was usually crawling with *Sex and the City* tourists and was now empty. Fuck, this was already weird. I bumped into the two girls from 2C on the stairs. They were hauling suitcases, ready to hunker down at a parent's house upstate.

I laid down on my couch as the sun disappeared and wondered what to do now. I let the darkness fill my apartment, without turning the lights on. Unnaturally quiet. Not even the usual street noise. Hmm, with bars closing tomorrow, maybe this meant I would be able to sleep through the night? Above me in 4B, the top floor, was Louie. He was a bartender and kept bartender hours. He also had various roommates who worked at night, so every night between nine and eleven o'clock t I heard the frantic footsteps of people rushing to get ready for work, and I heard those same footsteps return at 5 a.m.

Those footsteps sounded like a herd of buffalo in this 120-year-old building when you were trying to get some sleep. A few years ago, I went up there to see if he could maybe buy some slippers, but he showed me that he already had them. It's just the way the acoustics in the building were configured. And since we both lived in rent-controlled units, I would need to get used to the noise, because neither of us would ever move. Nope, not ever.

It turned out that Louie was a very nice guy and invited me to the bar where he worked for a drink on the house to make up for the noise. Louie's bar, the Oxford, turned out to be a great little old-time dive not too far from the apartment. In fact, it had become one of my regular stops on my barfly outings.

I sat up. That would be the perfect place to spend my last night of freedom.

At around 11 p.m., I made my way a few blocks over to the Oxford. I wasn't sure if there would be people in it, and I was half hoping it would be empty, because I was literally risking my life for a drink tonight. There still weren't a lot of people on the street, save for the usual drunk NYU students, who would come out for Covid-laced cocktails if they were two-for-one on a Monday night.

I walked down the few steps between a Korean fast-food outlet and a Dunkin Donuts and pushed open the door. There was just one couple sitting at the very end of the dark bar. Chris Isaak's "Wicked Game" was playing on the jukebox. The perfect place to hide from Covid.

The bar was nothing fancy. Used to be a speakeasy a hundred years ago and then was turned over to the Mafia to run. A long, basic wooden bar with some tables and chairs along the wall opposite. Enough room in between for two people to walk side by side. I'd heard that a hedge-fund manager had bought the place to prevent anyone from turning it into an upscale hipster paradise.

"Max! *Bienvenue!*" Louie greeted me from behind the bar and reached into the beer cooler for a Stella. "Cool?"

I nodded and sat in front of him. "How goes it, Louie?" Beer was opened and placed in front of me. Barfly was home.

He shrugged and raised one of his thick eyebrows. "Not expecting much business tonight. People are scared shitless, huh?"

I nodded. "Maybe they should be." I didn't know why, but for the first time I noticed that Louie didn't have any visible tattoos. Maybe the only bartender with virgin skin. Bartenders in New York veered between tatted muscled men and women anda tatted older, out-of-shape men, depending on the venue. Louie was just . . . normal. Thin but not muscled, a face that could be warm or threatening, depending on the lighting. His eyes were like mood rings, sometimes dark and colorless and sometimes full of life.

"You're not scared?"

"I'm too stupid to be scared." If I were really smart, I would be following CDC protocols inside my safe apartment. "How about you?"

He shook his head. "Covid don't scare me. I been through worse."

As I downed my beer, I wondered, *What could have been worse?* Maybe he'd been in the Army? He didn't look that old, maybe thirty-something. But one thing I had learned from my barfly tours of talking to strangers is that you never knew what people had been through. People in New York always had stories.

"Like what?" I asked.

Louie smiled and shook his head again. "I'm too sober to talk about it, and you're not drunk enough yet to hear it, buddy."

I wasn't sure if I wanted to hear it, but I ordered another beer anyway.

The couple at the end played Patsy Cline's "Crazy" on the jukebox and tried to do a slow dance, but they looked a little too drunk to handle it. So they finished their drinks and paid their tab.

I needed to fill the silence with innocuous conversation. "What are you going to do when this place shuts down?"

Louie grabbed his rag and wiped down the end of the bar. "Same thing as everyone else: Sit on the couch and wait till it's over."

"Are they going to offer takeout drinks during the day?"

He shrugged. "Don't know yet. It won't matter, I don't do daytime shifts. Your work close down?"

I nodded. "Furloughed today."

Louie stopped wiping, looked toward the door, and sniffed the air. "Shit."

The door opened as an older blond woman entered. Louie jumped over the bar and met her at the door. "I'm sorry, ma'am, we're closed."

The woman teetered on her heels. "No, it's not even closing time."

"We're closing early on account of Covid, sorry." Louie forced her out the door and locked it behind her. "Fuck."

Was she too drunk for the bar? I'd never seen anyone thrown out of here for being too drunk. "What was that all about?"

Louie jumped back over the bar and pulled out a couple of shot glasses and a bottle of Tuaca. "On the house."

We downed our shots. He poured another two. "Mark my words, shit is going to get crazy." We downed the shots. "She had Covid. Could have given that shit to you. She should be in quarantine or a hospital."

"How could you tell?" I ordered another beer.

He pulled a Stella out of the cooler. "I can smell it. It's a very distinct sour-milk-like smell. She reeked." He reached into his pocket and pulled out a pack of cigarettes. "Mind?"

I shook my head. "I didn't know Covid had a smell." I'd never heard anything on the news about a smell.

He lit his cigarette and exhaled the pale-blue smoke away from me. "Maybe it's just me. I'm really sensitive to that kind of stuff."

Sounded a little crazy to me, but this was one of the stories you lived for in barfly country. "Have you always had this . . . talent? Maybe you should help out at the testing centers?" I laughed.

He nodded very seriously. "I know, I really should. We'll see."

At the very least I was glad I passed the smell test. "So, are you drunk enough to tell me why Covid doesn't scare you?"

He smiled and pulled a beer out of the cooler for himself. "Almost. Covid isn't going to kill me. That I know."

"How do you know that?"

He took another drag on his cigarette. "I'm immortal."

I wasn't sure how to take that. I didn't know him well enough to understand his sense of humor. "How's that?"

"I'm going to live forever if I want to."

"Like a vampire."

He pointed a finger at me. "Bingo."

I nodded calmly while trying to process this new information. Was he fucking with me? Why would he do that? But at the same time, I had only known him to be a nighttime creature. Or was he one of those strange people who like to cosplay a vampire lifestyle? That would make more sense, although I'd be disappointed if that were true. He's always seemed to me way too cool to fall into some odd fetish like that. But as I had always thought, you never knew what kind of shit people in New York were up to.

"Smelling Covid, is that a vampire thing, or is it just a you thing?"

He tilted his head a bit and his face tightened up. "Well, it's like this. If you were about to enjoy a meal, but your food smelled bad, you probably wouldn't eat it, right? It's kind of like that."

He was so earnest. I had a good BS meter, and it was all out of whack with Louie. The story was obviously false, but he believed it with his heart and soul.

"Explain to me how it works. I only know vampires from movies."

He rolled his eyes and took a swig of his beer. "Don't go by that Hollywood bullshit. Real vampires are totally different. We don't spend all of our waking time trying to suck up people's blood. Mostly we do normal people stuff. About the only thing that's true is that we can't go out in daylight, or we burn up. Something about our chemistry or enzymes that's missing from our blood. The skin can't protect us from the sun. Also, in order to become a vampire, you have to agree to become one. You can't just turn an unsuspecting person. Oh, and we don't have to sleep in caskets. I mean, you can if you want to, but it's not, like, mandatory or anything."

Damn, he's got a whole fucking backstory. I noticed that he did have pale skin. But fuck, everyone in New York had pale skin. "Why did you agree to become one?"

He took a last drag on his cigarette and put it out in his beer.

"Another pandemic. I had the Spanish flu. It was a death sentence back then. When faced with your imminent demise, you make some crazy choices." He threw the beer can in the garbage. "Hopefully it will be better for everyone this time. I hope it doesn't get that bad. Look, I'm gonna close up, so I'm going to have to kick you out."

"Sure, no problem." But now I really wanted to hear more. He really seemed to believe this story.

As he led me to the door, he told me, "Come up to the apartment anytime if you want to know more, okay? I'm just a little sad tonight, is all."

The next few weeks, I hunkered down in the apartment as the world quickly descended into Covid Hell. I spent my time battling New York's unemployment system to make sure I could get some of that federal stimulus money, checking and then avoiding all the Covid news, and trying to get an Instacart appointment that wasn't five weeks out. I ventured out once in a while to wait on the lines to get groceries and spent all of my allotted time in the supermarkets freaked out over the people who couldn't wear their masks correctly.

I started to get emails from friends and coworkers. "Send prayers to Elaine from marketing, she's in the hospital. . . ." "Our cousin Marie hasn't been able to get out of bed for a week straight. . . ." "Would you mind contributing to Sharon's GoFundMe? Her husband is on a ventilator. . . ."

In between all this I would Google vampires of New York. Mostly I got back fiction—stories about alleged vampires, to slash fiction about people fucking them, and a shitload of TikTok fetishists who had gone to the lengths of finding a dentist who would install fangs.

About a month into lockdown, I woke up with a scratchy throat. Fuck. Was it those idiots in the supermarkets who always wore their masks at half-mast? I tried to schedule a test, but I couldn't find an appointment in the current decade. I could wait in line for a walk-up, but I couldn't stomach the idea of waiting in a line for hours with a bunch of potentially sick people.

Maybe it was time to visit my neighbor upstairs. Could he really smell Covid? I was that desperate. But I didn't want to be rude—I hadn't talked to the guy in a month, and just knocking on the door for a Covid sniff seemed . . . abrupt. I looked around the apartment—maybe I could take a bottle of wine and a couple of rolls of toilet paper. Yep, nothing said friendship more than toilet paper these days.

I waited until the sun set, and when I started to hear footsteps stirring overhead, I knew it was time to make my move.

I knocked on 4B.

A twenty-something woman with long pink-and-black hair opened the door. A new roommate? Girlfriend?

"Hi." She eyed the toilet paper in my hands.

"Is Louie in? I'm your downstairs neighbor Max."

"Max? Really?"

I nodded.

"That's his dog's name too."

"Dog?" I hadn't heard any barking.

"Max!" Louie called out to me from the hall, a small beagle in his arms. "Good to see you! Come in and meet your namesake."

"My namesake?"

The girl let me in the apartment. I noticed all the walls were painted dark red. Blood red? These people were serious. The apartment was a three-bedroom, much bigger than my cozy one-bedroom. But a top-floor unit with all these windows? Shouldn't they live in a basement apartment? I guessed that when it came to rent-controlled apartments, you didn't get that picky. I walked toward Louie.

"You can take off the mask here," he said. "No worries in this place."

The girl abruptly turned and stared at Louie.

"Yes, he knows," Louie told her. "Don't worry, Max is cool. It was him that gave me the idea for the dog. Max, this is Vanessa, another member of the nest."

Nest? I presented my toilet paper and wine. "Didn't want to come empty-handed." I slowly lowered my mask and waited for a verdict.

Louie did a quick sniff. "Dude, it's okay: You're clean."

I was relieved. Kind of. But maybe I was only "clean" in make-believe vampire world. I handed Vanessa the wine and toilet paper and took the cute dog in my arms. "My namesake?"

Louie slapped my arm and nodded. "Totally! This was genius! I been thinking about what you said to me that night in the bar—you know, how we could really help out, but, you know, we can't just go around sniffing people. So we got a dog, and we tell them that the dog has this ability to sense Covid in people. And bam! They believe it!"

A tall, graceful older woman with short gray hair walked out of one of the bedrooms. "Max the wonder beagle has a 100 percent accuracy record. The problem is that eventually it will catch up with us." She approached me and nuzzled the dog. "I'm Annie."

Louie threw his hands up in the air. "Debbie Downer in da house."

Annie looked at me. "We've been getting calls from all kinds of agencies to train their dogs. We've even gotten a call from the local news. We can't have any publicity." She turned toward Louie. "None."

Louie nodded. "True. But we should push it as far as we can."

Vanessa took the dog from my arms and sat on the sofa in the living room. "So much easier in the old days. People didn't question it so much as long as it worked."

"Pre-internet, all of this was much easier," Annie answered.

Louie checked his phone. "Look, we got to get rolling, we have four hospitals to hit tonight."

"Hospitals? Aren't the people in there already sick?"

Louie nodded. "We don't check patients—we triage the staff. That's about the only thing we can do at night. Testing centers only open during daylight hours." Louie put the wine on a table. "Max, we have to run, but come up this weekend and we'll open your wine."

I was a little freaked seeing the three of them earnestly sharing this fantasy, but I was also totally fascinated at the same time. I really liked hanging around them, but could I be friends with people who were convinced that they were vampires? The one wrench in this was that it seemed like Louie could actually smell Covid. Maybe that was just a

Louie thing and not a fake-vampire thing. I needed to know more. I needed to find the fake plastic fangs on his nightstand so I could reassure myself that they were just acting out a harmless fetish. At the same time, I felt even more empty than usual. I didn't even have a fantasy life that I could feel that passionately about. They were genuinely interesting people—I would go back up there on the weekend.

For my next visit, I was still thinking I should bring something, but what to get a nest of cosplay vampires? A meat dish? I didn't have much on hand. *Fuck it, I'll make a batch of tollhouse cookies,* I told myself.

After sunset, I waited until I heard footsteps above me and got my cookies ready. I also heard the echo of sharp heels on the stairs going past my floor up to the fourth. I heard a knock on the door, muffled voices, and then a door closed. Did they have other visitors? I decided to wait an extra thirty minutes. I didn't want to interrupt any vampire business.

A half hour later, when I entered 4B, I did a double take as their guest got up to leave.

"I'll be back," she told Louie and Annie. "I never take no for an answer."

The blond guest threw a wrap around her shoulders and hustled past me out of the apartment without acknowledging me.

I looked at them in stunned silence. "Was that . . . Madonna?"

Annie rolled her eyes. "Her second time here."

I handed the cookies to Louie. "Does she know about you guys?"

Louie smiled. "Yep. She keeps begging to get bitten. Bitch wants to live forever."

"How did she find out?" I'm caught up in the moment, forgetting that they are not actual vampires.

Louie shrugged as Max the dog padded out of the kitchen. "We're creatures of the night. We're in clubs all over the place, and someone probably said something to someone else, and Madonna's also a creature of the night. Someone probably said something to her and she started stalking us. Literally following us home from the clubs or wherever we were."

"You're not going to do it?" Why not make Madonna an official fake vampire?

Annie sighed. "Can you imagine what a nightmare that would be? She'd be on Instagram every night showing off her fangs and telling the world who she wanted to bite. She'd be a freaking nightmare for us. And not only that, but this would also go on literally forever."

"Publicity is obviously our worst nightmare," Louie added. "Even though we don't want her, she still talks about us on her social media."

Annie opened my package of cookies. "That doesn't bother me. As long as she's not one of us. She just sounds more deranged than usual. No one really believes we exist, so we like it that way. In fact, you don't really believe us, do you?"

I stuttered, not knowing how to respond. "I . . . do mostly."

Louie smiled. "Dude, I get it. No one believes in Santa until he shows up in your chimney. You need to see the fangs. No one believes until they see the fangs."

Annie took a bite of a cookie. "Mmm, these are really good. Trust me, you don't want to see the fangs. Not unless you absolutely have to, *n'est-ce pas,* Louis?"

"Can't argue with that," Louie agreed. "We can't just make them pop out, there has to be a very willing participant ready to go, and then, bam! But we appreciate being able to be open with you. It's nice to just sit and be normal with visitors."

How convenient that their fangs can't be shown. If I told them I wanted to live forever, what would they do? Better not push it and put them on the spot—I liked being around them. "I really enjoy visiting with you."

Louie let Max down off his lap. "Well, visitors is kind of what we call normal people."

"Why's that?"

Louie looked at Annie. "Do you want to explain the whole guardian-of-the-planet thing? You're so good at it."

Annie put down the second cookie she was about to bite. "It's pretty simple. A true vampire considers themselves a guardian of the planet. We have this code to protect it as much as we can. For instance, this is why we pitched in to help during the pandemic. We look at normal people like you who have a finite lifespan as visitors. You're here for a little while and you're gone. We're here permanently, so it's kind of up to us to keep the place in working order."

Not quite the bloodthirsty nihilists they were made out to be. I really liked my new humanist fake-vampire nest. "Where's Vanessa?"

Louie shook his head. "She's currently recovering from a bout of sickness in bed."

"What happened?"

Louie grabbed a cookie. "Vanessa is a nurse, she's the one who got us into the hospitals. The one she's working at is so full that they have people in gurneys out in the parking lot. So, she goes out there to check on them. . . ."

"Check? More like prey on them."

Louie ignored Annie. "She sees a young guy who's not well off. Most of the people in the hospital are older or already sick people, but there's this one young guy, and she feels really bad because he smelled of death. So she makes him the offer."

"And he said yes?"

Louie nodded. "But he's full of this Covid. Right after she turned him, she gets full-on sick to her stomach from his blood. She'll be okay, though."

"Glad to hear that."

How could they be making this up? Amazing.

Annie stood up. "She's had plenty of experience."

After Annie left the room, Louie looked at me. "Vanessa was my nurse way back when. Pandemics always bring in an influx of newbies. Always. Which reminds me: Annie! We have to get going!" Louie began clearing the table. "We have to go visit the guy Vanessa turned. He's going to have a lot of questions."

By the end of April, you could feel people getting restless. In New York, there were news reports of groups of people meeting in secret for parties or religious services. How can people be so goddamn selfish and stupid? It made me even more scared to do my usual trek for groceries. It meant that many more people may be carrying around this virus. That many more idiots with masks at half-mast may be unknowingly spreading this thing and making it worse for everyone. I was starting to feel the restlessness as well, like this thing would never end.

As vigilant as I tried to be, I made some mistakes and let my guard down. I forgot to bring a mask to the laundry room in the building, and there were two other unmasked people doing their laundry. Well, it was only a couple of people, so I grinned and beared it. A few days later, I picked up a food order at a Thai restaurant, and I went inside to pay without my mask. These were the small incidents that haunted me on April 30 when I woke up and felt out of it. My body was achy, like I had a flu. When I got up to pee, I had to steady myself. It was a chore to walk. I needed to return to bed. Maybe I should make some tea? I didn't have the energy, so I went back to sleep.

But I couldn't sleep, because I couldn't stop coughing. I had it, I was sure. By noon it was hard to breathe. It felt like an elephant was sitting on my chest. There wasn't any part of my body that didn't hurt. I wondered if I could get to a hospital. The thought scared me, because I would have to go in an ambulance and I had seen on the news that they were in short supply. What would a hospital do, even if I could get there? Put me on a gurney in a parking lot? I was trapped here. Adding to all of the physical pain, I felt so very, very alone. There was no one I could turn to, no one to call for help. I had made my loner bed, and now I might die in it.

I needed some pain pills. With all of my strength, I walked into the kitchen and found some Advil, took the max dosage, crawled back to my bed, and tried to sleep and forget about my sad life. All of those barfly stories I had collected, what comfort could they bring me now? I got a few moments of sleep here and there.

Sometime later, I heard knocking at my door. "Max? You okay?"

It was Louie. But I couldn't answer. I was worn out. I wasn't sure how much longer I could put up with this. Every moment was a measured painful breath without any respite. I slid back into a fitful sleep and dreamed about Vampire Madonna on a killing spree at some dance club.

I woke up to more knocking. I wasn't sure what time it was. I strained my neck to look at my phone, but it was too painful to move that much. I heard a loud noise, a pop from the front of the apartment. A shadow entered my dark room.

"You okay, Max?" Louie turned the light on. He stood in front of me with a crowbar in his hands.

I shook my head. "Bad," was all I could say, but I was overwhelmed with gratitude for him.

Louie sat on the edge of the bed. "Yeah, I smelled that shit from way upstairs. Figured you were going down."

Was I really that bad off? "Fang time?" I asked. As a joke. Sort of.

"I don't know, I don't know. It's kind of a big deal. You have to give it some thought. Remember, this is not reversible. You will not ever see the sun again. You will never have children. You may get bored for years at a time. I made macramé plant holders for, like, a decade."

I nodded. He was talking like it was all true. My entire nervous system upped into panic mode. He must really smell a bad case on me.

"Also, if you have big dreams for your life, you should probably kiss them goodbye."

"Huh?" Dreams, macramé? I closed my eyes. I didn't have the energy to figure out what he was talking about.

"The thing about human life . . . for visitors . . . is that you're on a schedule. That schedule has a definite deadline. Everything a visitor does is because you only have so much time to get it done. So everything you do, every single day of your life, from birth, is set to this ticking clock. Every single thing, whether consciously or unconsciously. My experience is that when you take away that ticking clock, nothing seems to matter as much. Not everyone is suited for that kind of change."

But that kind of decision was beyond me now. It seemed a luxury. I wasn't sure I had a choice. I was laboring for breath wondering if my own deadline was near. Was I about to die in a room with a fake vampire?

I opened my eyes and found myself staring into Louie's wide-open mouth. His shiny white teeth stared back. This was happening. Was he going to pretend-bite me? Were there fangs? I wasn't sure. I thought I saw a couple of very pointy teeth, or maybe they were just incisors. My eyes were playing tricks on me. He leaned into my neck, and I shut my eyes again, waiting to feel teeth against my neck. I felt a slight nick and then heard him sniffing. I waited to feel a puncture or a pinch—something. I didn't know what would happen except maybe I would escape what seemed an imminent death. I couldn't think much more about it; I didn't have the capacity to imagine beyond a bite; I didn't want to. But still, I felt no bite. I opened my eyes and Louie's mouth was closed in a smile. Did he do it already?

"They went back in. That usually means you will not need my services. I think you will actually pull through this. But you got to see the fangs! Now you're a believer, right? Let me fix you some tea."

Did I see them? I must have. I started to tear up again.

Louie was right: I did pull through it. And the ultimate barfly story became my own.

The night a vampire knocked down my front door to rescue me from Covid.

15

WHAT YOU WISH FOR

by Beau Karch

It was the end of the second week in March 2020 and the talk in the office that morning was all about Covid. A few days earlier, New York state recorded its first two deaths from the disease. Or was it a virus? Rumors swirled that the city government was considering what was being called a shutdown, which meant closing the office and having each of us work from home.

As I walked to the restroom in the midtown Manhattan office where I worked, I noticed there were fewer people than usual. The floor was usually a bustle of activity, with young real estate brokers high-fiving one another over new sales and the older brokers yelling at their team members for anything from a minor slip-up to a lost client. Because I was a writer in business development, I was rarely in the line of fire, but I also didn't get the massive rewards when deals paid off. I was slow and steady and that was fine with me.

I took a deep breath, opened the door to the restroom, and sidled up to the row of three urinals, taking care of business at the one farthest from the door, guarding my personal space. Never take the center urinal if you have a choice—standing next to someone while urinating is usually awkward, but, in this environment, it could potentially be deadly. As I stood there, I noticed one benefit of this Covid scare: The restroom was spotless and it actually smelled . . . nice. I mean, it smelled like antiseptic,

161

but that was preferable to the usual stench of our facilities. And I didn't blame the janitorial staff. They did their jobs and did them adequately, but young brokers who are always on the make tend to be a little sloppy when it comes to bodily functions. At least that was my experience.

I heard the door open and looked up to see Axel strolling in, taking the urinal next to me, breaking the unwritten code of the men's room and what we were starting to call "social distancing."

"Hey, Billy boy," he said. I hated when people called me that. My name is William.

Axel could be amusing, even funny, in small doses, but not one-on-one. He was only a few inches shorter than me but had what they call a Napoleon complex — always trying to get the upper hand. On top of that, he had the intense personality of a salesman working on his next commission, even when there was no commission to be had, because, as he said, "You never know when there might be some kind of payoff for cultivating a relationship."

His presence was like sandpaper against my skin, because he was predictably unpredictable. Was he going to be friendly in that schmoozy kind of way or was he going to be passive-aggressive and insulting? Or both? I forced the last drops of piss out of my body, wanting to get away before he said it.

"So, this is where all the dicks hang out."

Too late.

I rolled my eyes, zipped up, and heard Axel snicker as I made my way to the sink to wash my hands. My plan was to rinse them quickly and dash out before Axel could catch me, but then I saw it: a freshly printed sign stuck to the mirror. It must have been posted by the building management. The sign looked to be instructions on . . . how to wash our hands?

"What's that?" Axel startled me as he appeared over my right shoulder, like Candyman in the mirror.

The words on the sign were starting to sink in. "I guess we're supposed to wash our hands more thoroughly, you know, to make sure we're not transmitting the virus. It says here we have to wash for twenty seconds, and if we need help counting to sing 'Happy Birthday' twice to ourselves."

Axel looked at me. "You're not actually going to do that, are you?"

I looked down at his hands, imagined the coronavirus racing around his fingers and thumbs, and shrugged. "Seems a bit . . . much."

Axel rinsed his hands briefly while singing the riff from the Beatles song "Birthday" for about five seconds, wiped his hands on his pants, and, as he walked out, said, "I think I'm just going to lick a pole on the train and get it over with."

After the door closed behind him, I turned on the water and lathered up. I didn't sing "Happy Birthday," but Axel's riffing had planted an earworm of "Birthday" in my head. The song played around in my brain and, before I knew it, more than thirty seconds had gone by. When I pulled a few paper towels from the dispenser, I noticed it: a crisp twenty-dollar bill sitting on the counter. Had Axel put it there? Was it some kind of elaborate prank? I wasn't sure, but I rinsed the bill in the sink, wrapped it carefully in a paper towel, and took it back to my desk. If Axel asked about it later, I'd give it back to him. If he didn't, then I guess it was just my good luck.

That day, the firm announced it was closing our offices, temporarily, and that we should all make plans to work from home until further notice. I was in the middle of a project and had one final meeting with a group of brokers and facility managers to discuss our plan to pitch a prospective client. We were in a medium-size conference room, unsure about how to sit safely around the long table, so we decided to leave every other seat open, which wasn't that different from what a group of men do anyway.

"I think we should be okay. As long as we crack the door a bit."

"Yeah, nobody sneeze or laugh or anything."

"Or talk for too long."

"That's going to be hard with this group."

We chuckled, then stopped immediately, knowing that we had already violated the "no laughing" rule.

I looked around the room. "If someone sneezes, I'm out of here." No one laughed.

That was my last day in the office. A few days later, bored with this "work from home" arrangement, I tried the "Birthday" trick again in our bathroom at home, wishing for a return to "normalcy." I don't know what I expected, but nothing really changed.

By that time, the government had released more instructions about what to do to avoid catching Covid. My wife thought some of them were ridiculous, but I didn't want to get sick so I tried them all: cleaning heavily touched surfaces, avoiding groups of people. Then, in early April, the CDC issued its latest recommendation: Wear a mask to prevent the spread of the virus.

As I went through my morning ritual of cleaning our kitchen counters, I noticed my usual cleanser had been replaced by . . . something else.

"Honey, what's this spray bottle under the kitchen sink?" I yelled to my wife, Bobbi, who was working at her makeshift desk in the living room. "Where's my Formula Fantastik?"

"They were out at the grocery store, so I mixed some vinegar and water for you to use. Try it."

I was irritated that my Formula Fantastik wasn't here. "Did you check online?"

"They're out everywhere. Just try what I made for you. White vinegar is a natural disinfectant."

Angrily, I sprayed the concoction on the counters and started wiping. I usually wipe from right to left, but, because I was frustrated and not paying attention, I wiped from left to right. It cleaned the counters all right, but I wasn't sure if it was killing the Covid virus, and that made me feel itchy the rest of the day.

That evening, Bobbi and I went out for a walk with a friend. Before we left, I remembered the new CDC recommendation and retrieved from the hall closet a respirator mask, one that I'd used when we painted our apartment last year. It was thick and had two valves on its sides.

Standing near the front door, Bobbi looked at me as if I had just gotten my nose pierced. "Why are you wearing that old thing?"

I lifted the mask so she could hear me. "The CDC says wear a mask when you're out with people. This'll prevent any viruses from getting in my nose or mouth."

She opened a drawer in the foyer table and pulled out a package of KN95 surgical masks. "If you're going to wear a mask, wear one of these. You look ridiculous in that respirator."

"I don't trust those masks."

"Why?"

"You got them at the Korean deli, the same place where you got that ginseng powder that gave me a rash. I've heard about counterfeit masks that don't do anything. I'll stick with the respirator."

Bobbi shrugged. "Have it your way. I'm wearing one of these."

While we were walking in Central Park, me breathing heavily through my mask, I overheard our friend tell Bobbi that the government was providing more than $1,000 a week in unemployment benefits to try to keep the economy afloat. Even trapped in Manhattan as we were, and its related high cost of living, that sounded like a pretty sweet deal to me. I mean, a guy could do worse.

When we got back from our walk, still wearing my mask, I washed my hands while singing "Birthday" to myself, more out of habit than anything else. I then cleaned the counter with the vinegar, again from left to right because it had worked well earlier, before removing my mask and wishing I could somehow get that government unemployment money.

The next day, I got a call from my boss and a representative from HR. I was let go from my job—a reorganization, they called it. I was disappointed, naturally, but then it hit me: I was now eligible for unemployment. My wish had come true. But how? Could it have something to do with the hand-washing ritual, cleaning the counter with vinegar from left to right, and the mask? Or was it something else? I knew enough from playing fantasy sports that I couldn't rely on a small sample size—more experimentation was needed—but, at the very least, I was sure I had tapped into some kind of magic that would not just protect me from Covid but could change my life.

I bought a journal and wrote down the various things I had done to protect Bobbi and me from Covid. After trying various combinations and reading about rituals and incantations online, as well as consulting a collection of old Doctor Strange comic books, I came up with the following list:

> Spell of Containment: Clean countertops with the vinegar and water potion, wiping from left to right.

> Spell of Protection: Wear the respirator mask when outside (and sometimes inside), washing it carefully with the vinegar and water potion.

> Spell of Purification: Wash hands often using soap and water, singing two verses of the Beatles' "Birthday."

As I performed these rituals on a daily basis, I found that more of my wishes were coming true. After being annoyed by all the people in the park, I wished the city were less crowded—suddenly, the city emptied out. I wished for more nature outside my kitchen window, where I toiled on my computer looking for work—and more birds appeared. I even read that dolphins were spotted in New York Harbor. Sure, there were people dying from this damn virus, but I was thriving during the pandemic and, as a bonus, remained Covid-free. Thanks to my newfound magic, I felt invincible.

By early May, things had deteriorated in New York—the subways were shut down overnight to allow for extensive cleaning, the governor closed schools for the rest of the academic year, and the state of emergency in New York state was extended through mid-June. More than 300,000 had died from the coronavirus worldwide. And yet, my rituals allowed me to thrive. I even tried to wish away Covid altogether, but the magic didn't seem to work on such a large scale, as if there was only enough for Bobbi and me.

My magic would be put to the test one day when I was going to the grocery store, wearing my mask, latex gloves, and a New York Mets cap, with a bottle of Purel tucked in my front pocket. Purel wasn't magic, but it would keep my hands clean if the gloves broke.

On my way into the store, someone who was texting on his phone bumped into me. I stopped and looked at him, debating whether to throw a hex on the guy.

The guy muttered, "Watch where you're going, asshole."

Then I saw who it was. "Axel?"

"Yeah?"

He didn't recognize me. I took off my hat and lowered my mask a bit.

"Billy boy," he said. "Is it Halloween already?"

Shit. Why did I stop?

I pulled my mask back up. "Just trying to stay safe. You don't wear a mask?"

He grinned like the Cheshire Cat. "Don't believe in 'em. Fresh air and sunlight are what keep me healthy. Not dressing up like the Invisible Man."

He punched me in the arm. Hard. "You must be a man of leisure, sucking off the teat of the government while you're looking for a job."

I rubbed my arm. "It's okay."

"Well, you're better off, in my humble opinion. Some people just aren't cut out for corporate life. See ya in the funny papers, Billy boy."

I glared at Axel as he walked away. Guys like that always seem to get whatever they want. And who was he to walk around without a mask like he was so special? Without thinking, I muttered five words to myself that I would later wish I could take back.

"I hope you get Covid."

Two days later, I found out Axel had been infected and hospitalized. He recovered eventually, thank God, but he was in the hospital for weeks. Even after he was released, Axel had the symptoms of what they called long Covid and had to go on disability.

After I heard the news, I tried to stop the rituals—to throw away the bulky mask and use the KN95 masks, stop singing "Birthday" when I washed my hands, and go back to using my Formula Fantastik instead of the vinegar and water—but I couldn't, especially with everything I was seeing on TV and the internet about how so many more people were getting sick and dying from the virus.

The magic was the only thing keeping Bobbi and me safe, and I just couldn't let go of it. On the other hand, I couldn't take the chance that I would misuse this power and hurt someone else, so I decided to be very careful. I stayed indoors and didn't interact with anyone except Bobbi. I meditated, sometimes three times a day, so I wouldn't lose my temper and wish something bad on someone like the president, Dr. Fauci, or, God forbid, my wife. I lived like a monk, but, instead of a monastery, I stayed in our one-bedroom apartment on the Upper West Side.

This went on for more than a month, and during that time I grew increasingly irritable. Was I going insane? Bobbi couldn't help but notice, and she encouraged me to stop with the rituals and go outside with her, get some fresh air, maybe go for a walk in the park.

I resisted until Bobbi suggested in late May that we head uptown to hear some Broadway actor sing from his balcony. This was during the time when, at seven o'clock each night, people in the city would hang out of their apartment or office windows and scream, bang pots and pans, and blow horns in support of doctors, nurses, EMTs, and other first-responders. It was loud, it was raucous, and it was one of the few highlights of my monastic lifestyle. But going uptown—to stand among what I was sure would be a crowd of people—that nearly paralyzed me with anxiety. And yet, I was desperate for something different. I said yes.

I meditated five times that day and listened to soothing music on my phone. I stayed away from the news. I even avoided spicy foods. I didn't want anything to upset me that night. As we got ready to leave, I went through my usual rituals. Bobbi shook her head at me as I put on my respirator mask.

"William, you don't have to wear that thing. We're going to be outside and we won't be close to anyone else. They say you can't get Covid as easily outside."

"I don't believe that. Besides, this mask has kept me safe so far."

She harrumphed at me. "It's embarrassing. Look, if you insist on wearing something, at least try one of these KN95 masks. You won't look so crazy."

I grimaced. "I told you, I don't trust those."

Bobbi shook her head again. "I checked on the CDC website. These are legitimate. That old mask of yours isn't even sterile anymore."

"No, thanks. I'll stick with what I know."

She shrugged. "I'll take an extra one if you change your mind. It's hot out and you'll roast in that heavy mask."

"Fine."

We headed up Broadway, and, as we walked silently, I kept my eyes focused straight ahead, not letting anything distract me from our journey uptown to hear the actor Brian Stokes Mitchell sing "The Impossible Dream."

When we arrived at the corner where Mitchell lived in a nice apartment building, there was the usual clatter of pots and pans and air horns. I checked my phone. Sure enough, it was seven o'clock. I let out a sigh of relief when I saw that the people who had gathered on the sidewalks and in the median were spaced apart, not crowded together. My anxiety level was already high—it was the first time I'd been outside in weeks—and I didn't want anything to annoy me and cause me to do something rash. I just focused my thoughts on keeping Bobbi and me Covid-free.

As the sound died down, a handsome man with salt-and-pepper hair, wearing glasses, appeared from a third-story window and waved to the crowd. A cheer rang out, and then he started to sing "The Impossible Dream." As he performed, the people around me grew still. I heard myself breathing deeply, just letting the words and the music flow through me. He looked at something behind me. I followed his sightline. Behind us was an ambulance that had pulled over. The two EMTs next to it shouted and pointed to Mitchell, and he nodded back to them.

I felt a tear well up in my eye, and as it touched the top of my mask, I took it off and rubbed my eyes with my sleeve.

16

ONE LUCKY WOMAN

by Annie Rourke

Jacob had a routine in bed—right hand here, left hand there. A kiss here, followed by a caress there.

There was nothing wrong with the routine—each element was nice enough on its own—but once Madison realized it, she couldn't un-realize it. Couldn't un-know the routine.

The same moves.

In the same sequence.

Every.

Time.

She might not have even noticed, but they had little else to do these days. Stuck in quarantine and working remotely with no one else to talk to in that small, quiet apartment.

In the early days of lockdown, Madison had done what everyone did. She watched TV ravenously, pointing and screaming at the screen, hoping for a hint of when it would all be over. She talked on the phone for hours—her mother; her best friend, Dani; a couple of coworkers. Then she'd gone a little overboard, diving into rabbit holes online, following one crazy tidbit after another. First, she was convinced Trump had somehow done it all on purpose—in order to declare martial law and delay the election. Then it was suspicious statements by Bill Gates—billionaires know things, after all—but after groans and eye rolls from not just Jacob but Dani and her mother, she'd pulled back. Stopped the endless internet searches and just concentrated on watching TV to make sure she got her information from more reputable sources.

But then Jacob got quiet. Even quieter than normal. Which was saying something.

Over dinner, she confronted him.

"Is there something wrong?"

Head shake.

"You haven't spoken to me all day. Several days, in fact."

Shrug.

"Did I do something?"

One-shoulder shrug.

"Are you going to tell me?"

Jacob just rose from the table and walked quietly into the bedroom. She followed.

"Was it . . . I didn't fold the towels the way you like?"

Head shake.

"Oh, I know! I stepped out of the shower before I dried myself off. I know, I know, you told me to stand *in* it and . . . wait, that's not it?"

Exasperated head shake.

"Can you mime it out for me? Can I buy a vowel or something?"

Madison giggled a little, but a look of disdain from Jacob and she clammed up.

"Look, you're going to have to tell me. I genuinely don't know why you're mad at me."

"I don't like having the TV on all day, okay?" he said. "You never even asked if I wanted to watch all that."

"I mean, we're in the middle of a major historical event, a worldwide pandemic, like nothing we've ever—"

"—There's nothing we can do. Why listen to all the arguing and nonsense? And you're *constantly* talking to someone on the phone. Do you even notice that I'm here? Why isn't it enough that we're here together?"

"It is! I just . . ."

She wanted to say, *It's normal to want to know what's happening. To talk to people. To engage with the world.* But she knew she could never say that to him. It was that word. Normal. He would take it badly.

So she backed off. She turned off the TV. Let the calls go to voicemail. And he was right, it didn't really matter if she followed every new development. She had no control over it anyway. No one did.

The traffic light changed, the "walk" signal blinked. No one stepped off the curb. No one raced across the intersection. Madison sighed, turning away from the window.

Jacob was playing one of his video games—with headphones, of course, so as not to disturb her. This was how they filled their days now. Sometimes they read. And they had sex. Always in the bed. At the same hour. In the exact same way.

That's okay, she thought. *I can fix this. I'll just change things up myself.*

That night, as Jacob reached for her, she gamely flipped around, trying to throw a little mayhem into the proceedings. Something unexpected, even a little risqué. But he just gently maneuvered her back to the Routine in that quiet, endlessly patient way he had.

Madison stared up at the ceiling as he went through the motions. In exactly the way she knew he would.

Knowledge isn't power. It's boredom.

It's not like she could say something to him. She hadn't been able to say something to him—about anything—since she found out about the incident.

It was early days and pre-pandemic, back when she could happily ignore world events.

Madison and Jacob had gone on a double date with Dani and her new boyfriend. It was all going well until Jacob got a nosebleed—something he was prone to—but it'd been dealt with and Madison thought they'd all moved on. Until she went to the ladies' room.

"You know he hard-core vapes, right?" Dani said, wheeling around to her as they waited in line.

"He does what, now?"

"The guy literally got a nosebleed out of nowhere!" Dani threw up her hands as if case closed. "And, I mean, you have to smell it."

"Smell what?"

"That, like, sickly-sweet scent."

"That's his shampoo."

"Oh, sweetie."

Madison's gaze drifted down the hallway and across the trendy Asian-fusion restaurant to the table where Jacob and Dani's boyfriend still sat, awkwardly making small talk. How could she be in a relationship with someone and not know he was doing this? Not know he had a wildly addictive habit? Why wouldn't he just tell her?

That weekend, Jacob had gone down to see his dad at Princeton, but Sunday night, as a welcome-home, Madison had brought him up to the rooftop of her building for a romantic dinner. A little picnic. It was quiet, secluded, with skyscrapers rising on one side, expansive sky and water on the other.

Just the two of them. On top of the world.

Madison had looked over at him. "I know your secret."

Jacob was shaking salt onto his steak. The salt shaker paused. "You do?"

"You don't have to hide it from me."

"I wasn't sure. . . ."

"I mean, don't get me wrong. I don't love that you vape."

"Oh."

Short pause.

"I thought you meant this."

He stretched his arm across the space between them, palm up, and she could see the long scar down the inside of his forearm. It wasn't a jagged, sideways thrashing at the wrist like people who might just be considering it. This was a long, follow-the-vein, digging-into-the-flesh attempt. He'd been in the bathtub, drunk, hoping the booze and warm water would leech the life out of him faster before his dad happened to return. But, like everyone in that family, his father was a punctual man.

Why hadn't she noticed? But how many people actually study the inside of someone's arm?

He'd already told her the story—or part of it, anyway. His former fiancée, Amy, had cheated on him and broken off their engagement. Madison had thought the whole thing was ridiculous—they were still in college, and who gets engaged in college anymore? But they were high school sweethearts, had been together ages, and Jacob had been devastated. Madison just didn't know *how* devastated and that he'd spent a year in a facility.

"I'm so much better now, though."

His hand flipped over and came to rest on her knee.

By lunchtime the next day, Madison was tucked into a small café booth with Dani.

"I've never known anyone who tried to kill themselves," she'd whispered, hating herself for it. Hating that this was an issue for her.

Dani just shrugged. "So? Now you do."

Madison sat back, thinking about it. Thinking about whether this was just a part of growing up. Dealing with people who had painful histories, allowing them to grow and move past them. Could she really not handle this?

"But don't you see? Now I can't break up with him!"

"Were you *going* to break up with him? He's, like . . . the perfect boyfriend. He treats you like a freaking queen."

It was true that Jacob had been everything she'd said she wanted. A man who would *cherish* her. Who *wanted* to be in a relationship—not play games, not play the field. She'd wanted communication and connection. She'd wanted grand gestures.

And then, there he'd been. Smiling at her from his profile picture. He was handsome, sweet, even a little shy. He'd asked for her number and then used it. He'd called instead of texting. He'd given her a single red rose on their first date and hadn't expected her to go back to his place. He'd held her hand, listened to her stories, and actually wanted to get to know her.

He didn't even drink—he'd quit after the incident—and when they'd gone to the same restaurant, and he'd ordered the exact same thing, she'd teased him. He'd just smiled and winked at her. "I know what I like and I like what I know."

She'd giggled, practically hugging herself with the joy of it. Because what he liked was her.

Yes, she decided, right then and there, gazing across the café table at Dani. She could handle it.

And that seemed to release her. To free her to give herself over to him completely.

Madison thought she couldn't be happier—that there was nothing more she needed, Jacob was the ideal partner—but then she'd gone out of town for work. When she landed back at JFK, a man walked up to her and handed her a single red rose.

"You're one lucky woman," he'd said, smiling.

"What?"

Then a woman did the same thing. Then another man. And a little girl. There were eleven in all—each one a perfect stranger, handing her a red rose and saying, *You're one lucky woman*. Finally, there was Jacob, waiting for her with the last rose. It was like something out of a rom-com and she was smiling, surprised. Overwhelmed, really. And absolutely enchanted.

"I am a lucky woman!"

Not long after the Rose Parade, Jacob had moved into her place.

Then Madison learned what a great guy he really was. Always doing thoughtful, sweet things for her. Like the day she came home and found all of her furniture had been rearranged because he understood that she needed his help. She hadn't even had to ask. He could just see a better setup for the apartment.

She'd picked up her phone one day to find that Jacob had shuffled the order of her apps and sorted the many emails in her inbox into corresponding folders.

When she'd worked long hours, he'd run her a bubble bath. "You need this. It'll take that edge off."

And when she'd put off doing laundry, he did it for her, taking the opportunity to rearrange her dresser drawers because her things had been in *such* a state.

Madison stared at the neatly folded piles of underwear in her drawer.

She'd spun around. "You know what? Sometimes I don't plan my laundry days out in advance. I live on the edge. I'm wild like that!"

Jacob cringed at the sarcasm in her voice. He stared at her, hurt and shocked. Then he just turned and walked out of the room without another word. In fact, after that, he hadn't spoken to her for an entire week—his sensitive, perfect soul so wounded. Quietly shuffling around the apartment, unappreciated, attacked. It was torture to her, this silent, strained recrimination. This martyr act. She'd finally broken down and apologized.

She'd started kissing boys in bars. Cute, young, fun ones. She hadn't meant to. It just happened. On those nights when she was out with Dani—away from Jacob and his overbearing presence in the apartment—when she was being foolish and drinking and not thinking about all of the wonderful things he did for her. Not at all. And after a few drinks—the freedom of being messy, loud, and disordered washing over her, the beautiful irresponsibility of it all—she would catch an eye, smile a little.

She knew she was looking for someone to fix it for her. But wasn't that the problem? After all, she already had a man who fixed things for her. And Madison was just beginning to consider the irony of this—that maybe she needed to change some things about her life, about herself—when the world came to a screeching halt.

The pandemic. Lockdown. That tiny apartment.

Just the two of them.

And his sex routine.

There were other routines. Immediately after dinner—not a half hour later, not in the morning, as was her usual way—she was required to stand by him at the sink and wash as he dried, inspecting each and every plate and fork to see if it passed muster.

Jacob made a little *tsk!* as she handed him a bowl. Then he sighed. Then he put his tea towel down. He tilted the bowl into the light. He reached up to slowly scrape at something she'd missed.

"You need to actually look at it to make sure it's clean."

She tossed a cup into the sink, splashing soapy water onto the counter and his neat little pile of dishes. "Then clean it your damn self!"

He settled in next to her, under the covers. His hand reached over to rub her arm. Up and down, up and down.

"Oh, my God, if you try that damn sex routine on me, I swear to God, I will scream!"

"Excuse me?"

She sat up. "Your stupid sex routine. It's the same thing in exactly the same way. Every time!"

He sat up as well. "I know what I like and I like what I know."

"It's fucking psychotic! Do you know that? It makes me want to rip my skin off. I actually *cringe* when you touch me."

Jacob snatched at his pillow and stomped out of the room to the sofa.

Madison sat at the window, staring down at the sidewalk. A plastic bag drifted up, meandered from side to side a bit, then floated back down to the concrete.

She turned and stared across the room to the back of Jacob's head. He was sitting on the floor, playing one of his video games, his little vape pen next to him, the haze of smoke hanging in the air above him.

Her lip curled into a sneer. How could a man so infuriatingly fastidious have such a disgusting habit?

She peeled herself away from the window and marched across the floor, then stood blocking the TV. Her TV. Which she'd been forbidden to watch, though he played his video games on it all day long. Which was, *of course*, just coincidence. Not the real reason he'd refused to let her watch the news.

Jacob looked up, sliding the headphones off as she pointed at him.

"You know, every time you pout, every time you punish me with your silence—just shut down and refuse to engage at all—it's not you being *oh, so hurt*. It's you being emotionally manipulative. But you should know something. That only works if I give a fuck!"

He stood up and stomped off to the bedroom. The door slammed shut.

Dinner was spaghetti and meatballs. She picked up a bottle of red wine, caught his eye, and smiled smugly. The cork made a satisfying *pop!* as she pulled it loose. Then she poured a glass, the wine sloshing over the lip and spilling onto the counter.

"Would you look at that? I spilled the wine! Oh, *nooooo!*"

She left it there, the little red puddle glistening in the overhead lights, and plonked down in her seat. She took a long gulp from the glass and smacked her lips. "*Aaaaah!*"

Hunched over his plate, Jacob glanced up at her. "If you think you're being cute, you're not."

"Oh, my God, he speaks! Ladies and gentlemen, we have witnessed a miracle! Will wonders never cease?"

"Your behavior is completely unacceptable."

"What're you, my dad?"

"No. Because *I'm* actually here."

Her breath caught in her throat.

It was mean. The kind of thing he never said to her. Even his voice was different. Low and quiet. Like a dog emitting a faint growl of warning.

For a moment, the only noise was their forks clinking on their plates. Madison looked down, rolling the pasta around in the sauce. When she looked up again, he reached for his glass of water and she could see his long scar, the bumpy white border that split his forearm in two.

"If you're upset, you could always check back into your little facility."

It was nasty, really trying to hurt him, and the kind of thing she never said to him. To anybody. She saw him flinch, an actual physical reaction, and there was a long pause.

"You know, it's a shame that I'm the one with the scar. . . ." Jacob leaned back, his eyes burning as he regarded her across the little table. " . . . when she was the one who deserved to be punished. She was so disobedient."

He stood up and walked to the bedroom, slowly, methodically. Madison stared at his empty chair, breathing in and out.

She grabbed her mask and her phone, stumbled through the front door, and jabbed at the elevator button.

It was a beautiful evening in Manhattan, but there was no lively conversation from outdoor cafés, no loud music. No joggers enjoying the refreshing drop in humidity. Just the slap of Madison's soles on the pavement as she dashed across the empty streets, not bothering to check whether a car was coming.

She threw herself down on a park bench. In the distance, she heard a rumbling, a noise slowly growing in volume. Up and down Manhattan, there was clapping and cheering, echoing off the buildings and down the street canyons. It was seven o'clock.

She waited for the tribute to subside. Before her, the Hudson languished, wide and still. She looked down at her phone. Her mother was in the Hamptons, quarantining with friends. Dani was somewhere on the Connecticut coast with her family. They'd be in the middle of dinner.

Madison tipped her head back to gaze up at the clouds. She closed her eyes.

Then she looked back down at her phone and pulled up Google. She typed "Amy Highgrove HS."

It was a ridiculous thing to search, a "Hail Mary" heaved into cyberspace—she didn't even know the woman's last name, only the schools they'd both gone to—but as a picture popped up on her screen, Madison gasped.

This Amy had gone missing seven years ago. It was the end of the summer, just before her junior year of college.

The ages matched up. So did the high school and college.

But still. This couldn't be Jacob's Amy.

Could it?

Madison's thumbs flew over her phone, her fingers trembling as she typed in his name and Amy's.

Nothing.

She clicked on a local news story about the disappearance.

His name was nowhere in it.

She scrolled through Amy's social media—friends posting pictures and writing how much they missed her, that they prayed for her to come home.

No Jacob. No mention of a fiancé at all.

Madison sighed and raised her head, staring across the cold steel water to New Jersey. She stood up and took a few steps toward the apartment.

She stopped.

She turned around.

Then she pulled up the news article again, scrolling down until she found what she was looking for. A quick search and she had the phone number.

He likely wouldn't be at his desk, but . . .

The number rang and rang. It wasn't 911, but wouldn't a police department pick up at some point? Finally, an automated voice came on and she listened to the menu, punching in a few buttons. The phone rang again, the loud, rhythmic chiming like a clock ticking off the seconds.

Voicemail.

"Uh . . . hi, Detective Collins. My name is Madison Howard and I saw your name in a story about the disappearance of Amy D'Angelo? I had a strange . . . well, a question about someone who might have been involved in your investigation? A fiancé, I think, or . . . well, I don't know, and I know you guys are dealing with a whole lot right now. I really, um, appreciate all your support and hard work during this difficult time and, uh . . . okay."

She left her number and hung up.

The police were on nonstop shifts, being called out to Covid emergencies, putting themselves in harm's way trying to deal with desperate citizens, overrun hospitals, a rising death toll, and she was asking for a callback on a seven-year-old cold case she had no connection to but, hey, just as a courtesy, because her boyfriend made a strange, possibly threatening, comment after she'd made fun of his struggles with mental health?

She trudged back to the apartment.

"—even recognize her anymore."

She could hear him in the bedroom, talking quietly on the phone, but, apparently, he hadn't heard her.

"I just . . ." Jacob sighed heavily. "I'm really concerned about her, Catherine. She's not herself. It's the isolation, I think. It's hard on everyone right now, I know, but she's really acting so uncharacteristically. I'm actually . . . I'm a bit scared for her."

He paused.

"Right. Yes. I will. Definitely. No, thank *you*. Of course. Bye."

He hung up.

"Talking to my mother?"

Jacob whipped around to see Madison standing in the doorway. He crossed the room quickly, placing his hands on her shoulders. "I'm just concerned about you."

She didn't respond, and he leaned down to gaze into her eyes. "Are you okay now?"

"I'm sorry for what I said. About your . . ."

He pulled her into him. "It's been a rough time. This would put a strain on the strongest of relationships. We'll get through it. Let's just not talk about it again, okay?"

She muffled an *okay* against his chest. Then she let him pull her to the sofa, where she sat, snuggled up against him as he flicked on the TV.

That night, when he reached for her, she acquiesced, lying there silently staring up at the ceiling as he moved through his routine.

Madison yawned and rolled over to see Jacob sitting on the edge of the bed, looking down at her phone. He picked up his head, looked her in the eye, and raised his hand. There, on her phone, was Amy D'Angelo smiling sweetly at whoever had taken her picture.

Madison sat up slowly, considering whether to try to make up a story. But what could she possibly come up with?

She lifted her chin. "Is that your fiancée?"

Jacob frowned. "What? No." He lowered his arm. "My fiancée went to a different school."

"But you said—"

"Yes, we dated in high school, we just weren't at the same school. It's why we chose to go to college together."

She blinked a few times, unsure of what to say.

"I knew Amy D'Angelo," Jacob said, gesturing vaguely at the phone. "I heard about what happened, of course. It was really sad, but I barely knew the woman. Madison, what is this about?"

Her mouth opened and closed. "I just . . . the name . . ."

"It is a fairly common name."

"I know! I . . . oh, God, I'm so sorry. I just . . ."

"What is wrong with you?" Jacob stood up and took a few steps across the bedroom floor. He was shaking his head—but whether in anger or confusion, she couldn't tell. "You do this. You know you do! I mean, do we even need to go into all your ridiculous conspiracy theories on Covid? And you thought that guy, the, uh . . . Dani's boyfriend. You convinced yourself that he was cheating on her and he wasn't!"

"What? He absolutely was!"

"No, you *thought* he was. You had suspicion, nothing else."

"When she confronted him, he totally ghosted her!"

"Probably because he thought she was nuts! She was happy with that guy! You *ruined* her relationship."

"No, I—"

"You take a little bit of information and you create some crazy story in your head and then convince yourself you're right. And you're not!"

"I . . ."

"Why? Why do you do this? Do you just need drama or something?"

"I don't . . . I don't know! I'm just . . . having a hard time being here, in quarantine. Just us. In the apartment."

Jacob looked down. "You cringe when I touch you."

"No! That's . . ." She scooted forward and hopped off the bed. "Okay, yes, I said that. But only because I was mad."

"Because you're unhappy with our sex life."

She exhaled, collapsing back on the bed. "Well . . . it would be nice to change things up once in a while. I mean, even just the order of things."

"I haven't exactly been inspired lately, have I?"

"Ouch. Jeez."

She peered over at him and he lifted up an eyebrow.

"Fine. Maybe I deserved that. But this is good, actually! We should be able to talk about this stuff. We need to. We're going through this crazy thing together and I guess it's made me a little crazy, too, but we need to be open and honest and say what we feel and not, you know . . . not clam up. I mean, this is the most you've spoken to me in weeks! I need human interaction. You can't just refuse to speak to someone for days on end!"

Her voice was beginning to rise and she stopped, making an effort to stay calm.

Jacob nodded. "I know. I can work on that. I will work on that, okay? I promise."

"Thank you."

"And . . . other stuff, too."

She looked over at him, a small smile creeping up her face. "Are you going to scroll through the *Kama Sutra* or something?"

He chuckled a little. "Something like that."

"Oh, God, I'm not doing any weird porn stuff."

He laughed again. "Hey, you brought it up, not me."

She stood up and crossed the small distance between them, reaching up to put her arms around his neck. "I do love you, you know."

He pulled her in. "I know. I love you, too."

The Hudson was cheery, the sunlight sparkling off the little ripples as Madison walked along the edge, chatting on the phone with

Dani. It was a good catch-up, with Dani complaining about her family and Madison describing the creepy post-apocalyptic landscape that Manhattan had become. It got her a full twenty-five blocks. Then her mother called and Madison hung up with Dani. When she switched over, her mother sounded out of breath.

"Oh, Maddie! I'm so glad to get you. Are you okay?"

"What do you mean?"

"Where are you?"

"Just walking around. But no one's near me. I've literally passed, like, one other person and they were yards away."

"Sweetie, I'm just worried about you. Jacob says you've been acting really erratically. I know the isolation is hard, it's hard on all of us, but—"

"It's fine. We just had a misunderstanding. It was nothing."

Madison's phone beeped again, interrupting her mother's reply.

"—hurt yourself."

"What? Oh. Hang on. Let me call you back, someone else is calling."

It was an unknown number, but she clicked over.

"Ms. Howard?"

"Yes?"

"This is Detective Collins from the Highgrove Police Department."

Madison stopped. "Oh! Oh, my gosh, I . . . wasn't actually expecting you to call me back."

From the other end of the line, there was a long exhale. "Yeah, it's been a bit nuts around here. We're stretched pretty thin at the moment."

She felt stupid then—irresponsible, even—to be wasting this poor man's time in the middle of all this. "I really appreciate you taking the time to call me back."

"You know, that case has just never sat right with me. Sometimes they just . . . they haunt you. And Amy D'Angelo . . ."

The detective sighed again and Madison could hear it in his voice, hear all the nights he hadn't slept, the way he'd never been able to let it go.

"I'm so sorry."

"You had a question about someone involved in the investigation?"

"No, it . . . I thought my boyfriend had been engaged to her, but I had the wrong Amy."

"She definitely wasn't engaged."

"Okay, so there you go."

"What's his name?"

"Jacob, but it was a different—"

"Morrison?"

A breeze drifted in, cooler than it should've been.

"You know him?"

"He's your boyfriend?"

"Yeah."

"Hmm."

Madison paused a beat, waited for the detective to continue. When he didn't, she took a breath.

"Were you looking at . . . was he . . . ?"

"I never actually spoke to him. You know, it's a missing-persons case, not . . ."

His voice faded out and Madison finished the thought for him. *A homicide.*

"So . . . Jacob wasn't involved?"

"Well, he was in England when Amy disappeared. Leeds, if I remember correctly."

"What? Why was he in England?"

"Junior year abroad or something. As I said, I never spoke to him directly. Just his father. And, honestly, I might've taken a closer look, to be honest. Her friends said they thought he had a thing for her. But kids that age, there's rumors . . . who knows."

Her throat was so dry, Madison's voice cracked when she spoke. "Can you tell me what happened?"

"You mean to Amy?"

"Yeah."

"I wish to God I knew. She left for school, made it to the dorms, that we know, but the rest . . . Part of the problem was that the dates were hard to pinpoint. Her parents never heard from her that night, started calling her friends, but then there was some footage at a convenience store not too far away that looked like her. That was two days later. So, that was considered the last sighting but, *aaahhh* . . . I was never sure it was her. It was really low-grade footage, grainy and out of focus. . . . I don't know."

"No one saw her in the dorms?"

"She was there early. For field hockey. It wasn't the start of the semester yet so the dorms were pretty empty. She never went to the practice, though, and if you're there expressly to practice with the team, why wouldn't you?"

There was a short pause.

"Can I ask you something, Ms. Howard?"

"What's that?"

"What made you call me?"

"I don't know, to be honest. My, uh . . . Jacob was engaged to a woman named Amy and I thought—"

"It wasn't Amy D'Angelo, I can tell you that. But I have no idea who else he might've been seeing. As I said, I never spoke to the guy."

"Right. Okay. I understand. Thank you for your time."

She hung up just as a text came in:

Dinner on the rooftop tonight

Madison lifted her head slowly, her gaze following the graceful stretch of the building across the street, the sun glinting off the hot glass, all the way up to the top.

He was waiting in the kitchen, glass of wine in hand.

"For you, my dear."

"Thanks."

Jacob turned back to the counter and flipped open the lid on her old picnic basket. "This is a new start for us. We're going to find a way to be happy now. Both of us."

"Yes."

He wedged in the wine bottle. As he lifted his hand out of the basket, the bumpy white scar on his forearm hovered in her line of sight. "I made us lasagna. We're on an Italian kick right now, I guess, huh?"

Madison nodded, taking a sip of wine as he pulled a long, serrated knife out of its holder. Opening the refrigerator door, Jacob leaned in and grabbed a loaf of garlic bread.

"I thought about what you said and, you're right, we should talk," he said, sawing through the garlic bread, the soft *thunk!* of the knife hitting the cutting board. "We can talk about Amy. If you want to."

He tucked the slices of garlic bread into some tinfoil and threw it in the basket. Then, at the last second, tossed in the rest of the loaf and the knife. "Can I get you to carry the pan? I've got the plates and . . . oh, hang on."

He turned and reached back into the refrigerator for the butter.

"I found a picture of you in Leeds."

Her voice was quiet but Jacob stopped, his arm hanging awkwardly in midair. But it was only a moment. He reached in and grabbed the butter. "And why were you looking for pictures of me?"

"You covered your tracks well, I'll give you that. It took a deep dive and it wasn't even your social . . . some friend of yours who visited. You were sitting there, smiling, in a pub!"

Jacob closed the refrigerator door quietly and turned around as her voice began to rise. "Did your father—the professor!—arrange a hasty exit for you? To get you out of town?"

"What?"

"There was no facility!"

"There *was* a facility."

She was nearly hysterical now. "Did you even try to kill yourself? That could just as easily be a defensive wound!"

Jacob exhaled patiently. "It was in Leeds."

"What?"

"The facility was in Leeds. You know, you might not realize this—or maybe you just didn't take it into account when you decided to do your little Nancy Drew thing—but there's still a lot of stigma around mental health. So, yeah, my father didn't want the whole town knowing I tried to off myself when my fiancée broke things off."

"Oh, yes, and you were so distraught that you met your buddy for a night out in the local pub! You, who allegedly never had another drop of alcohol after the *incident*!"

Jacob exhaled again and shifted his weight. "I was there on a voluntary basis, I could go wherever I wanted. It's not like I was court-ordered to be there. We had told people I was doing a junior year abroad, so when my friend came into town, I met him out. And, yeah, I had a drink because I wasn't yet mature enough to accept that certain things trigger me. It's a lifestyle change that's not easy to make in your twenties. But it's nice to know what you really think of me."

"I—"

"This is exactly what I was talking about, Madison! You're doing that ridiculous thing you do! You take a little bit of information and you just blow it up into some insane conspiracy theory. You totally convince yourself of something that has no basis in reality whatsoever!"

"But I—"

"I don't know what to do anymore! I'm trying my best here. You want to talk more, I'm trying to do that. I made us a nice dinner to try to reconnect and you throw this at me?"

Madison looked down. Was she really wrong about it all?

"Now, could you hand me the silverware, please? Could you do that, at least?"

Madison nodded, reaching out and sliding the cutlery drawer open. She pulled out two forks and two butter knives.

"*Thank you.*"

Jacob whirled around, tossing the forks and knives into the basket and slamming the lid down. "This is the end of it now. We're not going to talk about this anymore."

He hoisted the basket off the counter. Then he seemed to reconsider. Putting the basket back down, he turned to her, reaching up to put his hands on her arms.

"You're going to listen to me from now on, yes?"

She nodded.

"Okay. Then everything will be fine."

He picked up the basket. Madison watched as he carried it across the floor. At the front door, he paused, leaning down to prop the door open with the picnic basket. Then he walked to the elevator to push the button. She heard his voice from the hallway. "Come up to the roof now. We'll have a clear view."

Slowly, her hand reached back into the cutlery drawer. Her fingers curled around the hilt of a large steak knife.

Because the thing was, she'd been a single woman in Manhattan for a very long time. She knew what she knew. And that guy was *absolutely* cheating on Dani.

"Yes. It's all clear to me now, my love."

She slipped the knife into her pocket and followed him out the door.

17

A VIRTUAL AGGRESSION

by Haji Freeman

Spring 2020

Josh was manager of the Customer Satisfaction and Strategic Planning Department at a major Northeast utility. He always opened the weekly Zoom call by 9:55. That Monday, June 1, as usual, Cheryl was the second person to Zoom in.

"Oh, my God, did you see the protests last night?"

"Yeah, it was sad," Josh said. "I mean, the violence after the protests was sad."

After a pause, he added, "And for such a good cause."

Cheryl was nodding. "I was proud of those young people. Until, of course, the looting started. But most of the looters didn't even look like Black Lives Matter protesters."

By now, it was ten o'clock and seven people were on the call.

Karen Pederson was an accountant approaching forty, who enjoyed talking about her yoga classes and spoke with near-religious fervor of the produce at Whole Foods. "One of my neighbors put a Black Lives Matter sign on her lawn," she said, "and somebody put a note in her mailbox that she better take it down because a time is coming, dot, dot, dot."

"That's horrible," Karen's sidekick, Janet, said.

Karen agreed. "I know. I was thinking of putting one on my lawn, but now I'm afraid."

It was a few minutes past ten. The group seemed to consider Karen's fear.

Another few seconds passed. A Black team member, Keisha, unmuted. "How do you think we feel? If you're afraid to put a Black Lives Matter sign on your lawn, how do you think Black people feel traveling through your neighborhood? Or, Lord forbid, if one of us wanted to buy a house on your street."

The pause that followed gave Karen a chance to respond. A chance to empathize with people she was afraid to champion with a lawn sign. But she wasn't up for it. More silence.

Keisha gazed at Bob's scowling face in his video box. His arrogance fired more words from her heart. "It's your silence that allows the vocal racists to get away with more egregious violence."

Derek, another Black employee, enjoyed Josh's discomfort, watching him frantically scan the video boxes looking for someone to rescue him. Derek wasn't interested. The death of George Floyd changed him. More than Eric Garner, Michael Brown, Sandra Bland, or any of the murders of other Black people by police, captured on video, since everyone now had a camera in their pocket.

Derek understood how old folks felt when they saw the picture of Emmet Till in *Jet* magazine. It's not that people back then didn't know Black men and women, boys and girls were being brutally killed without cause by white vigilantes and white cops—sometimes one and the same—before that picture. It's that sometimes one image can condense hundreds of years of terror into one big, ugly, pus-infected boil in the middle of your face and you got to do something about it. George Floyd was the Emmet Till of Derek's generation.

And Floyd's death hit Derek harder because of the pandemic. Here he was hiding out against an invisible menace to society when the real, visible menace was driving around every city and town in the country with a gun strapped to its waist.

No, Derek wasn't going to jump in and save Josh. Yet he did feel shame that, once again, Keisha was out in front of him leading the charge. She was a revolutionary. He was a gamer. She was out organizing and marching in the streets. He was fighting imaginary battles in a virtual war. He didn't know what to say to back her up, but he steeled himself for whatever it would take. Shit had gotten ridiculous.

Karen finally broke the silence, her voice dripping with pain, offense, and privilege. "Well, I'm sorry, Keisha." It reminded Derek of the fake apologies he used to give to his mother when he forgot to do his chores. "That I don't live up to your expectations. I'm doing the best I can."

Keisha's voice sounded gravelly. Derek imagined she was hoarse from chanting in the streets—he didn't know she had been tear-gassed the night before. Still, she seemed calm when she said, "Maybe if you didn't act like such a Karen . . . Karen, you could do better."

Josh saw the resting-bitch faces in the video boxes replaced by surprise and alertness, but the best he could manage was a cover-up. He blurted, "Okay, time to get to work. Let's start with an update. . . ."

Karen interrupted. "What did you call me?" Derek had never heard her so upset. She demanded, "Did you just call me the K-word?"

Keisha was clever. "That's your name. Karen." Somehow, Keisha said "Karen" in such a way that Derek knew everyone on the call heard it as "bitch."

It sounded like Karen slammed her palm against the desk next to her computer. "Did you just call me the K-word?!"

Mellow, as if she'd just emerged from a weeklong meditation retreat, Keisha replied: "That's your name, isn't it?"

Karen's face was red, tendons in her neck straining against her skin. She barked: "Maybe you wouldn't mind if I called you the N-word?!"

Before Josh cut the call, everyone looking at Keisha's video box saw her leap out of her chair. Then a window appeared: "This meeting ended by the host."

Derek's name appeared on Keisha's phone seven seconds later. "Do you believe that bitch?!" she shouted.

Derek regretted not saying the same thing as soon as he picked up the call. Then they would have said it in unison, kind of like a simultaneous orgasm.

Instead, he was reduced to a weak retort. "That's just what I was thinking." His words made him feel shame.

Angry, Keisha didn't seem to notice. "She threatened to call me a fucking nigger, Derek! On a business call. That white bitch is lucky we weren't in the same room—I would have choked her like I was a cop."

Derek knew he couldn't match Keisha's anger, so he went for play-by-play. "And Josh just disconnects the call! After he just said, 'Let's get to work.' What kind of shit is that?"

"I'm gonna get that bitch fired!" Keisha declared. "She can't say that to me. To us! How she gonna say that to a black woman in a goddamn business meeting!"

Derek considered saying, *She actually said 'the N-word,' which is almost as bad.* But he settled for, "This is fucked up."

"You're damn right it's fucked up. Everything else going on in the world, and I gotta be called out of my name at work."

"Yeah, but she literally said 'the N-word,'" Derek ventured.

"It's the same thing, Derek," Keisha said, making him feel stupid.

"I know. I agree with you, Keisha. It's just . . . she started talking about you using the *K-word* before she used the *N-word*."

Keisha exploded. "The K-word! What the fuck is that, Derek? That's some shit these privileged white bitches made up to make themselves feel like a victim when they're out here calling the police on us, getting us shot? You saw what that woman in Central Park did to that birdwatching Negro! She called the police on him when she was breaking the law! She lied about him threatening her! He was just looking at birds. Fucking Birdwatching While Black."

Derek felt like hanging up. How did he get in this? He was only trying to help. "Look, I agree with you one hundred percent, Keisha. Whatever you wanna do, I support you. But we gotta think about what comes next, and you know she's gonna bring that K-word shit up. That's all I'm saying. This has got to go up the chain now. We can't have another meeting until this gets resolved. Whatever you wanna do, I got your back."

"Thank you, Derek," she said, softer. "I'll tell you what I don't want," she went on, her voice rising again with every word. "I don't want no fake apology. They're always willing to fake-apologize, Derek. I'm not taking a fake apology. I don't wanna hear shit about no K-word. I'm gonna file a grievance against this bitch. I [clap] want [clap] her [clap] fuckin' ass [clap]."

"Natalie!" Josh yelled to his wife as he rushed into the dining room, where she worked. He had been in the adjacent living room during the disastrous Zoom call, strategically seated in front of the framed Monet copy by one of the artists Natalie was always befriending.

She looked up and removed her headphones, which had been playing ambient music to drown out the voices of Josh and his team. "What's wrong with you? You look worse than the time the Club Med van ran out of gas on the way to the resort."

His voice went up a register: "Stop teasing me with that!" Then, more gently, "I got real problems. One of my staff just threatened to call a Black woman on the call the N-word."

Natalie gasped, looking suspiciously at her husband. "No. How did that happen?"

"It wasn't my fault," he protested. "The whole thing escalated fast. It's not my fault the whole country's on fire! How do they expect me to manage an interracial team when the country's in the middle of a race war?"

"Josh," Natalie broke in, "what happened?"

Josh recounted the story as best he could.

Natalie, an attorney with a big data firm, asked, "Is it recorded?"

Josh's hands were sweaty. He hit his forehead with his palm. "Shit! Yes, it is. My idea in case we needed to look up something later." He ran a hand through his hair, and, with a conspiratorial look, wondered: "Maybe I should delete it?"

"No. That might be considered destroying evidence. Save it, but don't mention it unless somebody asks."

"Shit—destroying evidence," said Josh, crestfallen. "You don't think this could go to court, do you?"

Natalie threw a quick, pathetic look at her husband, then smiled. "Maybe you can get Karen to apologize before this blows up. I get that the Black woman said the K-word first, but I'm not sure that's even really a thing. You cannot, however, threaten to call somebody the N-word during a staff meeting. That's like taking your laptop in the bathroom on a Zoom call and taking a shit! You shouldn't even have to tell people that. See if you can get Karen to apologize."

Cheryl called upstairs to her daughter, "Frances, come down here."

"Ma, I'm studying. I'll be down in a bit."

"Frances, I told you to empty this dishwasher last night. Come down and do it now."

"Oh, all right, give me a minute." Frances stumbled downstairs in her quarantine outfit: hair in a wild bush around her head, blue Spelman College sweatshirt and gray sweats.

Cheryl was sitting at the kitchen table with her laptop and paper notebook beside her. As Frances reached up to put two glasses in the cabinet, her mother said, "White woman just called a black woman the N-word in my staff meeting."

"Get out of here!" Frances, out of habit, edited the curse word out of the phrase in respect of her mother. "This just happened?"

"Just happened. I'm waiting for my boss to call now. He's gonna want me to fix this for him, but he's gonna have to handle this one himself."

"What happened?" asked Frances, forgetting about the dishes and leaning against the counter.

After Cheryl described the meeting, she added, "And I used to like Karen. When Brian left, Karen encouraged me to apply as director. I asked about it, but corporate wanted a master's degree, so I didn't apply. Karen acknowledged that she saw me training Josh to do the job. But you can't teach smarts."

"So what happens now?"

"I don't know," Cheryl said, sighing. "He'll probably get Karen to apologize and that'll be the end of it. This all started because she was talking about putting a Black Lives Matter sign in her yard. Jesus, I don't know why she even had to bring that up, always wanting to be the center of attention."

"No, Mommy." Frances's eyes were wide. "You can't let her get away with that. That wasn't a mistake. She had 'nigger' at the tip of her tongue, ready to spit it out at the smallest provocation. Just like that white woman in Central Park. She's a nice liberal Upper West Sider until a black man asks her to obey the law. Then turns into that woman who lied about Emmett Till whistling at her.

Cheryl nodded her head.

"No, Mommy. She's got to go."

Cheryl's phone rang. She looked at the name, frowned, and picked it up.

Josh sounded cheerful. "How're you doing?"

"Not good, Josh. Not good."

"I know," he said with a sigh. "Tough morning."

"I can't believe what she said, Josh."

He turned guarded. "Who?"

Cheryl was indignant. "Who? Karen! She said the N-word."

"Yes," Josh admitted, "she *said* 'N-word.'"

"That's what I said!"

"But she didn't use the actual word. Just 'N-word.'"

Cheryl cut him off. "What're you going to do, Josh?"

Josh hesitated. "I'm not sure yet. I just wanted to touch base. Get your perspective. You know."

"Uh-huh."

"I thought what she said was wrong too."

"Who?" Cheryl demanded.

"Karen," Josh said. "I mean, maybe Keisha shouldn't have said what she said, but what Karen said was far worse."

"Far worse," Cheryl agreed. "What're you going to do?"

"I'm not sure. I'm planning to talk with each of them. Maybe ask Karen to apologize."

"That's not enough."

"You don't think so?"

"No." When Josh didn't reply after several seconds, Cheryl added, "Did you see how angry Keisha was?"

"Have you spoken to her?" Josh asked, furtively.

"No, but didn't you see her stand up before you ended the meeting?"

As he pictured it, beads of sweat formed in his armpits. "Yes."

"What do you think would have happened if we were all in the same room?"

Josh angled to take some control of the conversation. "Maybe it wouldn't have escalated if we were in the same room."

Cheryl snorted loud enough for Josh to hear.

"You think I should call legal?" he asked.

"You have to call legal."

"You think so?"

"Yes."

"And tell them what?"

Cheryl sighed. "Tell them everything, Josh."

Janet called Karen as soon as the meeting ended. "Hey, girlfriend."

"Janet. I don't know what just happened. Do you think I'm in trouble?"

The pause was indeed recognition that Karen was in trouble.

After a few beats, Janet said, "I don't know, but I've never heard anyone say the N-word in a professional meeting before."

"I know," Karen exclaimed. "I don't know what happened. I feel like I might throw up. It's everything going on. I wanted to help, then she called me the K-word, which pissed me off. Then, I don't know, I just kind of went there. Shoot, this is going viral, isn't it?"

"There's a chance," Janet admitted.

"I'm gonna look like another privileged white woman stepping out of line. Damn it!" she almost cried. "I can't get Amy Cooper out of my head. She lost her job when that video got out. What am I gonna do? Should I get a lawyer?"

"See if you can apologize first. That's the thing to do before you lawyer up. Try to squash it. Everybody's tense. Maybe put the sign up now. How can you be racist if you have a Black Lives Matter sign in front of your house?"

Karen was pacing while she talked to Janet. Her phone pinged, and she looked down at her laptop. "Hold on a minute. Bob just sent me an email, with the subject line 'Good for you.'" She read it out loud: "Dear Karen, I hope you're okay. You tried to reach out to that woman. Her tone when she called you the K-word was unforgivable. Call me if you want to talk. Bob."

Winter 2021

Derek didn't hesitate when he pulled up Keisha's number. He kept one eye on the blaring TV and scrolled to her name with the other. As her phone started to ring, he let both eyes loll back to the big screen.

She sounded bored when she answered. "Hi, Derek."

They hadn't spoken in six months, but he skipped any greeting. His voice came loud and fast. "You watching this shit?"

"Not anymore," Keisha said with a sigh. "I can't take it, Derek. I live by myself. If we're all gonna die, I want to be listening to my music and dancing. Not watching a bunch of crazy white men storm the Capitol."

"But guess which crazy white man I just saw running through the building?" Derek shot back, undeterred.

Keisha sighed again. "Bob."

"You saw him!" On the TV, a dozen Trump supporters banged on the door of the House chambers, with a reporter from PBS giving play-by-play like she was an NFL announcer.

"No, Derek!" Keisha shouted. "Are you fuckin' listening? I'm not watching that shit. Of course you saw Bob! Why else would you be calling me after all this time?"

Derek grabbed the remote and muted the rioters, gazing out his living room windows to the yard. His voice was low and hesitant. "I'm sorry for not calling. So much shit happened after you left. I planned to, but I didn't know what to say. Or if you even wanted to talk to me."

"You could have asked how I was doing, Derek." There were sobs in her voice. "You didn't have to be helping with my bills if that's what you were worried about."

"No, no, no, no, no," he chanted. "I wasn't worried about that. I didn't think you would even take money."

"You were right." She sounded offended. "So why didn't you call me? I thought you were my friend."

Derek hung his head. Should he hang up? He stuttered: "I . . . was ashamed, Keisha."

Curiosity came through in her tone. "Ashamed?"

He stuffed his tears and sounded angry, like it was her fault. "I should have left with you, Keisha! It was fucked up what they did. Trying to force you to accept her apology. I was proud of you when you quit!" He paused. "And . . . I wanted to leave too. Noelle even said she could do more shifts if I didn't find something right away. But . . . Keisha, I was afraid."

"Derek," she said coldly. "That's fucked up."

"I know. I know," he said, trying to placate her. "I—"

"No, you don't know. You should at least listen to what I have to say, since you didn't have the balls to call me when I needed you."

Derek sat back on his black leather sofa with his forehead in his hand, studying his slippers. He was silent.

"I cried for days," Keisha said. "You know my mama's in Detroit. I ain't got family here. Your wife was offering to support you, but you didn't pick up the phone and call your friend who quit because some bitch called her the N-word?"

Derek had read *The New Rules of Marriage,* so he said slowly: "I knew your mama was in Detroit. I hear that you cried for days. My wife was willing to support me. And still I didn't call my friend who quit 'cause some bitch called her the N-word." He sighed. "Keisha, I felt ashamed for not quitting too."

Would it have been easier if he had called after she quit and told her he was staying? He doubted it.

Neither spoke for some seconds. Eventually, Keisha broke the silence. "Okay, so you saw QAnon Bob run into the Capitol."

Derek's head was still in his hand. "Yeah, I'm sure it was him. But it doesn't even matter now. I should have called you. I'm sorry."

"Now you're apologizing too?" Her voice had a hint of the playfulness he had heard in the many conversations at each other's cubicles before Covid.

"I understand what I did wrong, and I truly regret it, and would do different next time."

"You could still resign."

He couldn't tell if she was teasing him or not. "After today, I might be ready," he said, standing up and clicking the TV on again. "I'm sorry to have bothered you, Keisha."

"Before you go," she jumped in, "how's Cheryl?"

He exhaled. "She had a stroke on Labor Day."

Keisha gasped. "Oh, Derek! That was the perfect reason to call me."

He rubbed his temples. "I would have called you if she died."

"Well, that's a consolation. Did anyone get kidnapped since I left?"

"No," he replied, "but Josh's wife kicked him out."

Keisha's voice went up a notch. "How do you know?"

"Janet told me." Derek stood and started to pace the room again. "She's been calling me since you left."

"Oh." The syllable conveyed volumes.

"It's not like that. She even encouraged me to call you. She wondered how you were doing. But she heard through the rumor mill that Josh's wife was having an affair with a partner at her firm. I'm told she kicked Josh out but kept the house."

Keisha chuckled.

"And Karen must think she won because I left?" Keisha asked.

"I'm not sure. Janet was close to her for a while after the incident. She thinks Karen hates herself for taking Bob's support but won't admit it. Janet stopped talking to Karen because she said Bob had started to radicalize her. According to Janet, Karen felt so bad about being called out for sounding racist she actually became racist to justify how bad she felt. Does that make sense?"

"Something like a self-fulfilling prophecy," Keisha said.

"I guess." Derek was standing before the screen, scrolling through the TV stations on mute. They all showed scenes of the Capitol riot.

"What happened after Cheryl's stroke?"

"Her daughter left school to care for her. I think she'll be okay. I talked to her after she got out of the hospital."

Keisha paused. "I'll give her a call. I hope this mess doesn't give her another stroke."

They were both quiet. Derek wanted to go back to watching the news.

18

THIS LITTLE LIGHT

by Kathleen Scheiner

Her last real-life session had been weeks ago. Hazel toted her garbage downstairs in the elevator and sunk it in the bin of her building's courtyard. There was a squawking above her in the twilight, and she craned her head back to see three parakeets flying in a circle but never rising above the rooftop. A dirty cage sat near the recycling and trash bins with its door open, and Hazel imagined their owner had let them out. Perhaps some magical thinking on their part, believing the parakeets would be happy with the other wild birds.

Right after she saw those parakeets, her headaches got bad again, worse than she could ever recall. Perhaps as crushing as the very first one that had hit her when she was nine, clearly demarcating the line between sunshine on her shoulders, hair swinging free in the breeze, and the sour darkness of her bedroom, where she spent most of her years till late adolescence. Hazel remembered the tinfoil fixed to the windows to keep the sunlight out, all color stripped from the walls of the room. When she was in the grips of one of those headaches, light and bright colors made her want to die. A spot of orange would lance her brain like a surgical instrument.

They never did figure out what was going on inside her head after countless MRIs, tests, and appointments with specialists. The doctors' best guess was that the headaches were migraines, and they prescribed painkillers that would knock her out until the pain left. Eventually, Hazel outgrew the headaches and leaned into something else that existed in her mind. She knew things she shouldn't. She could tell her parents when an unexpected check was coming in, pick a trifecta for her dad when he bet on the horses, or suddenly have an urge to study the night before a pop quiz.

With the resurgence of those headaches, Hazel drew the curtains in her little one-bedroom apartment in the Village, wanting to close herself up in darkness and avoid the painful colors. New York had become a different city from all the years she'd lived there. Barely anybody was outside on the street, which usually teemed with people— tourists in bright-colored clothing, soft bodies, and comfortable shoes moving oh so slowly among the gutter punks and colorful street people. Instead of a backbeat of chatter and traffic noises, there was now a constant wail of ambulance sirens overlapping and a rare pocket of silence when she noticed how loud the birds were.

Then Hazel heard something different outside her window—it was cooing. She parted her drapes and saw the orange eyes of pigeons as they roosted on her fire escape, as well as the black beady ones of a crow that stood out like midnight in the mass of gray bodies. That was peculiar.

Hazel couldn't help but think that they were hungry. With no tourists, no humans on the street, they had no pretzels or hot dog crusts to feast upon. In the twenty years she'd lived in her apartment, Hazel had never seen so many birds massed together on her teeny-tiny fire escape. And they never mingled together.

She found some crusts from a pizza box that had been sitting on top of her stove the last three days and put those on a paper plate for the birds. They barely stirred as she opened the window and maneuvered her screen out of it so she could place the plate outside like a postal worker delivering mail. The birds descended in a mass of feathers, the bigger pigeons muscling out the smaller ones to peck at the bread. But the crow was even more fierce, lashing out at the pigeons with its cruel black beak before selecting the fattest crust and flying off. An omen for sure—was she the crow or the pigeon? Or maybe even the parakeet? It made her nervous.

Her psychic skills didn't qualify her as an essential worker. But tell that to everyone else. Suddenly, Hazel's website became inundated with requests for bookings. Her server shut down at one point because of all the traffic directed to her site.

This was not the norm for her. She squeaked by in New York with about twenty-five regular clients and would occasionally get a few more through word of mouth who might contact her in a crisis, then stop showing up once things had righted themselves. Usually, her inbox didn't see much action, and most inquiries dried up once Hazel quoted them a price. Sometimes before the New Year, journalists would contact her wanting predictions, but that's not how Hazel operated.

Her sessions took place in her living room, where she had a giant bookcase that covered one wall. The different shelves had doors on them, and she would hide her TV and the daily clutter of life behind them when she had a meeting. On the wall near the window was a dark-blue tapestry with the different signs of the zodiac displayed in white. Hazel didn't particularly like it, but her clients seemed to appreciate a sign showing that they had entered another realm, and this served the purpose.

Hazel preferred meeting face-to-face. She believed the energy was better then, but she wasn't going to let anyone risk their life for a reading. Not that there weren't some who would try.

Hazel had run a few sessions on Google Hangouts if she really trusted the person and thought she had a good connection with them. The amount of strangers who were filling up her inbox now, though— how would she ever handle them? She could run a Celtic cross or past-present-future layout of tarot cards and give out a few pointers based on them. Or she could cast birth charts and see what transits were occurring or had just passed. Those were the tools she most relied on when she first started her business after 9/11, when everybody was mourning and looking for answers. But then she learned to focus on her client's energy, finding that her work was most special when she could help someone. If she was near them, she could sense what they needed.

Hazel's phone kept pinging, vibrating so hard atop her glass-topped coffee table that it nearly fell off with the movement. Messages scrolled by in a large font, since her eyesight was so bad. Everybody wanted help.

My mother died of Covid. Can you connect me to her?

What's going to happen—when will we be able to go outside again and stop scrubbing down our groceries?

I can't stand my children. I'm afraid I'm going to hurt them.

It was too much. Hazel had been avoiding the messages, the emails, the abyss of need that radiated out from her phone. But then an innocuous text scooted by—something lighthearted and flip: *Hey, Leia said you're really good. i'm going crazy right now not being able to see my customers. just want to talk to somebody. i can venmo you.*

Venmo. Hazel had it on her phone, but she had never used it, thinking of the app as a millennial thing while she was proudly Gen X.

She figured she could get by for a few months until the pandemic came to an end. The government had given her $1,000, and she didn't have to pay rent right now with the state of emergency, but those bills would eventually come due.

She could feel a pulsing start behind her eyes and knew how the pain would soon balloon into something monstrous, making her remember a scene from her childhood.

Her father had come home from work grumpy and barely looked at his wife when she said, "Hazel had another really bad one today," meaning a migraine.

Hazel's father twitched the newspaper tented out in front of him, making a noise like he was trying to drown out her mother, while he rocked back in his easy chair.

"Did you hear me?" her mother repeated.

Her father sighed and put down the newspaper. He shoved his reading glasses to the top of his head and looked at Hazel laying prone on the couch and then at his wife with watery blue eyes.

"Hazel is going to have to learn how to tune out these sensations," he said in a cool voice. "Life is uncomfortable. If she focuses on every ache and pain, she's going to be miserable. Hazel needs to just chew up some aspirin and get on with her day like everybody else. I'm not going to have her be some silly Victorian girl shut away in her room with the vapors."

Stiff upper lip. Oh, how Hazel tried. Her mother sent away for water from Lourdes and used it one day when Hazel lay on the couch with a real thumper so bad that she asked her mother to turn off the soap operas she liked to watch. Hazel felt something wet on her forehead and then her mother's slippery fingers as she traced the shape of a cross.

"Oh, Virgin in heaven. I see you. I see you. You've marked this child for something special."

The pain was bad, like a stake through Hazel's eye, and she fell asleep soon after. Later, she asked her mother what she had seen.

"On the wall above the couch, I saw a reflection of the Virgin Mary. She's your protector. She's a miracle coming through you."

There was pleasure and pain in the memories now that both her parents were dead, and she knew that, in their own peculiar ways, they only wanted what was best for her. They both had been right. She was special because she was sensitive, and she did have to learn how to tune out all the overwhelming sensory information so it didn't break her. Along with the lesson that life was uncomfortable, her father had also drilled into her that nothing came free. Hazel knew she had to do something about this pandemic—pay attention to the signs—rather than wallow in pain and fear inside her apartment.

The waves in her head rolled through her body and seemed to transmute into a tingling in her fingertips. She picked up the phone and quickly tapped out: *3:30 tomorrow? give me your date of birth, time born, and place if you know it and i can draw up a chart.* A thumbs-up emoji came her way, and Hazel took the phone with her to the tiny dark bedroom. She slipped it under her pillow and pulled the duvet over her head, locking out any light before falling into a tunnel of sleep.

When she woke the next day, still with a bit of a headache, Hazel was more hopeful than she had been in weeks. Maybe it was because her schedule had flip-flopped into a normal one. After the upheaval of the past few weeks where she worried the nights away and slept during daylight hours, Hazel found herself up at dawn with a fresh, clean start in front of her. She remembered the appointment she had impulsively made for later in the day and decided to lay in supplies.

She needed a candle to set the mood and could probably stand to clean up the junk that had accumulated on her couch and table. Hazel realized that would be in the background unless she moved her computer, and she really didn't want to do that. The ghost of the headache was still there, threatening to come back with a vengeance, and she was looking for easy solutions.

Hazel found her cleanest dirty clothes and took a red bandanna out of her sock drawer and tied it over her nose and mouth. The CDC and the New York government wanted everybody to mask up before going outside or encountering another person, and this was all that Hazel had. The medical-quality masks were reserved for the health-care workers, and the homemade kinds she had seen online were priced outrageously.

Hazel took the stairs rather than using the germy elevator. Her headache had dwindled down to a dull throb. Manageable. Outside it was a gray, slushy April day, saving her eyes. The paper plate she used to serve the birds had drifted down to the sidewalk after they ate the crusts weighing it down, and beside it was the stiff, cold body of a parakeet. Her heart breaking, Hazel picked the dead bird up with the paper plate and put it in the garbage. She used the flat of her hand to shade her eyes and looked up at her fire escape. The birds were still up there, congregating on the railing outside her living room window, and they watched her, their coos sounding like the clucking of tongues.

She turned her back on them and headed to the bodega on Seventh Street that she sometimes used for emergency items. She passed one person who moved onto the actual street to avoid walking next to her on the sidewalk, like she was the boogeyman. It made Hazel laugh to think that somebody found her scary. Her, all five feet three inches with soft curves, red hair, and size-6 feet.

She was only one of a few customers inside the bodega and was surprised to see sheets of plastic draped over the front of the cash register stand.

She got herself a shopping basket and concentrated on collecting enough supplies so she wouldn't have to leave her apartment for several days. Into the basket went coffee, sour cream, tomatoes, onions, and pita bread. She roved the tight aisles and marveled at how much wasn't available at the bodega. Usually, the shelves were packed tight with canned goods and all sorts of oddities, but there was so much empty space now.

Above the ice cooler, she saw what she was looking for: candles. They were cheap religious votives, not her preference. But she picked through those, shunting aside a green St. Jude and something for the lottery, until she saw one that was pink, but she couldn't quite reach it.

A woman with deeply tanned skin and curly hair, lank with a sheen of grease, bumped into her. Hazel's nostrils flared at the dank, unwashed stink of her.

"Give me some money, would you? I'm starving," the woman said, and the deep-violet aura Hazel saw around her drove fear into her heart.

"I got babies to feed."

Hazel was still up on tiptoe reaching toward the candles, and she started to shake, panic taking over her body.

"You want this?" the woman asked, towering over Hazel, and she plucked the pink candle from the shelf and put it in Hazel's basket, nice and easy like a basketball player.

The proprietor of the bodega came from behind the plastic-sheeted checkout counter, saying, "No money. No money. I want you to leave." He was barely taller than Hazel, but he pointed an authoritative finger toward the door.

"But I'm hungry. Help me, please. We all got to stick together now."

Hazel caressed the candle and noticed a fragrance wafting up from her basket; the wax was scented but not obnoxiously so. She turned the votive over and saw an image of the Virgin of Guadalupe on it.

"Lady, will you help me? I'm hungry. I'm hungry."

Looking up from her basket, Hazel asked, "What do you want to eat? I can buy you some food." She just wanted to get rid of her and make sure the woman didn't chase her back to her apartment.

The woman took off down the aisle, and Hazel hustled to the checkout counter.

"I'm ready to check out," she told the bodega cashier.

The man took his place behind the counter, suddenly much taller than before. Was there a platform that he stepped on? A small rectangular space had been cut out of the plastic sheeting, and she handed her products through it, while the man rang her up. Hazel heard the slip-slap of footsteps, and dread rose up in her. The homeless woman came up holding a box of Cinnamon Toast Crunch cereal and a two-liter bottle of A&W Cream Soda. It was a bizarre combination, but Hazel handed the items over to the cashier without comment.

"No money," he said again.

"I'm only buying her a bit of food," said Hazel nervously. "No money."

He rang up her purchases and bagged the items separately. Hazel handed the woman the lighter bag with her soda and cereal in it. "Here you go."

"Thank you," the woman said, and that made Hazel blush with embarrassment and shame. She hadn't done this to be charitable; she bought the items to get rid of the woman.

Chastened, Hazel went back to her apartment, taking the stairs up to the sixth floor. The new client had texted their birth information while Hazel slept, so she plugged that into Time Passages, her favorite astrological software for casting charts. She realized she didn't even know the sex of the person as she typed in their data and then held her breath as the chart appeared before her.

It never got old seeing the blank canvas of a star chart, perfectly round representing an individual, until twelve pieces of pie were carved into it and then populated with planets. Right away, Hazel could see this was going to be a difficult chart. There was a stellium in Leo, which was the eighth house, giving this person a focal point that was most likely sex-based. Someone into role-play and performing. Mercury and Neptune were conjunct there, which made her shiver. The eighth house was also death and transformation, and that was even scarier for Hazel to contemplate. This particular Neptune-Mercury aspect was something she associated with cult leaders.

Hazel downloaded Zoom, a video-conference software that she had been hearing so much about, and scheduled a meeting with the new client, her fingers jittering a little on her mouse. The person accepted her invite right away, and Hazel found it hard to swallow. Somewhere in the back of her mind, she had been hoping they would be a no-show, just a drunken text sent during the day.

She sighed before getting her space ready for this appointment and then herself. The apartment got a cursory cleaning, and then she hit the shower for the first time in days. With steam rising up around her, Hazel found the last bit of her headache was receding. She was weak and wrung out from it but also purified in a way. After her shower, she dressed in a fancy gold lamé dress because it was the only thing she had that was clean.

The last time she'd worn the garment must have been a year ago when she went to a seers' event in Bushwick, which had turned out to be a bust for her. She remembered everybody being so young and hip, while she, standing in the corner with a plastic cup of white wine, felt like a grandma, some relic left over from Studio 54.

To make it different this time, she blow-dried her red hair. The handkerchief hemline of the dress fluttered around her ankles, giving Hazel an urge to dress up even more. She ended up putting on a full face of makeup and her favorite amethyst ring before sitting down in front of her computer at 2:55 p.m., ready to begin her session.

She clicked the link in her calendar, which brought up a video screen where she could only see herself. Hazel lit the candle she had bought at the bodega and turned it around so the image of the Virgin of Guadalupe faced the screen. There was a prayer written on the back, which made Hazel smile when she saw some of the words: "Obtain for us sweet hope in the midst of the bitterness of life, burning charity, and the precious gift of final perseverance."

She remembered the prayer cards her mother collected at church, and the times she had found them in various novels in her childhood home. Scandalous novels like *Lace* and *Tropic of Cancer* where the prayer cards marked the sex scenes. Of course, Hazel couldn't talk about that with her mother then, but it seemed like a secret communication they had where she would read those parts, then replace the card and novel in the bookcase.

She gripped the edge of her desk as the computer's screen divided into two, with her face and a black square next to it. The black square flickered and then the face of a young woman with big gray eyes and long pale hair appeared. "Hi, hi, hi," she said enthusiastically. "I'm so glad to see you. I'm dying right now being stuck in the house."

Hazel cocked her head, grateful. This was no cult leader. "I'm happy to see you, too. I'm Hazel." She felt awkward and fumbled for what to say next. "So I've got your information, and I drew up your birth chart. This is the first time I've ever used Zoom, so forgive me if there are any glitches. I usually do in-person sessions."

"Will that affect my reading?" the woman asked.

The in-person meetings helped Hazel because of the tells she could see in her clients. She could pick up on when they were nervous or if they needed a push toward different behaviors. But at the same time, those meetings would take something out of Hazel, deplete her somehow so she was a shadow of herself.

The woman's warm smile beamed through the screen, and Hazel didn't want to let her down. She said confidently, "No, I don't think so. What's your name? I never got that information in your texts."

"Oh, God, sorry, sorry. It's just been crazy, you know. Who are you? Who am I? My mind's been spinning out of control. But it's Catalina. Catalina Ward. A lot of people think that's a fake name, but I never saw the purpose of hiding myself."

"A fake name?" Hazel asked. She looked at the chart on her screen and squinted her eyes. Was there an adoption that she hadn't seen? A crime?

Catalina laughed and flapped her hand. "Oh, I'm a dancer, and most of the girls take on a stage name. I think it makes it easier for them to separate work from real life." Catalina took up a hank of her wheat-colored hair and curled it around her finger.

"I've never heard of that," said Hazel, as she heard pecking behind her. "What kind of dancer are you? Broadway?"

Catalina laughed, and though she was years younger than Hazel, she said, "Oh, no, honey. I'm a stripper. I take off my clothes for a living."

Aha! Eighth house explained, thought Hazel. She turned behind her, expecting to see a pigeon at the window, but instead a sad, bedraggled green-and-yellow parakeet pecked against the glass, desperate to be let in.

"Excuse me a moment," she said and rushed toward the window, opening it. The screen was still out, and the cold wind whooshed in. Hazel held out a finger and was overjoyed when the parakeet hopped onto it. "Hey, little fella," she said. With her other hand, she shut the window and came to her desk, the parakeet still on her finger.

She faced the computer again and blew out a breath of air. The parakeet winged from her finger to her shoulder and sat there, making bright peeps, as she sat down again.

"How cute," said Catalina. "You don't keep it in a cage—that's so cool!"

Hazel laughed. "It just flew in my window. I guess I have a new pet." She went back to her Time Passages app to pick up the thread of her conversation before she was interrupted. "I was looking at your chart earlier and worried that you might be a cult leader with your eighth house, but I'm glad to see that's not the case."

Catalina dropped the piece of hair she had been twisting and fiddled with the large silver hoop in her ear instead. "A cult leader, really?" She nodded her head as if she were considering a career change. "Yeah, I could see that. I grew up in a really religious household. I actually thought I got the calling when I was eight, that God was talking to me."

There was a glow on her shoulder where the parakeet sat, and Hazel felt a smile tug at her lips. Out of the corner of her eye, she saw the bird's bright-yellow bill. "Then what happened?"

Catalina laughed, throwing her head back and showing off a long, slender neck. She wiped tears from her eyes. "I found out I couldn't be a priest. I could only be a nun. And I didn't want any part of that."

Hazel smiled. With a Leo eighth house, the woman had to perform. She couldn't be a shrinking violet or she'd go mad. "Makes sense. So, Catalina, what can I help you with today? Do you have any particular questions you want to ask me?"

Catalina drummed her fingers against something—Hazel recognized the sound—and then she said, "I'm sure you're getting lots of *When is this going to end?* And my question is somewhat related to that. I'm a dancer, and there's a certain energy, a spark, a touch that I can't live without. All my clubs are shut down, and I don't really like the idea of risking my life to give a lap dance. But I've gotta do something with this energy or I'm going to explode. I'm going crazy right now."

Hazel pulled up the current transits going on in Catalina's chart and saw Mercury moving through her third house of communications, but later in the year, the planet would swing back toward the eleventh house, that of hopes and dreams, friends, associations. Hazel narrowed her eyes.

"I see something in the future, where pressure must be released. You've got to find an outlet. And for some reason, I think it's got something to do with the internet." She felt the parakeet twisting its beak in her hair, almost like it was nuzzling her.

Catalina's smile turned dour. "I want to dance, not do sex acts onscreen. I don't want to be a cam girl," she said in a dark voice, all goodwill suddenly gone.

Oh, no, I've lost her. The parakeet tugged at her hair, and Hazel turned her head to see the candle's flickering flame. The guttering wick made a popping sound like it was trying to catch her attention, and Hazel touched the glass jar, hot to the touch. She saw that the heat had warped some of the words of the prayer, making the letters form new ones. Most of the words were nonsensical gobbledygook, but she was able to pick out two words that were close together: ONLY FANS.

"Have you ever heard about OnlyFans?" Hazel asked. "That's the message I'm getting."

19

THE PIGEONS' PANDEMIC: A LOVE STORY

by Laura Vural

April 1, 2020: On a Hell's Kitchen Terrace, in New York

"I apologize," I said to my love, her eyes dark, darting, refusing to look at mine. The wind rattled the terrace bars as we looked down from the twenty-eighth floor to our home, the park we'd just come up from.

She cleared her throat and bobbed her head forward, away from me.

"Please stop pacing and look at me," I asked Parmesan, a.k.a. Parma, called that for how she devoured balls of grated cheese under the outdoor tables of the pizza shop across from our park. But she wouldn't, or couldn't; she just turned away, bobbed again, and walked the six or so steps it took to bump into the glass apartment door.

"I know times are tough, but I promise we will survive."

This time Parma pivoted to face me and tapped her claws, a signal that she'd try to stand still long enough to listen. Honesty was demanded. I could never sidestep the truth.

"I screwed up," I confessed. "I knew you were right behind me with family, ready to surround our human friend, on her usual bench, with a bag full of dinner crumbs. But for some reason I froze, fixated by her toes, usually socked, but today they were naked, a crackled peanut-shell brown. I fantasized taking a tiny nibble, maybe just a taste."

Mindful that Parma didn't want to be on the terrace in the first place, I stopped explaining and listened to her rant. "You're ridiculous, Pita," she cooed. Pita was the name my human friend gave me the first time she saw me savor the crumbs of the soft folds of the round Greek pita bread. The woman on the twenty-eighth floor was one who proved, like others in the park, that many humans were good beings, not the evil haters of pigeons that Parma and her family believed them to be.

Parma flapped her feathers in frustration. "Even the children you love so much," she went on, "get joy out of chasing us from our meals, sometimes hitting us with sticks."

Instead of defending my human friends, I was distracted by my mate's vibrating, as she fluttered her wings faster and faster. It drove me crazy, not her impatience, but rather because it was so sexy. I had to fight the instinct to flap and "clap," what we pigeons call "making love," jumping upon her back right then and there. I knew she didn't share my love of humans. It was a constant source of tension, but Parma was my one, my only, my mate for life. And I had to finish my story.

"Listen," I went on, "less and less people are coming to the park to feed us these days. I should've made a path so everyone could feast, but when I shook myself out of my human toe fantasy, it was too late."

Parma didn't want to listen or wait for the human to come out. I danced around her, showing off my hip-hop moves, hoping for forgiveness. Annoyed, she finally broke her silence. "Pita, my human-loving birdbrain . . . you were only looking out for yourself. Before you even had a chance to act on your stupid fantasy, the other flock came and stole your old woman's crumbs." She was right. The invading pigeons were the palest shade of gray, only getting darker with hints of purple from their napes to their necks to their crowns. While lighter than me, they bore black stripes, widening on their right wings. Parma's family's markings, like most pigeons, spanned feathers evenly on both sides and showed their superior lineage, they contended.

The way I looked at it, no matter how light or dark, no matter the width or shape, striped on one wing or both, we were all proud descendants of rock pigeons, the first domesticated birds, even honored by humans in ancient Egyptian cave art. We rock pigeons are revered for our strong magnetoreception skills, an internal GPS used as a compass to be able to fly places and return home with ease. Both Parma and I were born in the park, so we were never trained to use our GPS. However, generations of her kin learned how to navigate and traveled miles across rivers and fields without trees. They passed down stories of their journeys to their children, who still possessed the high-and-mighty attitude of "educated" pigeons, looking down on indigenous urban birds like me.

Earlier, just before we flew up to the terrace, after the fiasco with the old woman's toes, we had the same argument we had almost every day. "My father says," and Parma would imitate her father's coo, a low almost-growl, "that Pita's family never earned their stripes or gave their lives fighting human wars with no rewards. His infatuation with humans is a sign of ignorance." And he'd add, "Your mate's markings are only on his left wing and can hardly be seen against his darker-gray feathers."

My angry tone would get higher, like a sparrow's, so I tried to keep calm. "What difference does it make if I have a great-great-great-great-grandfather who delivered messengers during WWII?" I'd argue. "All us pigeons live in the same park, side by side with the humans. We should celebrate what we have in common and understand and respect our differences, bird to bird . . . and bird to human." But Parma couldn't quite get there.

"Humans feed us, but they don't love us," she'd say in defense of her dad's point of view, in our nest, on a windowsill, in any alleyway. "He's right. Your obsession with humans distracts you. . . . And, like today, you often get the last crumbs. But . . ." my love would quickly add, " . . . you're curious about ev-er-y-thing," she added, lingering on every syllable. "And . . . you always make me laugh." She giggled. "You can charm humans better than anyone else, which means I will never starve. And . . ." she singsonged as she wafted, "you're a great clapper."

I fluttered, I flapped, flew a few feet above her, full of joy. No matter what her father said, no matter her own prejudices, she loved me. I lowered myself just close enough to tickle her back with my feathers. We rubbed our heads together and I was in ecstasy, but the drumming circle playing on the other side by the park interrupted our moment. And I was getting hunger pangs. "Let's go up and see my friend on the twenty-eighth-floor terrace," I whistled to Parma. "It's almost that time for her to come out to feed us." Parma pouted but agreed, flying higher and ahead of me.

So there we were, on the terrace, still waiting for a feeding. It was getting late, the sun was still out, but not for long. Parma felt trapped, pecking at the concrete terrace floor, searching for any undiscovered crumbs. I had to say something to relax her. "Parma, I love you so *muuuuuch* . . ." I sang out, "*soooooooo* much more than I ever could love any human."

She froze, gave me a hungry stare. "So stop waiting for your mammal woman. I'm out!" Before I could say anything else, Parma was expecting me to follow, but I wanted to wait a little more for my friend.

Soon the percussive pounding began, as it had every day, from every rooftop, at 7 p.m., like clockwork. During this time, my female friend would come out a few minutes before the noise began and we'd have our quiet time; sometimes I was alone, other times with Parma. She fed, we ate. She talked or sang, we cooed. I did not know why the humans started banging pots, cowbells, or metal spoons between the terrace bars, but my ears burst and my feathers ached to flee.

I wanted to, but I couldn't wait a second longer. Besides the painful noise, I was getting too hungry. Most important, I didn't want to lose sight of my precious Parma, so I jumped up to the railing facing the Hudson River and took off to the park to be with my beloved mate.

My plan was to fly straight back to our nest, made of twigs from the white birch trees, abandoned candy wrappers, and shoelaces left around DeWitt Clinton Park. Our home had been wedged in the metal roof beams atop the red-bricked bathroom shed since before I was born. Besides my mother's comforting *"mrrrroooo, mrrrroooo,"* my first heard sounds were listening to the human children's laughter between toilet flushes. Their voices tickled my ears, and sparked my imagination. Every day, after feedings, I tried to picture what the children looked like singing on the swings or cheering goals on the soccer field. My mom was precious to me, but those unseen humans were my first love.

When the park lights shined on our nest, my mother would school my brood of brothers and sisters huddled around her plump breast with words of wisdom. "People, young and old, are the ones who feed us. We eat what they throw away." She didn't say whether it was an act of kindness to feed all the birds who lived in the park, or if it was a lack of values, wasting cherished food, but I was grateful.

As I flew from the terrace across Eleventh Avenue to catch up with Parma, my mind drifted to the day, over a year ago, the day after my mother left this earth, but also the day I met Parma. I'd cried throughout the night, but the next morning I knew it was time to leave the nest, to learn even more about the humans, not just for their crumbs, but to understand the world beyond the park. My brothers and sisters had already left the nest a while ago to find their mates, so I was alone listening to the human children's screams of glee. I poked my head over the metal bathroom roof and saw humans and birds crisscrossing one another throughout the park. In my head, I heard my mother's coos, giving me the courage to take my first solo flight to forage for food and play with the children, the way I'd always imagined.

My dream came true as soon as I landed on the playground. A crowd of kids gathered around me. "You're it!" the chubby one with the glasses shouted, and they all chased me from the jungle-gym slides to the handball court, and back again. Even though I never had my turn to be the chaser, I enjoyed running in circles, but the humans soon got bored and I was alone again, but not for long.

The first time I saw Parma, she was also by herself, under the green-painted wooden slats they called a bench, between the iron arched legs. She was shaking. It seemed like she was getting up the nerve, just like the little girl in the yellow shorts, swaying her weight and braids back and forth, fixated on her friends' rope turning, for the right time to jump in. The pretty pigeon shimmered, metallic hues of violet, fuchsia, chartreuse, from her breast to her head. Her feathers were so light and soft; the stripes of gray had slight swirls and stretched across both wings and her belly, a blending I'd never seen before in my pigeon family nest. Mesmerized, I got up my own nerve to flit over and flirt.

"I'm hungry, are you?" I asked.

"Starving" was all she had to say. And we've been together ever since.

As I flew back to our nest, I replayed those first moments together over and over, planning the rest of my apology. But when descending onto the Fifty-Fourth Street park entrance path, I got distracted by a human male wearing all-sky-blue shirt, socks, and baseball cap, walking his dog, only a tiny bit bigger than me, wearing a similar blue shirt to that of his man friend, but with holes for four legs. I wondered if any pigeons ever dressed up like humans.

Waddling behind, I hoped the man would sit on a bench, eat a falafel pita sandwich or a bran muffin, and leave leftovers before the sun set. I'd coo loudly for Parma to join me and we'd feast. But the man didn't stop, just kept talking to the air, screaming through the light-blue mask on his face: "If I can't bring my son and my dog with me, I'll just stay here in Hell's Kitchen! You stay in Brooklyn. This lockdown shouldn't last much longer."

Again my mind wandered. I had heard tales of Brooklyn, from another human-loving pigeon who frequented the midtown park. Paisano, named by his Italian human friend, was a carrier pigeon and a distant relative of Parma's family. Her cousin thirteen times removed came from generations living in a Flatbush penthouse coop with scores of siblings, uncles, aunts, cousins, and a fifteen-year-old great-great-grandfather. It was almost unbelievable, as the oldest pigeon I'd ever met was the ripe old age of six. Paisano was my favorite of Parma's family. We shared our love of people and also joked about birds, squirrels, dogs, and rats, and even our human friends.

Meanwhile, a symphonic barking of altos, tenors, and sopranos from the dog walk beckoned the leashed canine. He jetted so fast that he startled his tall friend, who tripped, his mask falling to the ground. The man found his balance but left the mask behind.

"Paisano, do you want to share this cloth or its strings with me?" I asked, though I wasn't sure how we could tear it apart.

"Nah. You need it more than me," Paisano said, talking while an abandoned McDonald's french fry hung from his beak, like humans do with cigarettes. "Take it to my cousin. Parma'll love you for it. I know how she complains all the time about the winter cold, even in the spring." He laughed. "Besides"—the carrier pigeon stuck out his right shank, showing the tube clipped to his leg—"I'm here to work."

While I was anxious to bring Parma the mask, "clap" a little, and go out for a makeup dinner, I was curious to know more about the message Paisano bore. Thankfully, I heard Parma's cooing coming closer, but before we reunited there was a sudden gust of air, scores of pigeons of all different markings and shades coming in every direction, from the newly leafed spring trees, from three-story roofs, thirty-story windowsills, and from the wooden buildings by the piers. Parma landed by me first, then another pigeon, and another.

Without saying a word, Parma's beak and mine met. We both dived at the same morsels—crushed orange Chee-tos—gobbling them up as fast as we could. Before I asked Parma to go back to our nest, even more pigeons descended around Paisano. The carrier spoke for all to hear. "Paz, the old human who feeds you every day, also trains the Fifty-Second Street carriers. Listen to her. She will help us."

Paz, hunched, inched and zigzagged between all the types of birds. "*Hola*," she said to everyone. "I'm here to read the message being sent to all the flocks." First, she reached into her bag, threw crumbs to the crowd, then held out an individualized portion, just for Paisano to peck out of one hand as she bent to reach his leg with the other. Parma and I stood as still as we could, touching claws, watching the old woman unclip and unscroll the paper, pausing after reading each line.

The virus will kill humans. Humans will blame pigeons.
Pigeons are not bats! Pigeons are not rats with wings!
Meet tomorrow 5 p.m. Port Authority by the NJ Transit Gate!
Pigeon Power!

The next day, we were off. Our circles got wider as we soared, not as high as the clouds, but above the buildings where the humans lived and shopped. Each block, we multiplied, with flocks from city neighborhoods I'd never heard about. There were so many pigeons so close together in flight, the sun's light could only flicker through our feverish flapping. I had to admit it was so beautiful. There had to be at least a thousand of us, a glorious gaggle in a winged chromatic spectrum of grays, as well as browns and whites, all flying with purpose.

As we flew down Ninth Avenue, I tried to just focus on following Parma's lovely layers of tail feathers spread out like a fan. Even though I'd seen beautiful birds with marvelous markings, my life mate still was the only one who turned me on. Besides yielding to Parma's seductive passion to fight pigeon prejudice, I'd also hoped the adventure would give me a chance to see more humans in action. But as I looked below, there were no people on sidewalks going in and out of stores, eating on the run, and only a few cars, buses, and trucks driving on the streets. It was a disappointment, nothing like the thrilling midtown hustle and bustle with plentiful foraging opportunities that the more traveled pigeons had described about their journeys to midtown.

Parma looked back to make sure I was still behind her. "Pita, stay close. This is no time to get distracted."

I shouted back the obvious. "Parma, I can see you and look around at the same time!" She knew, like every other pigeon on earth, that because our eyes are on the sides of our heads we have 360-degree vision.

"We have to get to the gates together so the trainers can let us all in at the same time! Our strength is in our numbers!" Parma screamed. She'd said those exact words to me a thousand times in our nest that morning, between my many, many attempts to mount her, the way I loved to start our day.

"C'mon, birdie, we got time," I cooed, hovering above her.

Parma resisted. "Not now, Pita. I told you. I know it's spring, but I'm not ready for breeding! Today is about letting our voices be heard!" Even though I was ready to have baby birds, to be a father, I had to be a patient partner and show that I was down with the cause.

Still in flight, I was amazed by all the Times Square neon lights blinking below, wanting to freeze and memorize the multicolored flashes of words and pictures. It was abandoned by humans, but I could imagine the crowded blocks full of tourists, of all different sizes and colors, walking the streets, discarding food of many flavors and textures for gourmet feasts. Focusing back on Parma, I promised myself to take her there after things got back to normal.

As we flew closer to the Port Authority, I couldn't help but worry about what was going to happen when we all invaded. Hopefully, we wouldn't scare any good people away. Maybe, if I was lucky, besides making Parma happy that I was fighting for justice for all pigeonkind, I'd make some new human friends, and they'd feed us tasty leftover snacks.

"Look!" Parma whistled. "Paisano's flying into the terminal, onto the bus ramp! Let's go do this!"

I'd never seen my love so excited. It was finally her chance to let the humans she was taught to hate know how much pigeons deserved respect. Ever since we were together, after a person yelled, kicked, or shooed us away, Parma would strut away indignant, puff up and proclaim, "Humans should honor us just like their beloved bald eagles or red-breast robins!" So, flying in formation, with so many other angry and determined pigeons, I realized that Parma was not being overly sensitive. She was not alone in her feelings, especially now that we were being blamed, with no scientific proof, for humans suffering and dying from the virus.

We sailed between the steel girders onto the winding ramp, ascending to the dark, dank and fume-coated bus parking spots. Paz, my park friend, and other animal-rights activists were already there, holding the heavy doors open for us. Hundreds of protesters flew into the waiting area just inches above the floor, some waddling by habit, to pick the crumbs by people's feet. I wondered if Parma would be right, if the prejudiced humans would stop spreading all those lies about us, if we showed up as a united force of pigeons with our bird-loving allies.

As we waited for more protesters to join us, and if the humans waiting for their buses wouldn't interfere, I wanted to feast first. I saw a man in a wrinkled business suit brushing croissant flakes off the Dunkin' Donuts bag on his lap. Before I could put one claw in front of the other, Parma slapped me with her princess warrior wing.

"That's not why we're here," she scolded. "Don't you get it? These humans are not our friends!" Ashamed that foraging was still more on my mind than protesting, I turned to offer another of my frequent apologies. Parma didn't want to hear it and put her wing up to my face, then snapped, "We're supposed to line up with Paisano and the humans holding the signs," my beloved instructed. Of course, I obeyed.

We both stood steadying ourselves on one leg, warbling along with the humans shouting: "Pigeons are proud New Yorkers . . . not virus scapegoats!" Some scared passengers ran away, but others, used to seeing scores of pigeons at the terminal, didn't flinch, ignored our massive numbers, and kept reading their papers. But when a flock of spotted pigeons swooped in, they flew past the protesters, as if they had a completely different agenda. I wasn't sure if it was out of an extreme case of anti-human anger, or out of hunger or greed, but they surrounded and ambushed two little boys sharing a bag of popcorn, dropping more kernels on the ground than in their mouths.

"Mommy, Mommy!" the shorter one cried, "the pigeons are trying to eat us!" When I heard that, I took it as a joke at first. It reminded me of my delicious toe fantasy the other day. But what was about to happen was far from funny.

"Boys, get away from those disgusting birds! Don't touch them! They have diseases!" their mother shouted. The two bags strapped across her body, and two more bags in her hands, weighed down her thin frame. She was mean and a blamer, but she seemed to be struggling herself. I was hurt by her scorn, but almost felt sorry for the human mother.

"Parma . . . Pita . . . peanut . . . pasta . . ." Paisano's call snapped me out of my pro-human empathy. He waved his majestic wings, marked with what looked like a cluster of a king's silver crowns, signaling everyone to come closer to him and our human friends.

"People and pigeons unite," Paz and another twenty or so unwinged protesters chanted. I began to feel a new pigeon pride, and I joined the tweeting: "Kill the virus . . . not the pigeons."

Parma hopped closer, put her wing around mine, and our voices grew even stronger. I thought clapping was the most powerful way to express our love, but in that moment, I felt we were just as close. She'd helped me to discover a new admiration for my pigeon brothers and sisters.

"Parma," I cooed in her ear so she could hear me over the chanting and whistling. "Thank you for making sure I was a part of this. Maybe there is power in numbers."

"I love you too," she cooed back, then shouted, "The pigeons united will never be defeated!"

Some of the humans had stood from their benches and were pointing their phones at us. Paz was at a newsstand talking to a woman with a big camera on her shoulder. I wanted to get closer to hear what she was saying, but I froze—I saw masked police officers coming up the escalator in helmets, face guards, and vests marked NYC Animal Control Unit. They marched in straight rows toward us with nets and batons.

"Officers, officers!" the mother yelled, "these pigeons were attacking my boys!"

"Passengers!" a Port Authority cop barked through a megaphone. "Please leave the area. Go down the escalator and there will be someone to tell you new gate numbers for your bus."

As soon as the tired woman, her popcorn-eating sons, and the other passengers left the area, an animal-control officer blew a whistle, piercing our ears.

"Don't move!" Paisano commanded. "We have to stand our ground!"

More high-pitched sirens blasted, and the anti-pigeon battalion lunged at us, raising their nets and their batons. We tried to be disciplined and not move, but it would've been suicidal to be a sitting target. Instinct prevailed and we broke ranks, flying in all directions.

"Stay close!" I shouted to Parma. But I could not see where she flew to.

The cops attacked, striking pigeons on their backs who didn't take off in time. Our human allies, mostly senior citizens, did not let their age stop them from fighting back. Some picked up wounded birds, wrapping them in shawls. Others locked arms and stood in front of the cops to give the flocks more of a chance to fly away before the pigeon-hating humans scooped us up in their nets.

"Get the doors, get the doors!" Paz shouted to help us escape. I didn't want to leave without Parma.

I used my 360-degree vision to find her, whistling as loud as I could, "Parma, let's go—now!"

Some of the cops unclipped black plastic bags from their holsters and dumped captured pigeons in them, tying the bags closed to take them away. Others scattered what looked like birdseed on the floor. "Pita!" Luckily, I heard Paisano's voice screeching. "Don't eat them, they're poisonous!"

"Where's Parma?" I shouted back. At that moment, she was all I cared about.

Paisano didn't answer. He darted toward one of the nets, hitting its rim as hard as he could. He shook it enough to twist the net to the side. The pigeon prisoners fled, including Parma. My mate flapped furiously, disoriented, up to the ceiling and down again, up and down, then spinning. I was scared she was injured, that something was wrong. I hovered just under her, trying to slow her falling pace as best I could.

"It's okay, it's okay, I got you," I whistled. Parma finally slowed and followed me down to the ground. She was out of breath but nodded that she was okay.

"Let's get out of here!" I pleaded, circling around her to get her to follow me to one of the open doors.

"I'm not leaving without Paisano!" she said, and she took off to help her cousin.

218

The embarrassed cop who'd lost his avian detainees dropped his net, took out his baton, and went after Paisano. Parma and I flew to his aid, along with Paz, who used all her strength to swing her bag of crumbs against the cop's head. "Go, go!" the old lady shouted.

As he tangled with her, the three of us flew to escape, but another policeman chased us. Just as we got low enough to fly through the doors, the vicious badged man clubbed Paisano against the wall. My friend dropped to the floor.

"No, no, no!" Parma cried out.

I used my one-marked wing strength to block her from turning around to see her cousin's lifeless bleeding body. I helped propel her out of the gate, through the open space between the terminal girders, up to the darkening sky.

Later, safe in our park nest, we relived every moment of the protest and what led to Paisano's death. The harmonies of human and pigeon voices chanting for our rights filled my soul, but it wasn't our song of solidarity that replayed in my head. That moment was stolen by the pigeon-hating humans' sinister syncopated attack. Only the sounds of whistles, bullhorns, and the frantic screeching echoed in my mind. All I could see were the nets, the batons, and Paisano's bloodied head.

My beloved was cradled in my wings. I rocked her to the rhythm of the children's swings, creaking back and forth from the west winds blowing from beyond the Hudson River.

"I should've done something to save Paisano. . . ." Parma wept and wept.

"No, no, baby," I cooed. "You tried. It was the humans." I knew my words would not be able to soothe either the loss of her cousin or the defeat of the protest. "You told me how bad they could be, but I never imagined they'd attack us like that," I confessed.

I'd never heard Parma's coo so broken. "I knew they'd try to net us but didn't ever think they'd actually kill us," she whimpered. "How are we going to stop them from wiping us out? Especially now that our leader, Paisano, is gone."

I wanted to tell her that our human friends will use their science to prove to the world that we pigeons are not the source of the virus. Maybe when they find a cure, people will stop being so angry and scared of us. But I knew that would give Parma little comfort—she'd been skeptical of humankind way before their pandemic. Instead, I asked, "What makes a human hate so much they want to beat and kill?" Our unanswerable questions nested beside us.

Until that night, I chose solely to focus on the kindness of humans. I made excuses for their many wars, that they were always fighting against something evil. I'd never allowed myself to acknowledge the bad guys were also human. It was my turn to sob.

"Sweet Pita, you were also right. Not all humans are bad," Parma mind-read. "Paz and our friends risked themselves to save our lives." She nuzzled her head against mine. "We need to be strong for each other." My beloved's usual pitch was returning. My wings trembled.

We hugged for a long time, our claws crossed on the twig and paper floor of our nest. We hadn't eaten since before the protest, and both of our gizzards grumbled.

"How 'bout we go to the terrace for dinner?" Parma suggested, hoping that if I saw my human friend it would lift my spirits.

"Oh, baby, yes. . . ." I wanted to clap her right then and there, but I just gave my mate a few pecks. We shook out the tension in our grieving wings, and Parma led the way over the empty park field, lit for a night baseball game, but without any players.

"Oh, my!" Parma was surprised when we got to the twenty-eighth floor. "Your friend must have been expecting us!"

On the terrace, strewn across the floor's concrete bubbles, around the clay flowerpots and under the deck chair, were Parmesan and pita crumbs. Music, a pounding and slapping conga beat that made my claws tap and want to turn into feet, blasted from behind the glass door. For a moment I forgot how sad and hungry I was. My human friend loved that salsa music, so I waddled over to the glass door and saw her dancing with an invisible partner like she always did.

"Look, Parma, she's home!" As we gobbled up our favorite treats, the woman opened the door to greet us, but something was different. She looked like my friend, but her hair was longer, her eyes bluer, her voice more an alto than a soprano.

"Ahh! Pita and Parma, so glad you came," a younger version of our human companion said with a piece of paper in her hand. "My mother was worried about you. She saw the news about the Port Authority protests and wanted me to check if you were okay."

"I wish all humans were like this," Parma warbled with crumbs on her beak.

"Where's your mother?" I whistled, but the daughter didn't understand. Only people who took the time to study us could comprehend our coos. The mother human was just starting to figure it out, but the daughter was kind and read from her paper:

Dear Pita and Parma, While I'm in the hospital, healing from the virus, I know this disease is not from you precious pigeons. Humans can be so foolish and

*cruel. I just saw what happened on tv. I am so sorry
for the pain, for your losses.*

"Is she gonna be okay?" Parma looked up from the last
of the pile she'd been pecking. I didn't know—just wanted to
hear the rest of the note.

*My friends, look out to our river. She knows never to
surrender to the elements, to keep gliding even when
iced, even against the roughest tide. And so must you
two. Never give up your fight for justice or your love
for each other. My daughter will come until I get well.
Much love. Peace.*

The park drums summoned avian and human spirits alike, in
sync with the salsa music playing from the apartment. Parma and I
waddled to the beat and joined the daughter at the railing to honor her
mother and the call to never give up. The three of us looked to the river
below, then up to the sky, lit by the moon and park lights, to sing our
goodbyes to Paisano and the other fallen pigeons. Though she didn't
know the words, the daughter hummed with us, and we harmonized,
"*mrrroooo . . . mrrroooo . . .*" singing for her mother, our good friend, to
heal.

As the cooler winds rattled the terrace bars, Parma looked at me
with loving eyes. "Pita," she cooed. "It's time. I'm ready."

20

THERE WILL BE FLYING CARS

by Richard Jones

I'd been watching the clock all day, and finally the workday was over. I closed my laptop and walked out of my makeshift office. It used to be our extremely small guest room. If I stood in the center of the room, I could almost touch the walls on both sides. But that's Manhattan for you. We were lucky that we had two bedrooms and enough space to work.

I closed my office door behind me and plopped down on the couch. My wife was on the other end of the sectional, intently typing something on her computer.

"What are you feeling for dinner?" I asked.

"It's up to you," she said noncommittally, pushing the decision to me.

"I don't feel like cooking," I said, too exhausted by life to make dinner. "I guess let's order something."

For the past two months, this had been our daily routine. Wake up, work, figure out dinner, watch every television show that's ever existed, go to bed, and do it all again the next day. With more free time than I was used to, I did what everyone else did during the lockdown: made fancy cocktails, baked bread, and endured endless Zoom happy hours. Two months in, the novelty was wearing off.

I reached into my pocket and pulled out my phone. Instead of looking for a place to order from, I opened Facebook. I scrolled through my feed, more out of habit to shut off my brain. I stopped on a post from my mom.

> *Check out this video from when I was in elementary school. They filmed everyone in my class talking about what life would be like in 2020. I can't believe it's been 50 years!!!! Thanks, Pete, for posting this! Such good memories!*

"Did you see my mom's post on Facebook?"

"You know I don't look at your mom's posts anymore," my wife said sarcastically, not looking up from her computer. "Once she started posting about politics, I un-Friended her."

I laughed. The political posts and chain-letter equivalents were annoying. I clicked play anyway, interested to see what my mom said. I'd watched this kind of video before. They were always wildly off the mark.

My mom, always the optimist, appeared in the middle of the video and said that there would be world peace because every country would give up its nuclear weapons. The rest of the kids said everything you'd expect. The first kid said flying cars, which every person always thinks is right around the corner, but at this point it seems like it will never happen. A freckle-faced redheaded girl said that we'd all have robot helpers with us wherever we go. I guess that was kind of true if you counted the phones in our pockets. I recognized my mom's best friend, Barb, who now lives in Arizona and sells her terrible pottery to tourists. She talked about space travel and how we'd colonize the moon and other planets. The short clip ended with a kid in desperate need of braces talking about how all diseases would be cured and we'd all live past one hundred.

I sent my mom a text telling her how much I enjoyed the video and went back to my evening. It was pizza again for dinner. Then, before going to bed, we watched a reality show that we had recently gotten into, about pig farmers in Texas.

"Hey, buddy, you okay?"

I opened my eyes. The sun was high in the sky, and I squinted to see a man talking to me.

"My programming requires me to assist in the case of a medical emergency," another voice said, sounding almost mechanical. "Would you like me to call the paramedics?"

I rubbed my eyes, trying to figure out where I was. I had to be dreaming, but this felt so real. I had vivid dreams all the time, but none where I could smell the rotting garbage on the street and feel the sun's rays on my skin. I was standing in the middle of a street. The yellow lines in its center were barely visible.

The man to my left was slightly overweight and wore a dark-gray tunic. It was New York, and you see people dressed strangely all the time, but this outfit was unlike anything I had ever seen. Was he in some weird cult, or was this some new style I hadn't caught on to yet? And why wasn't he wearing a mask? Everyone in the city was wearing masks when they were in public. I realized I wasn't wearing one either. I reached into my pockets, looking for my mask, but came up empty.

I moved my glance to the other man with him. My eyes widened when I saw that it wasn't a man at all but a robot. It looked and moved like a human, beside the fact that it was metallic and not wearing any clothes. Something like the Terminator after his skin had been burned off. Sure, there are robots around here and there, but they're usually clunky devices designed to do one thing, like pick a package off a shelf or vacuum your house. This was a fully functional humanoid robot.

"Maybe you should get him help," the man said to his robot.

"No, I'm okay," I said. I wasn't, but I needed to figure out how I could wake myself up. This dream was giving me weird vibes, and I didn't want to be in it anymore.

"You sure?" the man asked. "You look pretty out of it."

"No, no. I'm good. I haven't seen a robot like that before."

"Really?" the man asked, tilting his head in confusion. "I've had him for years. It's the cheapest model that most people have."

"Ah, yeah," I said, not wanting to seem suspicious.

"Wait. Where is your companion robot?"

"He's in the shop," I said, trying to brush him off.

The man walked around me, the robot following a few paces behind him. "This city is going to hell," he said to his robot as they continued down the street.

I was on Park Avenue, in Union Square, Manhattan. This was usually a heavily congested area, but I was in the middle of the street. How had I not been run over yet? I looked in both directions—there wasn't a single car on the road. I ran to the sidewalk to avoid almost certain death before a speeding taxi inevitably hurtled toward me.

As I stepped onto the sidewalk, I spotted a woman, strangely wearing a tunic similar to the one worn by the man I had just spoken to. Like with the man, a robot walked a couple of paces behind her.

"Excuse me," I said, trying to be polite.

She looked up, surprised that I was talking to her. She pulled her purse closer to her body and stared at me suspiciously as she slowed down ever so slightly.

"What's today's date?" I asked, anxious to get any information I could.

"What?" the woman asked.

"The date. What's today's date?"

"May 6, 2020," the robot replied.

"Where am I?"

The woman stopped walking and looked at me, then at her robot. "Are you okay? Where is your robot?"

"Where am I?" I shouted, slightly panicked.

"New York!" she shouted back. "Where do you think you are?" she added sardonically as she walked away.

"Am I dreaming?" I shouted back. If you ask someone in a dream if you're dreaming, don't they have to tell you the truth? Isn't it like when a police officer is undercover, they have to tell you they're a cop if you ask?

The woman ignored me and darted away; her robot struggled to keep up.

I looked up and down the street, and still not a single car—yet there was incessant honking. I realized that the sound wasn't coming from the street but from above. I looked up, and there it was—a traffic jam a hundred feet above my head. Flying cars!

Each car had a long, thin body, roughly the same length and width as cars that I was used to. There were protective bubbles over the cars. They almost looked like convertibles with clear plastic shells on top.

Wasn't the whole promise of flying cars that you wouldn't have to deal with things like traffic anymore? Of course there was still traffic in New York! I could see the unmistakable yellow of cabs interspersed among the cars. I wondered if there were still buses, and if the subway still existed. And whether they flew through the air too. . . .

If I was capable of creating this crazy dream, I had more of an imagination than I realized. Then it dawned on me. Only a couple of hours ago, I watched the video that my mom had posted about what the future would look like. They say dreams are things in your life that you need to work through. I wasn't quite sure what I had to work through, but maybe I should go along for the ride.

I tried to remember what else they said in the video. Seeing a nearby Duane Reade pharmacy pulled me back into reality and grounded me in something I was familiar with. That kid with the bad teeth, who was now in his sixties, said that diseases wouldn't exist in the future. Going into a pharmacy was the perfect way to test out his hypothesis.

The automatic door opened as I approached the entrance. Luckily, that didn't surprise me—we had those where I came from too.

"Excuse me!" I shouted, being particularly bold by making a scene.

"Welcome to Duane Reade," the high school student working the counter said, not looking up, her robot a few feet behind her. She wore a blue tunic embroidered with the Duane Reade logo.

"Have all diseases been cured?" I asked brazenly.

"What?" the girl asked, looking at me for the first time.

"Diseases," I said firmly. "Are there any left?"

"What are you talking about? I'm calling the cops if you don't leave!" Workers at a store in the city had to have seen everything—she knew how to handle a crazy man shouting in her store.

"Okay, okay. But are there any diseases left?"

"Of course there are," she muttered as she picked up a corded phone that was obsolete years ago.

"Covid?"

"I have no idea what *ccoovviidd* is," she said, sounding out each letter.

"Covid-19, the coronavirus, the pandemic. That doesn't ring a bell?"

"No!" she screamed. She diverted her attention to the phone. "I'm at the Duane Reade on Park and Fifteenth. There's a homeless man in here, with some strange clothes, making a scene." She paused and listened to the person on the other end. She hung up. "The cops are on their way."

I wasn't scared of being arrested in a dream, but I didn't want to turn this one into a nightmare by my fear of being arrested. I had managed to get through college without being arrested for public intoxication, and I didn't want to see what I had missed out on, even in dream form.

I walked out of the store and back onto the busy street. Maybe this was a nice dream if Covid didn't exist, and I should enjoy being out and about. I had spent the past two months locked in our apartment, other than an occasional quick trip to the store, where I was terrified that I'd catch the virus. I'd keep my mask on and stay as far away from people as I could, and for a short time I washed everything that came into our apartment. The freedom that this dream city was offering was a nice change of pace.

Two out of three things from the video were true. I wanted to see about world peace and space travel.

"Hey, who's invading who right now?" I ask a man wearing a tunic and carrying a briefcase.

"Bug off," the man replied.

Bug off? Who says that? Another man, balding, skinny, wearing the same tunic, approached. "Are there any wars?" I asked. "Is there world peace?"

"Not since 1991, when the Gulf War ended," he said, not slowing his stride. "The entire world signed the Earth Treaty in 1996. Am I on a man-on-the-street television show? Where are the cameras? What do I win?"

I ignored him and looked south, into the distance. The Twin Towers rose in all of their glory. If 9/11 didn't happen, it was hard to argue that this dream world wasn't superior to the hellish one I came from.

"Hey, you!" I heard from behind me. I turned to see two police officers walking toward me. One had a black mustache, the other clean-shaven. Each also wore a tunic with a badge on his right breast and a gun holster around his waist. I pretended that I didn't see them, put my hands in my pockets, and whistled my way down the street.

"You with the weird clothes, stop!" A hand grabbed my shoulder, halting me.

"Were you the one at the Duane Reade bothering the cashier?" the mustached cop asked.

"Yeah, that's him," the cashier said, as she walked onto the street to identify me. I stood there silently, hoping I'd wake up at any moment.

"Are you on drugs? Or have you been drinking, sir?"

"No, Officer," I said nervously. "I'm sorry I caused a scene. I'll go."

"Not so fast," the mustached cop said. The other remained silent, his hand on the butt of his gun. "Why are you dressed like that?"

I looked down at my clothes. It was what I usually wore: jeans, a T-shirt, and sneakers. I guess I did kind of stick out compared to the tunics everyone else was wearing.

"Your ID, please," the other officer ordered, finally speaking.

I reached into my back pocket, and to my surprise I pulled out my actual wallet. I took my license out and looked at it for a second. It was my license, all right, bad picture, with my eyes closed. I handed it to the previously silent officer.

"Sir, are you really going to hand me a fake ID? It's not even a good one." He showed it to the other officer and laughed. "It's probably the worst one I've ever seen."

This was a dream, so I figured I might as well be bold. "Listen, I'm going to level with you," I started, trying to speak with confidence. Even though it was just a dream, I still wasn't comfortable talking to a police officer. In my nondream life, I felt guilty, even if I wasn't doing anything wrong. Just driving by a police officer filled me with dread. "I'm dreaming right now. So why don't you just let me go continue my dream in peace?"

The officers looked at each other, clearly confused by how I was acting. "Sir, we're going to have to bring you in."

"No, thanks," I said, before taking off down the street. When I was awake, I wouldn't call myself fast. So I wasn't quite sure what made me think I'd be a speed demon while dreaming. I didn't even make it thirty feet before they were on my heels. The mustached officer leaped through the air and jumped on my back, instantly bringing me to the ground. A moment later, handcuffs were around my wrists.

"This is a dream!" I screamed. "There is no such thing as a flying car! Or maybe there is, but I've never seen one. Robots aren't that good! Covid is a thing! Covid is a thing!"

"You have the right to remain silent. . . ."

Days later, I was still in the dream. Or so I thought. Or hoped. I was at Jefferson Psychiatric Hospital in upstate New York. They didn't arrest me but instead brought me to a hospital. I knew that I was going to wake up any minute in a cold sweat, and the memory of this strange dream would slowly fade away. I'd promise myself that I'd remember it, but when I got around to telling my wife about it the next morning, it would be all gone, or only fragments would remain. But that didn't happen.

Since I was dreaming, I decided to tell the truth. The steady stream of doctors that came in to try to diagnose me all heard the same thing. I am dreaming, and I come from a very different world. There were no such thing as flying cars and robots that everyone had. And there was definitely not world peace. The world was a mess and was dealing with this virus that had spread across the globe. The doctors all wrote furiously in their notebooks, and I could see that they all thought I was crazy.

They pumped me with all sorts of drugs and told me that they would make me feel better. I stayed in the hospital for close to two weeks before they transferred me to Jefferson. There, I shared a room with Gerald. He was a nice guy from Connecticut. I could never tell why he was there, but he listened to my story and didn't tell me that I was crazy. He was the only one.

I attended group therapy and met one-on-one with a doctor. I kept telling them that this was a dream, and I felt like I was talking to a brick wall. The medicine they gave me made me feel numb, but I refused to submit to the idea that I was making all this up.

All I could do was hold on to hope that I'd eventually wake up. But after the first month at Jefferson, I started to have doubts. Dreams don't last this long. Maybe I was sick, and I *had* made it all up. Perhaps it would be easier if I told the doctors what they wanted to hear. If I could convince them that I was better, I could get out and figure out how to wake myself up.

As I approached month six, I had my routine and started to tell the doctors what they wanted to hear, and there was talk about me being released.

An alarm blared through the room. I reached over to the nightstand, where my phone was sitting, and, like a caveman, tried to stop the incessant sound.

As I sat up, my bedroom came into view. Not my room at Jefferson, but my apartment. The old dresser that I bought after college was across from the bed; the new desk we got for my wife sat next to it. I was home—it *was* all a dream! I looked over to my wife, who was just opening her eyes. There she was, after six long months, beautiful as I remembered. I gazed at my phone: May 6, 2020. It was the right date! The day after I went to bed.

"How'd you sleep?" she asked, having no idea what I had just endured.

"I had the strangest dream," I said, getting up from the bed and walking to the window. "It was like the video my mom was in. I woke up in a world with all the things the kids predicted. It was crazy. There were robots everywhere. And there were flying cars. And—" I paused, opening the curtains to peer out the window. I jumped back as a flying car whizzed by. I looked at my wife, now panicked that I was losing my mind. "Does Covid even exist?"

ABOUT THE AUTHORS

Susana Aikin was born in Spain to an English father and a Spanish mother and is a writer and Emmy Award filmmaker living between New York City and Madrid. She has an MA in Creative Writing from the Manchester Writing School, United Kingdom, and has published three novels and a memoir: *The Weight of the Heart*, Kensington Books (2021), *Nadine*, Libros de Seda (2020), *We Shall See the Sky Sparkling*, Kensington Books (2019), and *Digging Up the Salt Mines*, Ishtar Press (2017).

Rebecca Baum is a novelist, ghostwriter, and content marketer. Her published novel, *Lifelike Creatures*, was longlisted for the Crook's Corner Book Prize Foundation's 2021 best debut novel set in the American South. Her ghostwriting has served founders of global nonprofits and mission-driven commercial enterprises. A native of Louisiana, she has lived in New York City for more than 20 years. www.rebeccabaum.com

Jocelyn Bystrom writes for pleasure, therapeutic release, and for the little girl she sees and stares at in the mirror who struggled in silence for far too long. "Unwelcomed Guest" is Jocelyn's first published short story. She has workshopped with Natalie Goldberg, author of *Writing Down the Bones*, Meghan Flaherty at the writersgrotto.org, Patrick Price, founder of askabookeditor.com, and The WriteWorkshops. Her newly completed manuscript is titled: FINDING HOPE, The Mind-Body Connection & Hope for Well-Being.

Laura Castro has had short memoir pieces published in The Sun Magazine's "Readers Write" section. Her poem, "The Return," was judged a "Notable Poem" in a Gemini Magazine Poetry Open. She worked 20 years in theater and later ran an afterschool "Coffee House" for teenagers and their teachers, which combined poetry, jazz, dance, and visual art, culminating in annual performances at New York City's Nuyorican Poets' Café. She taught playwrighting to high school students in the Find Your Voice program, which worked out of Lincoln Center Studio. Laura studied playwriting with Arthur Kopit and is grateful to have been mentored by Jeff Ourvan in The WriteWorkshops.

Taylor Days has been with The WriteWorkshops for one year. "An Iota of Harm" is her first published piece, and she's currently working on a memoir.

Ross Dreiblatt is an author living in South Florida. His first novel, *I Am Not Brad Pitt: And Other Stories*, was published in 2021. He has had numerous short stories appear in online literary magazines. He studied journalism at Hofstra University and fiction in John Rechy's master workshop at UCLA.

Haji Freeman is a poet and writer. His poetry has been published in an anthology by the Trustees of the Boston Public Library, and his non-fiction by the Boston *Globe*, Voice Male and Spirit of Change magazines. He is author of *Facilitating Fathers Groups: 22 Keys to Group Mastery* and has honed his craft at both Grub Street Center for Creative Writing and The WriteWorkshops. His first novel, based on the life of his great grandfather who escaped from slavery during the so-called U.S. Civil War, is forthcoming.

Derlys Gutierrez is an attorney in New Jersey. "Breathe With Me" is her first published short story, and she's also completing a time-travel novel titled *Don't You Want Me*.

Jessica Jiji is the author of two novels published by HarperCollins, *Diamonds Take Forever* and *Sweet Dates in Basra*, which were also released in Italian, and another, *How to Judge a Book By Its Lover*, that won the 2021 Indies Today Best Humor Award. Since the start of the pandemic, she has written more than a dozen screenplays, winning Gold Prize in the Page International Screenwriting Awards Competition, Semifinalist at the Austin Film Festival, and Winner of the Big Apple Film Festival. Skateboarding with her three sons is more than worth the 20 stitches and nine-inch metal plate holding her arm together.

Richard Jones, a technologist turned writer, is a former tech executive who discovered he prefers writing prose to code. "There Will Be Flying Cars" is his first published work. He is currently working on his debut novel and lives in South Carolina with his wife, daughter, and dog.

Beau Karch is a native Ohioan who has lived on the Upper West Side of Manhattan for more than 25 years. A business development professional, he has worked in the professional services and legal industries, academia, and theatre for most of his adult life. Part of the The WriteWorkshops community for the past three years, Beau recently completed a literary novel titled *Rounding Third*. "What You Wish For" is his first published short story.

Christopher Ragland has worked as a professional actor and voiceover artist for almost 20 years. After narrating more than 200 books, he finally decided to write one! With the amazing guidance of The WriteWorkshops, he finished his first novel, *The Social Contract*, last year and is hard at work on his second book. "At Least Five" is his first published piece, and he's thrilled to be a part of an outstanding group of authors. https://christopherragland.com.

Annie Rourke was for many years an Emmy Award-winning broadcaster journalist, who has transitioned to writing full-time. She's written two novels and is currently working on her third screenplay.

Kathleen Scheiner is an editor and writer living in Brooklyn, New York. She's written for *Publishers Weekly*, Scholastic, *Chime for Change*, *L'encran Fantastique, Toxic*, and *Penny Blood*. Her novel *The Collected* was published in 2013, and her short fiction has appeared in *Memoirs of Meanness, A New York State of Fright, Under Twin Suns*, and various Girls Write Now anthologies. See more at https://horrorfeminista.com/.

Heather Siegel is the author of two award-winning memoirs, *The King & The Quirky*, and *Out From The Underworld*, as well as the YA novel, *The Indigo*. Her creative nonfiction has appeared in numerous publications, including *HuffPost Personal, Salon.com, The Erma Bombeck Writers' Workshop, Entrophy Magazine, The Flexible Persona,* and *Paris Lit Up*. She holds an MFA from The New School and is the recipient of various accolades, including the Readers' Favorite Book Award 2020 Gold Medal in Women's Nonfiction, the Next Generation Indie Book Award 2020 Winner for Women's Issues, and the Goose Wickes 2019 Prize in Prose. Visit her at www.heathersiegel.net.

Brittany Sirlin is a middle school English teacher currently working on her first young adult novel, as well as several children's books. She's a member of the Society of Children's Book Writers and Illustrators and the National Council of Teachers of English. She has studied writing with both The WriteWorkshops and Quill and Cup. "Playing Dead" is her first published work.

Laura Vural is Founder and President of Listening and Visioning, LLC, and has for four decades championed the integrated arts approach of positive youth development. Currently a consultant for community-based organizations around the country, her work has earned numerous honors, including the Coming Up Taller Award from the President's Committee on the Arts and Humanities in 2005, for the best youth arts program in the country. She is also a documentary filmmaker, serving as an Executive Producer on "Harlem Rising: A Community Changing the Odds" (2020) and Writer/Executive Producer on "A Time for Activism" (2023) about the 1970 takeover of Ethical Culture's Fieldston School by students of color. She received an M.A. in Art and Art Education from Teachers College, Columbia University, and taught Collaborative Practices in Community Arts Education there. A proud mother and grandmother, Vural is currently writing her poetic memoir with The WriteWorkshops, tentatively titled *the invisible and blue of small things*.

Thomas Walsh has been writing and editing words professionally for many decades, highlighted by 22 years as an editor at *Rolling Stone* and RollingStone.com, and preceded by work as a reporter-writer (*Variety* and *Daily Variety* — TV, film, theater), a reporter-writer-editor-you-name-it (*Back Stage* — the performing arts), and an editor-writer (at too many sports publications to name, most of them defunct, some of them still at it, like *The New York Times*). After all that, "Full Moon Fever" is his first published piece of fiction. He earned a B.S. degree in communication arts (media) at St. John's University in New York, and he recently rejoined The WriteWorkshops, where he wrote, rewrote, and learned with much appreciation for five years.

Monica Wendel is an associate professor of composition and creative writing at St. Thomas Aquinas College. She holds an MFA in poetry writing from NYU, where she was awarded Goldwater and Starworks teaching fellowships. Her most recent chapbook of poetry, *English Kills*, won the Coal Review prize and was published by Autumn House Press in 2016.

Ashley Williams holds a B.A. in Creative Writing and Literature from Hofstra University. Born and raised in the Bronx, New York, Ashley has been studying with The WriteWorkshops for more than five years. Her two completed young adult novels spring from LGBTQIA themes. "Stuck On Me" is her first published short story.

ABOUT THE EDITOR

Jeff Ourvan, founder of The WriteWorkshops, is an attorney and literary agent with the Jennifer Lyons Literary Agency and the author of The Star-Spangled Buddhist. For more information on The WriteWorkshops, visit https://thewriteworkshops.com/.

Made in United States
North Haven, CT
15 March 2023

34135589R00143